The Pawnee War

The Pawnee War

A novel

By

Shawn J. Farritor

Also by Shawn J. Farritor
And available through Xlibris

End of Pawnee Starlight

Library of Congress Control Number: 2013916140
ISBN: Hardcover   978-1-4836-9589-1
               Softcover   978-1-4836-9588-4
               Ebook   978-1-4836-9587-7

Rev. date: 09/18/2013

To order additional copies of this book, contact:
Xlibris LLC
1-888-795-4274
www.Xlibris.com
Orders@Xlibris.com
141463

Contents

For my wife, Amy

~ Beloved ~

Historical Prologue

The Pawnee War was a series of skirmishes and confrontations between white settlers, Nebraska Organized Militia, and a detachment of U.S. Army dragoons in the early summer of 1859. The Nebraska Militia's march up the Elkhorn River Valley and parlay with the Pawnee on a windswept hill near the present site of Battle Creek, Nebraska, was unique in the history of the American West. It was the only time a territorial governor led armed forces into direct military confrontation with a Native American tribe. Nebraska Territorial Governor Samuel Black took this dubious honor and he remains the only Nebraska governor to command military forces on the field of battle.

The Pawnee War hastened the development of Nebraska as a federally recognized state. In many ways, it signified the birth of Nebraska as an independent entity. The territory was no longer just a passageway to the west. Nebraska Territory presented itself to the nation with a functional central authority capable of uniting for self-protection. It was worthy of statehood. Nebraska citizens would need this self-awareness and unity as the federal army abandoned most of the territories within two years to build up eastern forces to fight the Confederacy. The American Civil War loomed in the not too distant future and with the determination of that far bloodier struggle, the relationship between federal and local powers was changed forever. In addition, Sioux and Cheyenne warriors would attack the Overland Road in Nebraska in 1863. Nebraska was left to its own devices to counter this threat and the experience the militia gained during the Pawnee War proved invaluable.

In spite of all the disorganized marches, the exaggerated nature of the Indian depredations, and the militia chest-thumping, the Pawnee War was a serious affair. People died as a consequence of anger, confusion, and misdirected leadership of both the settlers and Pawnee. At least one white woman lost her life and an unknown number; possibly as many as a dozen Indians died or were seriously injured. Numbers of white settlers lost all that they owned, their livestock slaughtered and crops burned. All of the effected settlers faced the bitter decision whether leave or stay on their destroyed farmsteads and try to rebuild their life, perhaps starving in the process. Many, if not most, chose to cut their losses and return east. It would take years for the Elkhorn River Valley settlements to recover.

For the Pawnee people the conflict was even more of a watershed moment. Everything would change for them, from the greatest war chief of the tribe to the youngest cook fire girl. Under the leadership of *Petalasharo II,* the Pawnee settled into the Pawnee Agency, a tract of land located along the forks of the Loup River. At the time of the Pawnee War the bands were scattered both north and south of the Platte River. The Pawnee Agency had been established in 1848 but few stayed within its boundaries. The Fort Childs Treaty had granted the Pawnee land for this agency but the tribe did not seem to comprehend what had been agreed upon. Whether the chiefs intended to give up the people's freedom and comply with its strict terms can be debated. What occurred in the immediate aftermath of the treaty was very little. The only Pawnee band that complied and fully settled at the agency was the *Skidi.* It was not much of a sacrifice for them as the hills along Loup Rivers were their ancestral lands. The other bands were scattered across to southeast Nebraska and northern Kansas. The *Chaui, Kitakahaki,* and *Pitahawirata* continued to roam relatively freely. The *Chaui* maintained the traditional seat of power, the village of *Pah-Huku.* The whites, for their part, were at first indifferent. Neither the federal Indian authorities nor the local officials seemed to have an interest in making sure the terms of the treaty were followed. For a decade or so it looked as if the arrangement with its loosely enforced terms would work. Perhaps the whites and the Pawnee could live as friendly neighbors.

All of this changed after gold was found in the far west and near Pikes Peak. Miners and settlers traveling over the Overland Route to Colorado, Oregon, and California significantly diminished the ability of the American Indian tribes to live along the route. Towns and farmsteads popped up and the land grew more crowded. A second treaty was struck, the Treaty at Table Creek in 1857, and all legal niceties to settle the roaming Pawnee to their agency were sewn up. There were simply too many whites pouring into the west with dreams of a better life through farming for the Pawnee to continue to roam.

The burning of the ancient Pawnee village of *Pah-Huku* spun events out of control. The Pawnee War triggered the determination of the territorial authorities to see that all terms of the prior treaties, at least terms agreed to by the Pawnee, were observed. No longer would they be allowed to roam across Nebraska on pilgrimages to their sacred sites or to hunt game, even when food on the agency was scarce. Their hunts were to be strictly overseen by white officials and individual Pawnee would need to be given passes to leave the reservation. It was a terribly difficult transition that was only exacerbated by their proximity to the tribe's traditional enemies, the Sioux and Cheyenne. But that is the part in the story covered by my first novel, *End of Pawnee Starlight*.

Tribes and Indian terms referred to in their Indian names are italicized while tribes and terms referred to in their English names are not. Thus, *Petalasharo* is italicized while Man Chief is not.

This is a work of fiction based upon the tragic and heroic history of the times. Writing about the Pawnee people and their difficult experience in the history of our country has become a passion of mine. I hope I have done the Pawnee justice with my words. The founding men and women of our state were ambitious and proud. Sometimes they lived up to our highest ideals. Often they fell short.

Throughout the writing of this book, I found the excellent tribal history by George Hyde, *The Pawnee Indians*, constantly by my side as a reference.

I understand that even after the years have passed, there remains a great deal of anger and resentment over the Indian Wars and the aftermath. I have written this book hoping it finds a receptive audience. I meant it to be educational and entertaining. In my defense against anyone who is offended by my depictions or characters, I can only state that no offense was intended.

SJF, Grand Island, Nebraska

Map of Nebraska Territory, 1859

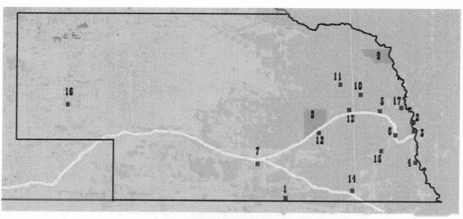

Territoral Border 1959	1. Pah-Hur / Guide Rock	11. Battle Creek
	2. Omaha City	12. Lone Tree
	3. Bellevue	13. Columbus
Modern Border	4 Nebraska City / Table Creek	14. Battle of Big Sandy Creek
	5. Pah-Huku Village	15. Lancaster
	6. Platte Bridge Crossing	16. Kusirr paa'u
Overland Routes	7. Fort Kearny	(Fortress Mountain /
	8. Pawnee Agency	Courthouse Rock)
	9. Omahaw Agency	17. Fontanelle
	10. Dead Timbers	

Incident at Battle Creek, Nebraska
July 13, 1859

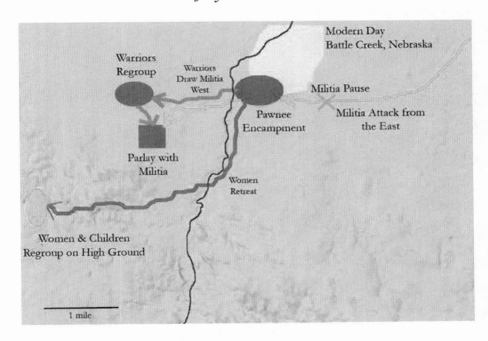

List of Characters

Entirely fictional characters in parenthesis

Pawnee

Petalasharo II a/k/a Man Chief — *Chaui* Pawnee Sub Chief/Great Chief

(Pahaat Icas) a/k/a Red Turtle — *Petalasharo*'s first wife

Petalasharo — I Late and legendary Great Chief

(Rulasharo) — *Skidi* Pawnee medicine man, *Petalasharo*'s father

Big Axe — *Skidi* Pawnee Head Chief

Sharitarish Malan a/k/a Angry Chief — Pawnee Great Chief

Sharitarish Tiki a/k/a Little Anger — *Chaui* Pawnee Sub Chief, son of the Great Chief

Horse Chief — *Pitahawirata* Sub Chief

Lechelasharo a/k/a Knife Chief — *Chaui* Pawnee Sub Chief

Tacopohana — *Kitakahaki* Sub Chief

Tahirusawichi — *Chaui* Medicine man

Sky Chief — *Skidi* Sub Chief

(Eerit Ta) a/k/a Seeing Deer — *Chaui* maiden

Whites

Bradigan O'Kelly — Organized Territorial militia officer, Lieutenant

John O'Kelly — U.S. Army regular, Lieutenant, Bradigan's father

Caitlyn O'Kelly — Army wife, Bradigan's mother

John Thayer	Organized Territorial militia commander, Colonel
Thomas Cuming	Territorial Secretary of State/Acting Governor 1854-55
Margaret Murphy Cuming	Territorial First Lady
Julius Sterling Morton	General Assemblyman/Territorial Secretary of State
Henry Leavenworth	Fort Atkinson post Commander/ Colonel
Mrs. William Hamilton	Bellevue hostess
Stephan Burt	Territorial Governor, 1854
Horace Greeley	Editor of the New York Tribune
William Richardson	Territorial Governor, 1855
Samuel W. Black	Territorial Governor, 1859-1861
Donald Fellows	Deputy of Fontanelle
Everett Fellows	Deputy of Fontanelle
Joseph Donovan	Barracks Instructor, Lancaster Settler, Militia 1st Sgt.
John Browz	Abolitionist
Charles Eastman	Nebraska Territorial Attorney
Fenner Ferguson	Nebraska Federal Judge
Samuel Allis	Pawnee Agent
Patrick Davis	Lancaster settler
Jim Goodrich	Lancaster banker
Jeremiah Garrett	Lancaster settler
Eliza Black	Territorial First Lady
Francis Depuy	Elkhorn settler
Sarah Depuy	Elkhorn settler
Jimmy Depuy	Elkhorn settler
Uriah Thomas	Elkhorn settler
Sheriff John Pattison	Sheriff of Fontanelle
John Schoer	Deputy of Fontanelle
Lawrence Robinson	U.S. Army Regular, Fort Kearny Colonel

The Edge of the Frontier

Chapter 1

September 31, 1824
Near the Council Bluffs, Along the Missouri River

From his father's teepee, *Petalasharo* gazed out across the field and trees sheltering the tribe's ponies, and toward the Spanish encampment. Their uniforms, flags, and standards flashed bright and colorful against the fading sunshine along the far hillside. The Indian boy had never seen Spaniards before, but he could see they were very different from the rough French trappers and austere American frontier regulars. Wearing light blue topcoats and glistening golden helmets, the lively cavaliers appeared brilliant in the evening sunshine. It was only close up an observer could see the hard wear the journey from Santa Fe inflicted upon their grime-ridden pantaloons and dusty leather chaps. Great fanfare and noise heralded their arrival the day before, and only toward nightfall had their tents appeared giving the impression the camp was settling down and they were nearing slumber.

The Spaniards encircled their encampment with trusted native allies who were no less colorful in their southwestern finery. The Indians were Utes, brothers of the fierce Comanche who lived like lizards in the desert on the far side of the mountains. Utes had always been allies of the Spaniards, and were therefore enemies of the Pawnee.

The boy wandered over to the edge of the Pawnee horse herd. He traveled much with his father and yet he had never gone on the warpath. Many of the grandmothers of the *Skidi* Pawnee thought he was odd but then he was not of their tribe. Pawnee yes, but his mother was of the *Chaui* band. With a *Chaui* mother and a *Skidi* father the offspring was sure to be singled out for jests and glances, but his mother had not been cowed by the women's whispers. She named him after *Petalasharo*, a man who had demanded respect. *Petalasharo* had been a great Pawnee and former Great Chief of the Pawnee Confederation. His name meant "the commander of men" and he had lived up to it. *Petalasharo* was conqueror of the dreaded Comanche and dispatcher of countless Sioux. It had been presumptuous to name him *Petalasharo,* as if her son had the fierce *Skidi's* blood pulsing through his veins. It was a hero's name for a bashful medicine man's son. She thought it might ease the boy's transition to live with his father's people.

The young boy and namesake to *Petalasharo* turned back toward his encampment where it stretched out over the hill south of the trader's post. His father, *Rulasharo*, brought him here, to Fort Atkinson, to witness the peace ceremony that was half sponsored and half demanded by their new American overseers. Last summer his father left the land of the Pawnee and traveled south along the great Missouri River to St. Louis, where he and other headmen of the upper river tribes were given gifts. The old redheaded soldier chief, William Clark, boasted the Americans would soon spread through the lands of all the tribes and everyone would live in peace. The Spaniards and their mighty king across the far water would no longer trade or war with the Pawnee. All trade should go through the Americans and the father in Washington would protect them. A Spanish war against the Pawnee would be a war upon the Great White Father himself. Clark promised the Pawnee would be treated as powerful allies and given many gifts, while the Spaniards would grovel before the soldiers of the powerful Great White Father. All of this was to be good, and the Great White Father would see how strong and friendly was the Pawnee Nation.

Within the Council Bluffs cantonment, set up high on the wooded crests above the Missouri, an even younger lad stretched his small frame to peer through a rifle port at the bright red and gold banners hanging limp in the late morning light. John O'Kelly was all of five years old. Taking quick advantage of his mother's brief distraction with John's younger brother, the boy ran to the redoubt to catch a glimpse of the world beyond the fort's walls. Beside him stood his father's immediate superior, Colonel Henry Leavenworth. The colonel wore the striking blue of the Missouri State Militia rather than the deeper blue of the federal army. He was tall and slim, seemingly too slim to last a prairie winter. No one doubted his grit however.

John looked up at the distinguished, gray-haired American colonel surveying the scene with childlike wonder. Leavenworth's eye squinted through an eyepiece as he looked to the Spanish delegation and the camps of the Pawnee tribes to the north. The colonel glanced down at the dark-headed lad and gave a friendly wink. The bashful boy looked down and ran off to find his mother

Colonel Leavenworth, federal commander of the cantonment, expected the Spaniards and he knew the Spanish crown's royal envoys never traveled light. They were guests of the United States government but they looked as if they were ready for a brawl. Nearly five hundred Indian mercenaries had accompanied a brigade of Imperial Spanish *cabelleria*. It was the largest Spanish military entourage to travel north of the Platte River.

The politicians in the east had organized the peace negotiations. The United States War Department hoped to flex federal muscle in this extreme western outpost. Thomas Jefferson had purchased the sprawling lands of great Louisiana more than twenty years before but American power and influence had been slow to creep into the hinterlands. Mixed populations of French and Spanish traders still fought with the shifting alliances of competing plains tribes. The Pawnee had been extremely aggressive raiding Spanish outposts in northern Mexico and the Great Basin. These raids grew so persistent the Spaniards leveled protests in Washington. The Americans had to bring the Pawnee under control. The Pawnee Confederation was at the peak of its power and masters of both banks of the Platte for four hundred miles upriver. Their complete control of the fur trade made them attractive allies for the American newcomers. The American plan was to make the Pawnee enter an accord with the Spaniards in exchange for American trading privileges and military assistances. If the tribe refused, they would be treated the same as their *Arikara* cousins a decade earlier, when a hasty alliance was struck with the *Yankotoni* Sioux, and an *Arikara* encampment was attacked and slaughtered. So far so good, the head chiefs of the Pawnee had been far more flexible than the diplomats had anticipated.

Colonel Leavenworth trailed his looking glass to the northwest and saw the representatives of the Pawnee Confederation making camp with their families. The Pawnee people were more than a single nation. They were a military alliance of four independent tribes. The mystical *Skidi*, the warlike *Kitakahaki*, the vigilant *Pitahawirata* and finally, the diplomatic and regal *Chaui*. Over the last century each tribe had put aside their squabbles to form the Pawnee Confederation. They became lords of the Platte River Valley. The colonel thought that it was good that the Pawnee Treaty had been drafted and agreed upon by the diverse Pawnee chiefs yesterday. It did not matter that their translators had not gotten into the details. The chiefs had struck their mark. At least half of the colonel's job was sewn up. But true diplomacy needed to continue. It remained necessary to convince the Spaniards, and their new friends among the Indians of the Missouri, that the American government had the will, and the power, to end thievery and depravations along the Santa Fe border.

The colonel was a career frontier soldier and it was his job was to keep the peace. His main concern lay not with the Spanish diplomats and their flashy royal guard but with their native irregulars. He was dubious about the Spanish diplomat's ability to maintain discipline and keep the tribes separated. At least Colonel Leavenworth had secured Big Axe's promise to keep the Pawnee in check. Big Axe assured him that the braves under his charge, two hundred and fifty *Skidi* and *Chaui*, would respect the peace of the Great White Father. They would respect this peace until the Calumet Pipe was smoked, terms secured with the foreign diplomats, and the Spaniards had returned to their Mexican provinces. The powerful brave, Big Axe, stated the Pawnee Great Chief himself, *Sharitarish Malan*, had given this guarantee.

The following afternoon long cedar tables were dragged out and taken onto the parade ground. The colonel himself directed the placement of each thick bench knowing that the Spaniards expected European precision and formality to be followed, even with frontier diplomacy. The Pawnee followed Big Axe and their great men proudly into the encampment of the white soldiers. *Petalasharo* trailed with the followers trying to keep his eyes upon his father. The women and children were unusually reserved due to the strangeness of their surroundings and the men were quiet and serious. This was not the Pawnee way. Their peace councils featured much feasting and dancing, but the boy knew many of the white man's ways were unusual.

As the Pawnee head chiefs were seated in the place of honor, to the right of Colonel Leavenworth and his guards, the Spanish delegation let loose a tremendous blast with their golden trumpets. A line of Spanish lancers entered the fort's gate and the attaché from Santa Fe was introduced. The boy noticed the Spaniards had not brought their friends the Utes with them inside the fort.

Petalasharo found what followed mundane, even had he understood all of the words. Many men stood and spoke through a series of translators and it seemed to drag interminably. Even the dignified chiefs sitting cross-legged between the white color guards shifted their weight from time to time and looked about as the sun traveled across the sky. *Petalasharo* noticed that there were other boys within the fort, both white and Indian, who seemed as bored as the Pawnee children. Gradually, as young children do, they timidly began to circle one another before the boldest among them spoke up and they began to tease and play. *Petalasharo* was drawn to a boy practically hidden beneath a brown forage hat. The Indian boy could not understand the other child's words but he knew they were close in age. The white boy had a floppy bushwhacker's hat that hung down low below his ears giving the boy the face of a willow tree. The white boy reached out and ran his dusty finger through *Petalasharo's* roached hair cusp. At first, *Petalasharo* shied away but then he began to laugh. Soon the Indian had snatched away the drooping hat and the boys were chasing one another through the crowd. They were off in a separate world, as children often find themselves, chasing and laughing and roughhousing.

Time passed quickly through those moments and the end of the council was announced by a tremendous blare of trumpets. Soon *Petalasharo's* father was dragging him out the gates but before the Pawnee had left the parade grounds, John had run up to his new friend and gave him his hat. *Petalasharo* looked up at his father in desperation! What did he have to trade? *Rulasharo* understood his son's concern and spoke softly to him. *Petalasharo* took off a leather-braided necklace with a stone-carved turtle pendant. The turtle was a powerful spirit animal to the Pawnee but the boy handed it over eagerly. Johnny O'Kelly looked at it questioningly. At first, he thought that it was a girl's present, but the Indian boy offered it so genuinely he took it and put the amulet in his pocket. It would be many years before his son would be given the opportunity to return the hastily offered gift.

Chapter 2

May 3, 1827
Pah-Hur Rock

A few years later *Petalasharo* and his father went on a spiritual pilgrimage to one of the sacred sites of the Pawnee, the sacred site of *Pah-Hur*.

"Surely this isn't it father?" *Petalasharo's* expression sank as he gazed up the dusty outcrop of rock that lifted out of the earth less than two antelope's leap from their horses. "My visions of *Par-Hur* were far larger. Why would the sacred animals gather here? There are much bigger bluffs on the prairie." *Par-Hur* was not a formidable butte by anyone's stretch of the imagination. But it was here, *Par-Hur*, the guide rock where *Rulasharo* brought his son. The Pawnee believed the sacred animals would gather in its shadow and discuss the matters of man. It was one of the most revered locations for the people. The three layered slate rock projection elevated twenty feet into the air and pointed toward the direction of the winter's setting sun. It was hidden along the low northern hills of the Republican River Valley and looked completely out of place. It was as if the chief of the Pawnee gods, *Tirawahat*, had lost the formation and dropped it on the spot by accident.

"Why wouldn't the animals gather here?" *Rulasharo* asked smiling at his son's disappointment. "Perhaps they should gather at the Fortress Mountain?"[1]

Petalasharo thought and said, "If I were a spirit animal I would want to hold my council on the top of a mountain closer to the star gods."

---

[1]   The Fortress Mountain is now known as Courthouse Rock in western Nebraska.

"It is good that you would like to be closer to the gods, but the spirit animals do not need to move to commune with the stars. Some things can best be seen from a distance. As night comes and we begin to pray, you will see of what I speak."

The boy set up a small camp below the lengthening shadow of the rock. It was in the darkest part of the shade cast by the setting sun where the Pawnee felt the spirit animals gathered by a mystical council fire. Father and son shared a small meal of dried antelope meat and corn bread. They watched as the rock pointed toward the sun as it disappeared into the earth. Despite a chill coming with the darkness, *Rulasharo* refused to start a fire. He assured the boy they had nothing to fear from the animals and *Petalasharo* was put at ease. He listened as the bird's songs stilled and the coyotes lifted their voices. The heavens were clear and the blanket of stars seemed to *Petalasharo* to be the most brilliant night sky he had ever seen. The two Pawnee mystics, father and son, felt blessed that night with good spiritual medicine and they engaged in a long quiet conversation.

"Father, what do the white men believe about our star gods?"

"This is a question best asked to a white man son, but I will answer as best I can. The white man believes his god is the only god that matters. He is strict and he says our gods do not exist. In their world, his god is our god too. The white man feels the Pawnee choose not to recognize the true god."

"Why does the white man believe that our gods do not exist? Even our enemies understand that gods exists for their people as we believe their gods exist for them."

"The whites, whether American or Spanish, believe the people exist for the god. The god does not exist for the people."

"Do the whites believe there is only one god?"

Rulasharo pondered for a moment; "It is something that has always confused me. I feel you must be a white man to understand, although I have met some *Kitakahaki* who claim to understand.[2] They only have one god but he is three gods—They have their great god and he is the father of their human god, Jesus Christ. They also believe in a spirit god who surrounds the first two gods and touches the white people with fire. All of these gods are one god."

---

[2] In 1827 a few southern *Kitakahaki* had converted to Christianity.

"Has anyone seen the spirit god burn people?" a wide-eyed *Petalasharo* asked.

"I have not heard this was seen by the whites, but it must have happened to their people in the past."

"These beliefs seem strange to me, father."

Rulasharo hugged his son, "Our beliefs seem strange to them as well. They have a book that tells them of their gods, especially their human god, Jesus. He is the favorite of the Black Robes."[3]

"It must be hard to believe in a god that you cannot see Father. I am glad that we have our star gods whom we see." *Petalasharo* continued, "I am glad we have our wind gods we can feel and the direction gods we can face. I am happy we have our spirit animals to help our people survive and give us medicine to cure our sicknesses. It is good to have *Tirawahat*[4] and the Corn Mother.[5] They show us their love in their daily gifts. I am glad our gods are in our life and are not as mysterious as the three gods who are essentially one god of the whites."

"It may actually be easier to believe in a confusing god than it is to follow simple gods. It is best if men do not understand their gods because when men become certain of the unknown they close their hearts and minds to other thoughts. *Petalasharo,* my son, always believe in our gods because you are Pawnee. The ways of the gods will always be a mystery to men and do not be led astray by priests, medicine men, or shamans who say they have all the answers. They are men and cannot know the ways of the gods. I tell you this again—men cannot know the ways of the gods."

Rulasharo looked up to the sky and his face was lit by the glow of the starlight. He continued, "We can never understand whether the gods are one or many. We must always remember that we are not gods but must pray there are gods because without gods all of our questions will go unanswered for all time. With gods in our universe we can hope they will someday explain our mysteries to us. Perhaps in this life or when our eyes close for the eternal night."

The young boy absorbed all of his father's words and kept them close to his heart. His beliefs in the Pawnee pantheon and the spirit animals, the Pawnee sacred bundles and sacred sites, never wavered. He remained true to his father's request, and the Pawnee beliefs, until the end of his days.

---

3   Jesuit missionaries
4   The greatest of the Pawnee gods.
5   The matriarch goddess –bringer of life and nourishment.

Chapter 3

August 20, 1832
Bellevue Trader's Post

Just over nine miles to the south of the Council Bluffs, along the east side of the Missouri River, nestled a low-lying meadow. Nearly a hundred years before, French fur traders set up an encampment to gather beaver furs harvested from the nearby marshes and streams. They called the area *Belle Vue*, or beautiful view, after its picturesque surroundings. The encampment had developed as a gathering place for white men and the neighboring tribes and the trading post prospered. With the coming of the American military and following the negotiations at Fort Atkinson, a small army post was established. Lieutenant John O'Kelly was assigned to this tiny garrison and within a year of his arrival at the post, he married the daughter of a trapper, Miss Caitlyn Murphy. The couple, in the best Irish Catholic tradition, set upon the task of raising a large and boisterous family.

Bellevue had become a large trader's outpost and a porter's storage paradise. Warehouses lined every street and, in the beginning, excess building material was common. Willows and cottonwoods lined both sides of the Missouri below the river bluffs. Suitable housing material, however, was less common as the lighter woods rotted quickly and most homes remained sod. O'Kelly was not content to raise a family in dirt. After three years John constructed a new wood frame home out of planking left over from docking material. The ash wood planks had been floated up river for the purpose of constructing docks for the burgeoning waterway trade. The lieutenant purchased the unused lumber at bottom of the barrel prices and went right to work. The family realized that while the two-room home was smaller and draftier than their old sod house, it was also drier and easier to keep clean. Caitlyn O'Kelly appreciated the novelty of being the only officer's wife capable of entertaining the ladies of the post in such style. She was delighted. Now they had room to entertain. Before the construction of the O'Kelly home, the ladies gathered at the enlisted men's dining hall or in the commanding officer's home for their quilting or poetry readings. The O'Kelly's new house had an additional function as well, a task that Caitlyn ranked as one of great importance. She took it upon herself to instruct all Catholic children in required catechism. They met three times weekly not including, of course, the occasional Sunday Mass at the Trader's Hall conducted by traveling missionaries.

It was indeed hard to be a devoted Catholic on the American frontier, Mrs. O'Kelly thought, but the children deserved to understand the tenets of the Holy Mother Church. Its teachings would serve them well in life whether among the heathens or misguided Protestants. Each Tuesday and Thursday she would sit the three children down at the rough-hewn wooden table for their lessons. Caitlyn would always start first, her eyes closed, head bowed:

> Angel of God, my guardian dear,
> To whom His love, commits me here.
> Ever this day be at my side,
> To light and guard, to rule and guide.

The young ones absorbed these lessons like small sponges, eager for the attention of their doting mother as much as for scripture. It was a happy and gentle time.

Lieutenant O'Kelly provided for his family through his military wages and the O'Kellys had settled down to a consistent and nurturing routine. The children played along the muddy streets and fished along the river, waving to the increasing numbers of river craft and steamboats. Indians and traders often conducted business along the river's edge. And, of course, the children watched the bustle about the docks. Thus, their lessons weren't limited to scripture. They often gathered down along the docks amongst the traders and Indians listening to tales of the frontier. The O'Kelly urchins quickly learned common greetings in *Omahaw*, Pawnee, and Otoe. As they grew older they learned the languages of the *Omahaw* and *Skidi* Pawnee who were most often swapping trinkets and food near the wharves. Unknown to the children, however, the economics of the fur exchange were rapidly changing. Shifting fashion preferences in far off markets like Boston and Paris cut back on the prices and profitability for the men who lived on the frontier. Confusion and frustration increased among both the white traders and their erstwhile Indian partners. Land was the new commodity and steamboats brought more and more immigrants and picked up fewer and fewer pelts and furs. A way of life was changing and no one understood why.

While the fur trade stagnated, the wharves and warehouses, buildings and pathways remained. Men of vision saw this infrastructure as a potential opportunity. Knowing the federal government was changing its role along the lower Missouri these men saw the abandoned buildings as potential depots to supply western outposts. This insight was hidden to many men at the army post and they grew anxious of reassignment. No one wanted to be reposted to an even more remote location such as the forts of Kearny or Laramie.

The O'Kelly family remained indifferent to the rumors whirling around the Bellevue Trader's Post. Caitlyn would only sigh. She knew they would go wherever the Good Lord and the Grand Republic could use a man of Lieutenant John O'Kelly's talents.

Chapter 4

Petalasharo watched the wounded Pawnee braves trudge into the village. Many grasped for water handed out to them by old men. The villagers were curious what fate had befallen them; the men looked as if an enormous prairie fire had smoked and bloodied their skin. They leaned heavily against one another's shoulders and lances, and the old ones gathered to hear the men's words. The tribe learned their warriors had won a victory from mumbled remarks. Most of the Pawnee were confused. The exhausted braves appeared far closer to men who had been ambushed and defeated than fighters returning in triumph.

Petalasharo sat on a fallen oak speaking with the younger warriors as they looked upon their recently acquired scalp parcels and replenished with dried jerky and water. Their eyes spoke eloquently of shock and disbelief; for there had never been a battle like it. The boy listened how the braves fought at the Big Sandy Creek, a dry gravel trench less than a hundred miles to the southeast.

The numbers involved in the combat were beyond counting. Rather than a clash that lasted minutes or hours, this fight continued on for five suns. *Upirikutsu,* or the morning star war god, had surely possessed the fighters, and drove them to insanity. No one could remember a prairie battle where warriors continued to fight, kill, flee and then return to fight again. It was a madness inspired by a sadistic god. They did not fight for game or horses, women or hides. They fought for land and they discovered in conflicts over territory, there is no retreat.

The Pawnee and Otoe had been gaming near the Otoe's large village on the Big Nemaha River. Some Missouri, Ponca, and friendly Osages were there as well. The trapping had been good further west, and the Indians were returning from trading at Bellevue. A wild call interrupted a hand game that the Sioux, their traditional enemies, were coming down from the north. The Indian allies were hot for their blood.

"How did they get so far into our territory?" Shouted the Otoe. "We must fight and drive them out!"

The Pawnee were quick to join the attack and a hasty alliance was galvanized. The number of braves grew to rival the leaves on the trees. As the Pawnee, Otoe, and Osage rode toward the Sioux the grass was trampled for miles by the pounding hooves.

At the crooked sand creek called the *Urutu Kaku* by the Pawnee, the battle was joined. The most reckless died first. The Pawnee had the advantage of surprise and poured into the Sioux encampment flinging arrows and hatchets in all directions. The size of the gathering was unknown but it was obviously very large. The camp's horse herd spread over the hills along the horizon. After the first moments of confusion, the Sioux rallied on the far side of the camp and counterattacked. Bewildered by the Sioux numbers, the Pawnee retreated and rode over the valley crest. The Otoe waited in ambush. The Sioux rode down a narrowing defile and were surrounded on three sides by archers and muskets. Their horses were slaughtered as the steeds found themselves unable to wheel and turn. The Sioux tumbled from their mounts and bodies were broken under terrified animals. Still, many Sioux came on. On this day they seemed to know no retreat. What was this insanity? Why did the northern raiders continue to ride into the valley in greater and greater numbers? Who could count them all? The sand creek turned into a red paste and the horse's bodies dammed the stream. The Sioux began to press the advantage of their numbers, yet the allies chose to fight as if they were amidst their women and food stores.

The battle had already provided plenty of war honors for the invaders, yet the Sioux chose not to cut and run. The first night came. The hills burned with campfires of the Sioux. The allies peered out at their antagonist's fires wondering why they had not left their camps. Had not enough scalps been claimed today?

The Otoe held a war dance and a big drum was produced to fill the darkness with their rhythm and chants. The Otoe sang songs of anger. Songs that would protect them from incursions of raiders bent upon pillage and destruction. This was their land and their songs would float among the hills. They had heard of what occurred to other tribes after the Sioux had invaded. The Otoe swore they would not be driven out. Never again would these trespassers enter this valley. If the Sioux would not leave this night they would not live to see the next.

As the sun rose, the tribes joined battle once again and the fighting was even more crazed and bitter. The Otoe rode into the midst of the Sioux and the fighting was hand-to-hand. As the warriors had killed one another, the Otoe ponies broke their legs as they twisted and kicked at the invaders. Yet the Sioux were relentless. They came and fought, retreated and died. They came, scalped, retreated and died. They came, killed, retreated and died some more. Madness was the only description and the psychosis continued until nightfall. With the darkness the battlefield was yielded to the scavengers of the night; hawks, crows, and wolves. Coyotes howled and fought over the dead and their voices joined the Indians' chants rising to the heavens. The Sioux campfires remained and maintained a silent and seething vigil.

The sun rose the next day and the Sioux returned. The Otoe, or at least those that remained, waited to kill them. This was not a battle for scalps, counting coup, or singing war songs. This was a battle to kill and die. Hardened by the madness, the Pawnee joined the desperate killing of the fray. Without the assistance of their Pawnee brothers, the Otoe would have lost the day.

After dusk the Sioux campfires remained. No one slept, understanding they were no longer in possession of their bodies or their minds. The war gods of the Pawnee, Otoe, and Sioux were now in control, and the following morning they flung the antagonists at one another again. The horses had all been slaughtered so the warriors ran on foot to the reddish brown Big Sandy Creek. They killed one another and when no one was left to kill, they warred upon the corpses, scalping the dead and defiling their bodies. As night fell, the survivors limped back to their camps.

The Pawnee stared out at the campfires in the hills and to their horror realized that the Sioux were not fleeing. Disappointed and confused that the Sioux refused to leave, the Pawnee braves thought only their retreat would end this madness. Many wanted to pursue such a course, after all, was this not the Otoe's fight rather than their own? *Tacopohana*, a young but crafty leader, now spoke to the Pawnee. All of the more experienced chiefs had been killed. With a cool breeze floating in from the north, *Tacopohana* spoke to his soldiers in the moonlight.

"The Sioux for whom we have been battling are not normal men for they are men possessed. Is it rational for a warrior to continue to fight in another man's land when there is no hope for victory? These warriors are not looking for scalps or ponies. They are looking for conquest. Fighting for conquest is a white man's curse and the Sioux have become so possessed. They have spent too many years with easy conquests and they must be taught our land will not be theirs. Conquest for land is not a war trophy like a scalp or a pony. Conquest for land gives no glory to the brave. It gives the glory to those who follow the brave to make use of his death and spoils he has won. The Sioux who will follow the ones we kill today will take advantage of our weakened condition. They wish to conquer the Otoe land. The Sioux have more warriors than we and they know they could succeed. Once that has been done, the Sioux will wish to conquer others and the Pawnee will be next. This is as much our fight as it is the Otoe."

The braves sadly nodded for there was little glory in this war of conquest. Why could people not stay within their own land and raid as in the days of old?

"Take up your great hearts my braves!" *Tacopohana* announced. "For tomorrow the Sioux will die rather than conquer! We will fight them in a new way and there will be no more mourning in our lodges."

The Pawnee listened to their new leader and adopted a new tactic. No one slept that night for they were too busy binding two bows together, overlapping one another so that the bows were far longer. They then spent time restringing the ends. Thus bound, *Tacopohana* taught them to lie on their backs, hold the bows with their moccasins, and draw the arrow and string with both hands. They could then launch their arrows great distances, easily reaching the creek bed from the heights of their encampment. As the morning sun appeared over the horizon, they found Sioux warriors waiting to battle along the creek among the corpses. This time their challenge was not met with a charge, but by a hail of arrows from unimaginable distances. The slaughter continued, but this time it was only the Sioux that died. Eventually the Pawnee surrounded the remaining warriors and captured the survivors who hid underneath the bodies.

The last Pawnee to die was *Tacopohana* himself, who was killed by a knife to the throat by a Sioux pretending to be dead. Enraged, the Pawnee decided no one should escape. They hoped to kill off the madness of conquest by killing all the Sioux. Enormous pyres were built and the survivors were burned to spare themselves from their disease. The Pawnee used dry brittle wood and stoked the flames to make sure the warriors died quickly. The Sioux gods made their braves suffer enough and the Pawnee had wanted these warriors to end their days mercifully. After the screaming had died down, the Pawnee and their few remaining allies looked out thankfully at the darkened hills. They understood that this had been a battle very different from anything before. Far from their helpless ones, there had been no reason to continue the fight. Far from their provisions and lodges, the braves from all of the tribes fought for no other reason than an inexplicable bloodlust. Surely it was a battle delivered by the gods. They would have to consult their medicine men upon returning to their land.

They needed to pray because this did not seem like a victory. In looking out at their smoldering pyres, the Pawnee knew nothing else could have been done—yet they still felt badly. The night oppressed them as if the gods of the cardinal directions were angry. The air smelled sweet with burnt hair and flesh. Their mouths were dry and the braves spit powdered stringy blood that had a salty tang. The salty tang tasted like guilt.

Petalasharo heard these tales and shuddered for days. The mothers and orphans keened the death cries for many nights. A few maidens, desperate with anguish, cut their wrists and ran to the river to rub sand into the wounds. They chose not to live without their loved ones. *Petalasharo* saw how horrible the effects of war were. Would he ever fight in a battle like the one on the banks of the Big Sandy Creek? In the future he would go on raiding parties and lead men in conflict, yet he was always tormented by the stories told by those exhausted young Pawnee braves. Nightmares of Big Sandy Creek lasted the rest of his life.[6]

---

[6] The Big Sandy Creek Battle probably took place somewhere in modern Jefferson County, possibly where the creek runs into the Little Blue River. Legend suggests that sixteen thousand Native Americans participated in the conflict resulting in three thousand Sioux casualties and two thousand Pawnee-Otoe-Osage casualties. Oral history relates that after the battle had ended, the Pawnee burned seven hundred captured Sioux.

Chapter 5

June 26, 1840
Bellevue, Nebraska Territory

"I am so proud of you Caitlyn! We have another son!" John exclaimed as he knelt by his wife's bed in the infirmary.

Caitlyn lay back cradling the infant with an enormous yet tired smile. "What shall we name him John? We are truly blessed. Our children are all fine and healthy!"

John wiped the perspiration from his wife's brow with a towel soaked in lavender water. He could see the joy in her eyes. "I have thought about this Caitlyn. If it was a girl I would have chosen Amy because we are blessed. It is a boy. We should call him Bradigan."

Caitlyn smiled looking into the baby's face. "Bradigan? Yes—Brady. I like that."

Territorial Nebraska

Chapter 1

June 30, 1852
Bellevue Port along the Missouri River

The packed steamboat station house smelled of human sweat and burned tobacco so Mrs. O'Kelly kept her scented handkerchief over her nose. Bradigan tried to bury his nose in a *Far West Quarterly* to avoid the eyes of their fellow travelers looking askance at his mother. He knew she did not mean to seem haughty in public but his mother always embarrassed him so.

It was a big day for the family. Bradigan, his mother, and sister waited for the steamboat to take him down the Missouri to St. Louis. Bradigan O'Kelly was a happy blonde-headed child who followed his older siblings in nearly everything. As everyone had grown up and sought their way in the world Brady had followed his father's lead and looked for a career in the military. He had enrolled in the army officer's training school and he was to report to Jefferson Barracks just south of St. Louis. The first academic muster was to gather on Independence Day but Mrs. O'Kelly's son wanted to arrive early to settle into his new surroundings. The young man was hopeful doing well could possibly lead to a spot being open for him at West Point. Attending the elite army training school had been his dream since he was little. But now, despite his mother's hovering and idle chatter, his attention focused upon the words as he read;

> "The indisputable advantage and idealism of the American Republic has a God given mission to complete; the divinity of the responsibility no less authorized by providence than the teachings of Christ, to spread our American virtues and

civilization to the far reaches of the New World; Life, liberty, and the true pursuit of happiness."

Jane McFee he thought to himself. She seems like a smart lady.[7]

A long, deep whistle from the dock announced the arrival of the steamship *Bertrand*.[8] Bradigan abruptly folded the magazine and stuffed it into his satchel. He hugged his mother, and buoyantly said his goodbyes. Mrs. O'Kelly handed him a ruby stone rosary and made a quick sign of the cross over his forehead.

"Bradigan remember to register with the parish once you arrive." His mother reminded him with a mist in her eyes. "St. Louis is a good town for Catholics. It is far more accommodating to our religion than this wild frontier. I remember my time there so fondly." Her eyes glazed over for a moment with a distant memory but she fought her tears and returned to the present needlessly adjusting his scarf.

"Yes mama." He said as he practically ran down the gangplank.

The steamer's great wheel began to churn the muddy water with determination as the great boat slowly backed into the open channel. With a tremendous grind and shifting of gears the boat reversed direction and followed the flow southward. His mother knew that it was down this river where her Bradigan would grow to manhood and become a soldier. The thought was not much of a comfort as she saw it disappear around a bend.

The trip downstream went smoothly and within three days Bradigan arrived at his destination. St. Louis had been built upon the fur trade. From that "soft gold" of beaver and otter pelts the city had developed a veneer of culture and opulence. Behind the wharves and large flat warehouses stood elegant French and Spanish styled mansions owned by prosperous merchants. He made his way through the crowded markets and hopped a supply wagon to the institution. The Jefferson Barracks could not have contrasted more from colorful and exciting St. Louis.

---

[7]   Jane McFee was a leading and early proponent of Manifest Destiny.

[8]   The steamboat *Bertrand* sank April 1, 1865, just north of Omaha on the Nebraska side of the river. The river channel meandered causing a controversy over the rights to its excavation in 1968 between Iowa and Nebraska. Its artifacts are now preserved in a museum at the Desoto National Wildlife Refuge.

The plebe shelters were drab functional buildings designed with absolute austerity. Most of his fellow students were as quiet and as cheerless as the dull environs. Bradigan soon learned his instructors were southerners who were instantly recognizable by their stern and arrogant accents and precise manners. A few had fought in the Texas Rebellion and then returned to pursue careers in military instruction. Bradigan found his professors unduly harsh and inexplicably distant. They seemed to treat their racing hounds, slaves, and horses with greater consideration than the young men under their tutelage. It was this oppressive atmosphere that Bradigan objected to. The tyranny quelled all of the young students' spirits as effectively as a cold pan of water on a frigid afternoon.

There was one exception to the heavy handed teachers, First Sergeant Joseph Donovan who taught practical engineering. O'Kelly related to the gentle and soft spoken former enlisted man. Unfortunately, the sergeant retired after O'Kelly's first year to go into farming.

O'Kelly's classes were difficult. Many nights, especially during the first few months, he cried himself to sleep muffling his sobs to hide the sound from his fellow plebes. It was not all terrible. He enjoyed the courses in language and history but the mathematics classes were nearly incomprehensible. He was easy going and quiet and made friends slowly but steadily. Still, he preferred to spend his time alone. He would often wander away from the barracks to feel the breeze on the prairie or watch the river flow southward. Along the riverbanks, Bradigan would occasionally run across hovels of escaped slaves fleeing to the north. He would give them food and a kind word but that is where his assistance ended. His instructors would not look kindly to aiding fugitives of lawful authority.

The first year plebes' mornings were spent in dreary lectures regarding the tactics of Alcibiades, Alexander, and Caesar while the afternoons were consumed with drill and equestrian pursuits. He was a competent enough student to continue progression in all his coursework, but O'Kelly was well aware his marks were in the lower tier of the class.

The seasons passed and then the years. He grew more comfortable in his surroundings and in his second year he was allowed to adopt and train a horse. The animal and its master became inseparable during his time off exploring the fields and meadows surrounding the academy. During the third year of his schooling, his mother died of cholera. He learned of it through a trader who remembered his family from years past. A letter arrived from his father confirming the news three days later. His father died the day after writing the letter. He arranged for three masses to be conducted with the local pastor and managed to secure a two week furlough to return home.

His return home was bittersweet as Bradigan took in all the changes. His father's old post had turned into a proper town site with streets legally platted out and organized. Bellevue had grown with merchants, craftsman, settlers and preachers. Gone were the rough fur traders and hunters and only a few settled "civilized" Indians braved the trip into the community. He looked out at the bustle of the town and thought his mother would have approved; a small Catholic parish had sprouted up at the edge of the market square. The priest came to visit the boy holding a small box. He said that John O'Kelly wanted Brady to have it. Inside was the small turtle pendant. It was not much of a bequest, but Bradigan held it close remembering the story his father had told him about how he received it many years ago.

Brady decided once his academics were over he would return home. He no longer dreamed of West Point. Bradigan thought he could enroll in the local militia. Surely the organized militia could use someone with his military pedigree.

Chapter 2

October 18, 1854
Bellevue, Nebraska Territory

A palatable hush descended on the town's grand Mission House. The nineteen-room mansion was owned by one of Bellevue's leading citizens, the Reverend William Hamilton. The reverend and his wife were desperate to make a good impression upon their dignified guests. Despite of the silence of the gathering, the stubborn hostess, Mrs. Rosemary Hamilton, desperately tried to refresh drinks and engage in small talk. But the gasps and moans from upstairs distressed and worried the visitors. The chairman of the town council, who had eyes on a lucrative political career, a fine man but prone to brusqueness, asked about the governor but it was understood that nothing more could be done. Sworn in as the first governor of Nebraska Territory only two days earlier, Francis Burt languished in the master bedroom desperate for a breath. Beyond the point of exhaustion his body twisted and curled while trying to get air into his lungs. His wife begged for him to take deeper breaths but it was simply to no avail. His hands and face continued to grow whiter and colder. His sad eyes would search the far corners of the room beyond the point of desperation. Searching for peace but knowing it could only be found in the grave.

The governor had caught a chill on the steamer heading up the Missouri River from St Louis. President Franklin Pierce's chosen one was a South Carolina Democrat who had never been west of Appalachia. He was not acclimated to the brisk northwestern wind that blew southward from the upper Missouri. As he and his entourage disembarked on the pier in Bellevue he felt a tightness and sting in his chest. Few onlookers noticed the slight rasp in his voice while the oath of office was delivered.

He delivered the solemn pledge with an air of authority but the man practically collapsed into the carriage with his wife close behind. The couple was delivered to their hosts' home where the new governor was immediately taken to the upstairs bedroom.

The following day the locals knew something was wrong when the governor's wife declined the invitations for the daylight gatherings. Like frontier provincials everywhere the elite depended upon their ceremonies. It was a tiny bit of civilization the gentry, shopkeepers, and politicians imported into the new territories. Claim club meetings, ribbon cuttings and gatherings were planned with precise deliberation. While the local politicians grudgingly rescheduled a number of events, the populace, particularly the ladies, stubbornly refused to cancel the ball. The grand inaugural ball had been scheduled to take place at the Hamilton's as their Mission House mansion had a full piano. The event shouldn't be too difficult for the governor as he simply needed to make an appearance.

The locals wanted to impress upon the new governor the obvious benefits of maintaining the seat of the territorial government in Bellevue. Why, no other city had so much as a boardwalk to stroll upon without sinking your boots in the Nebraska mud. While the citizens of Bellevue took pride in the churches, homes and streets that reflected prosperity and order, they were also a superstitious lot. The dreadful coughing and labored breathing filtering down to the front foyer could not be ignored.

As each couple arrived, Mrs. Hamilton reassured the guests that it was nothing but a slight fever, and the ladies and gentlemen tried to pretend as much. But just as the last guests made their appearance, the exhausted man died. The shattered first lady absorbed herself in the Book of Common Prayers and ignored the sincere condolences of the well-dressed strangers.

Everyone understood the significance of the man's passing.

Colonel John Thayer of the Nebraska Organized Militia expressed his sorrow to the hosts and removed himself from the premises as quickly as possible. He knew that he needed to return to Omaha City and inform the Territorial Secretary of State, Thomas Cuming, the new governor had died. Rather than have the South Platters of the Nebraska General Assembly appoint a temporary governor, the constitution made succession very clear. Thomas Cuming, who the colonel took as a pompous songbird, was the new governor of Nebraska Territory. Still, he did not want some other scoundrel to ingratiate himself with the secretary and steal his recently wrangled appointment as head of the militia.

The colonel glanced over his shoulder to motion for his aid de camp to accompany him and saw the senators and councilmen trying to catch a word. He politely but firmly continued on for he knew they were all creatures of John Sterling Morton, the speaker of the general assembly, and he knew he could not tally in Bellevue.

Colonel Thayer and his young second in command, Lieutenant Bradigan O'Kelly, rode north down into the cedar-lined hills hugging Pappio Creek. On the steep banks of the nearly dry stream they met with the color guard detachment that was to maintain its position between Bellevue and Omaha City to be given word before entering Bellevue for the planned inaugural parade. Sergeant Adkins was surprised to see the colonel ride off with his adjutant at that late hour but saluted each man in turn and offered his superiors a cup of coffee.

"There is no time sergeant," the colonel said. "Your men need to go to the Platte Crossing Bridge and then send word the regiment is not to leave Nebraska City absent my written order. Lieutenant, please prepare a dispatch." He continued as his aid searched for a writing instrument. "Sergeant, keep a guard on the ferries, allow no civilian traffic to cross to the south, not even Speaker Morton himself without my word. You don't need to give a reason just say military necessity. No more details. If old Julius Sterling needs to talk with his old friends in Nebraska City tonight he's going to have to get pretty soaked."

As Lieutenant O'Kelly hastily scribbled out a letter for the colonel struggling with the paper and pencil in the near absolute darkness, the sergeant looked confused.

"But sir, I figured we would march in the inaugural parade tomorrow?" The sergeant asked. "We just came from down south."

"Your orders have changed my good man . . . Governor Burt is dead."

Sergeant Adkins looked at his men. "Dead sir?"

"Dead sergeant and our men will not be needed for the funeral. It is more important for you to carry this message to Lieutenant Hawthorne that the regiment is not to leave Nebraska City. He is to listen to no one . . . the council, the sheriff, not even the federals without my word. The regiment must remain in Nebraska City while this mess is sorted through."

The sergeant uncertainly reached for the O'Kelly's dispatch and muttered, "Yes sir, but who is our governor?"

Thayer looked down from his horse and saw the man's consternation and decided to soften his words. "Sergeant, I really don't know. I

understand the men will be disappointed in missing a parade, but we
have the people to look after. The Nebraska Militia cannot be used for
an underhanded purpose. Governor or no governor I take no pleasure in
giving arbitrary orders. But trust me and obey me. I am your commander
and you need not lose sleep over who is my immediate commander. I will
see my militia through this." Thayer saluted and said, "Off with you now,
you have your orders."

Adkins offered a quick salute in return but the colonel and his aide
had already ridden off. They continued to ride through the night only
stopping at a settler's house for the colonel to check his timepiece. They
rode northwest up the Pappio Creek that snaked down the terraced levels
towards the shore of the Missouri River. Omaha City was nearly double
the size of Bellevue and constructed upon three terraces of bottomlands
that rose from the river's west side. Boasting a population nearing a
thousand citizens, the city owed its remarkable growth to the Nebraska
Ferry Company. The ferry company was the brainchild of a number of
Council Bluff investors although most locals referred to the businessmen
as accomplished Iowa swindlers. Chief among these alleged swindlers
were Mr. and Mrs. Thomas Cuming, a remarkably proficient political
and financial couple. While Thomas attained the office of secretary of
Nebraska Territory, quoting Homer and Pericles along the way, his wife
handled their investments. Marriage and politics had been good to them.

Bellevue profited heavily from the fur trade, and like the fur trade,
it was now in decline. Unlike the older town, Omaha City and its
thriving ferry company looked to the river for commerce. The river
and a half-baked notion the Illinois B & O rail line that terminated in
Council Bluff would somehow bridge the great Missouri River and begin
a transcontinental railroad.

These grand schemes were the furthest thing from the colonel's mind
as he and his sidekick stumbled through the dark. Only a few flickering
lamps maintained by the sleepy residents of Omaha City could be seen as
they made their way to the Herndon House.

"It is after 2:00 a.m. Sir. The secretary is surely in bed," protested
Lieutenant O'Kelly as they tied their horses to the hitching post rail
running along Farnham Street.

"Not Thomas." The colonel laughed as he made his way up the steps
to the Hamilton House. "For a man who doesn't like the spirits he is a
true night owl."

The pair met with the valet who motioned the two into the drawing room where, sure enough, the Nebraska Territorial Secretary of State sat speaking with the federal attorney, Charles Eastman.

The secretary's past was somewhat unknown. It was thought he had served with the quartermaster cantonment in Galveston Bay during the Mexican-America war. He had arrived in Omaha and immediately set himself working the ferry docks. He always seemed to have cash. The man was capable but his quick rise confounded his enemies. His most prominent and fiery foil was a fellow politician from south of the Platte River, Julius Sterling Morton. Morton was the opposite of Cuming in ways easily discernible. While Cuming spoke in grand abstracts referring quickly to obscure philosophers and ideas, Morton spoke and acted as a hard-nose practical farmer. He drew analogies from the soil, from the crops and seasons, from cyclical husbandry. His wealth was like his ideas, tangible and personal. He took precise notes with everyone in his debt whether that debt was financial or political. He expected favors to be returned.

Adding to the mystery of Thomas Cuming's past was the source of his wealth. No one was certain whether he was born into it, married into it, or created it on his own. There was even a shadowy rumor Cuming had killed a man in a duel after the war. He lived in the back of a Council Bluff warehouse with his wife who he had shipped in on a steamer from down south in the early 1850s. The couple had continued to flourish. In 1853, Cuming was mysteriously named to head the territory's weights and measures commission by the St. Louis inspector general and from there he slipped his way into the position of territorial secretary of state. Despite their wealth the couple lived simply, Thomas said in the tradition of Cato the Elder. None of his contemporaries knew, or much cared, how Cato the Elder would have lived. His abstractness created a distance among the simple citizens of Omaha City, but it also added an air of dignity.

Secretary Cuming noticed the officers enter while he was sitting by the fireplace enjoying a thin cigar. "Colonel Thayer? This is a truly unexpected surprise! Did the political elbowing down in Bellevue disagree with you so much that you skipped the ball?"

Secretary of State Cuming was a man pleasant to look upon by both sexes. He was a handsome dark haired fellow. Thomas kept his appearance quite precisely wearing his mustache in a thick Italian style and a sculpted goatee. Less than thirty years old the secretary had used his meticulous manners and lofty eloquence to negotiate his position within the hardscrabble game of territorial politics. When push came to shove however, the secretary never compromised his principals as a devoted Whig and an abolitionist. The man lived for Nebraska politics and there was no mystery behind where he stood on most issues. He absolutely detested the compromises the federal government carved into the Kansas-Nebraska Act and was distressed by every territorial legislator south of the Platte.

"Perhaps sipping from the secretary's own bottle will revive you." The territorial attorney, Charles Eastman, who looked well into his cups, offered Thayer a glass.

"You look chilled from your nocturnal ride colonel; please take a glass with my compliments."

"I don't mind if I do, Thomas." Colonel Thayer chose the bottle of Kentucky whisky over the glass and took a mighty swig. He then handed the flask to O'Kelly who politely looked for a glass in order to imbibe.

"These golden spirits will be the end of all of you boys, but please, let it not be said that I am a moralist." Secretary Cuming remarked in half jest. "John, please tell us what can be the cause of this late night visit. Was there trouble at the good governor's ball?"

"There was no ball, Thomas. Governor Burt is dead."

"He is dead, colonel?" Cuming clarified with a hint of disbelief in his voice, "But how can that be? Surely not assassinated?"

"Don't rightly know, Thomas." The colonel said as he followed O'Kelly's lead, picked up a glass, and poured a finger or two. "But he is dead and your rivals are scared. I have never seen old J.S. Morton paler in his life. Governor Burt looked healthy enough getting off the steamer but something terrible got into his lungs, died from consumption, near as I could tell."

"The dear man . . . we had shared a friendly correspondence." Cuming's face showed a deep concern as he suddenly asked, "Could they say I had him poisoned?"

Colonel Thayer nodded and began to speculate looking between both men; "You know they will, Thomas, what with Morton and his South Platters calling you a corrupt slave lover and all. J. Sterling does not think anything, even murder, is below you."

Eastman spoke up, suddenly sober and feeling the strength of his office. "They can say whatever they will, Thomas, we know the truth because we know you." The well sauced attorney hiccupped slightly and continued, "I will defect from the Democratic Party if such a vile charge is brought to my office. Regardless, the organic laws are clear, you are now our governor."

"Yes." Thomas said as the weight of the governor's office settled upon him. "I am now the governor; Nebraska has been spared a grand injustice. If Burt had moved the capital away from Omaha City, the territory would have been ruled by Morton and his plantation friends. Can you imagine dear friends, our territory governed by farmers and Nullifiers? Farmers have no sense of history behind the last fallowed field, no sense of imagination beyond the next crop cycle. A territory governed by farmers? Even the thought of it has always chilled my marrow. Nebraska deserves better men with visions of trade and robust commerce. Francis Burt would have sold the territory to these want-to-be slavers who are always looking to the earth. I will be a good governor as I was thrust in to this responsibility as a new Cincinnatus!"

Eastman was on his feet lifting his glass to the new governor. "Hail, Governor Cuming!"

Colonel Thayer raised his bottle and said with a smile, his position seeming secure, "You will be an excellent governor and the militia is with you, but let's not get ahead of ourselves. We have a lot of work to do before folks call you a new Cincinnatus." Colonel Thayer had to keep from rolling his eyes as he muttered quietly, "Whoever that fellow might have been."

Thayer ended up being right as to the amount of work that needed to be completed by the newly elevated governor. Thomas Cuming's brief and controversial administration was consumed by three enormous and consequential decisions. The first was to immediately commence the construction of the foundation for the territorial capitol building in Omaha. It was optimistically christened as The State House. The second was the series of reforms he enacted to centralize the frontier economy, close down the wildcat banks, and develop a political structure for the territory. The last was to build up the territorial militia in a single-minded determination to steer Nebraska away from violent sectional conflicts over the slavery issue he saw lay ahead.

The decision to name Omaha City as the state capital was the most controversial. The largest farmers' market towns and population centers lay below the river and the South Platters were livid. Led by their charismatic champion of agrarian rights, J. Sterling Morton, the southern state legislators broke off all debate on this single issue. They went about inciting a lowbrow scuffle within the chamber of the General Assembly and were strong-armed off Capitol Hill by the sergeant at arms and his boys. The most vociferous attempted to remove the government to Florence, a small developing town north of Omaha City. The Omaha City police and territorial guard overwhelmed the hamlet's outmatched constables and drove them from Florence in what amounted to a street brawl. The rowdies retreated to Nebraska City where they continued to conspire south of the Platte under the protection of Julius Sterling Morton.

Governor Cuming did not allow these distractions to stop his reforms in constructing a viable federal territory. He divided Nebraska into four enormous counties surrounding the four major population centers, Columbus, Nebraska City, Beatrice, and Omaha City. He closed down the local wildcat banks that were printing their own currency. The governor sent the militia out into the streets and rural passes to shut down the claim clubs that fed upon the dreams of recent immigrants in much the same way political gangs and machines exploited new arrivals in New York and Chicago. He promoted Thayer to general of the organized militia adding to the man's swagger.

Cuming continued with his eccentricities. He had read somewhere that Alexander the Great had slept with a copy of the *Iliad* under his pillow. Thomas bragged to his friends that that was fine for a conqueror but inappropriate for the builder of civilizations. His preference was the *Aeneid*. He would found Omaha the same way the fabled Trojan exile Aeneas found Rome. His quirks aside, he was a good administrator and most agreed that in the end, the young politician did what needed to be done. Governor Thomas Cuming created Nebraska out of anarchy and perched Omaha City at its pinnacle.

Chapter 3

September 24, 1855
Pawnee Agency, Nebraska Territory

Petalasharo had grown into a solid and stately young man, slightly given to a vanity only noticeable from his meticulous personal appearance and the feather headdress he wore on too many occasions. It was an odd trait too coming from a humble upbringing. He spent much of his childhood with his father's people but, in his heart, he remained a *Chaui* like his mother. She had been of the tribe and clan of the Pawnee nobility. His father, however, wanted him to learn the practical and necessary skills that the Pawnee *Akitaru,* or common people, had excelled at for centuries.

The *Skidi* of *Rulasharo* camped along the forested upstream bend of the Plenty Potatoes River[9], located forty-five miles, or the distance an average Pawnee messenger boy could cover in three good runs, west of the old *Chaui* village of *Pah-Huku.* Along sandbanks of the stream the young brave spent his days learning the rote songs and chants of an aspiring young Pawnee priest under his father's tutelage. With his lessons in tribal ceremony and theology, *Petalasharo* also learned the hunting skills necessary for the men to gather the tribe's food and skins. He learned to anticipate shifts in the wind and from which angle a hunter should approach a herd of buffalo or fidgety antelope. He became an accomplished hunter. The boy's education was exceptionally broad.

The Pawnee traced *Petalasharo's* lineage through his mother and she had been a *Chaui* princess. The tribe considered *Petalasharo* within that

---

[9]   The Middle Loup River is west of present day Dannebrog, Nebraska.

band's nobility. In the early 1850s the young boy fulfilled his destiny and returned to the *Chaui* village. He was immediately accepted within the *Pah-Huku* council of chiefs.

His vanity and dress, which had been much remarked upon by the *Skidi*, now simply seemed due and proper. Still, he remained popular with the commoners. He presented gentle affability and absolute earnestness. The young chief lacked pretentiousness entirely and just as many errand boys, criers, and skinners shared his lodge and his feasts as did chiefs and medicine men. His conversations were always quiet and sincere and his temperance was constant. He kept his hair long and unbraided. He favored buffalo meat to elk, and took to a simple reed mat rather than thick skins for bed. After he matured in adulthood, he preferred his first wife, *Pahaat Icas*, a quiet but stern woman, to her other younger companions. He never indulged in whisky, always greeted the dawn, and spoke to the stars and *Tirawahat* at night. He never skipped the devotions to the Corn Mother. Indeed, *Petalasharo* was remarkable even for a medicine man's son, as he never felt the need to regret his actions of the day.

For many decades an aging and reclusive chief led the Pawnee nation, *Sharitarish Malan*. He had been the principal chief since before the tribe struck their first great treaty with the whites in 1824. During his early years *Sharitarish Malan* had been a wise and virtuous leader, however, with age came dissolution. He had used the past decade to advance no other purpose then to consolidate his own power. So formidable with his fellow Pawnee he seemed to yield before the whites, giving in with whatever they asked and avoiding conflict. If the Pawnee would question his decisions he turned upon them with a vengeance and his anger was well known. The white men knew him as Angry Chief or Cross Chief, but the *Skidi* Pawnee name was more precisely translated as Malignant Ruler. He had been the Great Chief of the Pawnee confederation even though he rarely ventured outside the ancient village of *Pah-Huku*. Seldom did he gather in council but arrogantly sent his dictates to the bands through his well-chosen minions.

Some felt he was fearful of sickness. The Pawnee scattered after the terrible diseases that struck the villages in the late 1830's and since then he neglected to call them back in a gathering. The Angry Chief maintained his family and council in *Pah-Huku* despite the fact many of the Pawnee bands moved to the Pawnee Agency by the Loups.

He was reclusive with whites sending diplomats in his stead. For a time most whites did not know what *Sharitarish Malan* looked like but they could see his influence. Even Pawnee bands far from the *Pah-Huku* village referred to him in their parlays with whites, and the tribe knew he had powerful medicine. He sent their warriors on far-flung raiding expeditions to the south, stealing horses and slaves from the Osage, Comanche and Ute. When the warriors would return with the booty and herds, they would gather the ponies and bestow them upon the Great Chief. He would ignore the gifts and the Sioux would quickly steal the prized animals. It was a bizarre and irrational replenishment, but one that gave old *Sharitarish* odd satisfaction.

It was under this unusual and remote leadership the Pawnee people drifted in the mid-nineteenth century. The bands wandered with roughly half returning to the agency during the winter and half to *Pah-Huku*. Encounters with the whites became more frequent and less predictable. It was a road that would lead to no good end.

The Treaty of Table Creek

Chapter 1

June 2, 1856 Cincinnati, Ohio

Sam Black nervously bounced his silvered-tipped blue-ash walking cane upon his boot as he waited for Richardson to return with his report. Few events in America were as exciting as a national political convention and the 1856 Democratic Convention was more dramatic than most.

"Damn this confounded waiting!" Black thought as he tried to calculate whether the excruciating delay helped or hurt his chance to be named as a floor delegate. He poured himself another two fingers of bourbon but stopped short of taking a mighty swig. The handsome dark haired son of a Methodist preacher felt he enjoyed his liquor a bit too much for his own good, but he needed something to calm his nerves.

Samuel W. Black was a forty year old Pennsylvanian tenderfoot when it came to politics on a national scale. A veteran of the Mexican War he had initially been drafted into civil service by his old commander from the Mexico City Campaign, President Franklin Pierce. He was a tall gangly man with dark receding hair and a mustache that swept up into well-trimmed sideburns. Most thought Black was handsome although he constantly paled beside his delightfully bright and distinguished wife, the former Eliza Irvin. The two had married early in life but had not been able to spend much time together due to Samuel being called to service. The war ended successfully for the United States and, seemingly, for Lieutenant Colonel Black. Reports came back to his home state that Samuel had distinguished himself well. He was poised to enter a brilliant military career, but he wanted none of it. At the end of hostilities Black returned to Pennsylvania and dabbled in private business ventures. He was neither astute nor lucky and his savings dwindled. He and Eliza fought over money often. Black thought if he was allowed to devote his attention to investing full time his luck would improve. In addition, the man wanted to leave the army. He had seen too much in Mexico.

Samuel Black resigned his military commission but this did nothing to help the family's finances. He immediately felt he had made an error as his wife remarked she always thought he looked better in military rather than civilian dress. She patted him on the chest when she saw the look in his eyes and said, "never mind now, the republic will survive without you to protect it."

Black studied the law and although it did not suit him, he proved competent as a clerk. Eventually, he used his connections with his former commander to get himself an apprenticeship in a Pennsylvania probate court. Unfortunately, Black was never cut out to be a lawyer. He never was comfortable with the swagger and bombast of the courtroom. Unsure about legal niceties and the complexities of codes, canon, statutes, precedents, etc. etc., so on and so forth, he relied on his willingness to do whatever the higher-ups wanted and he hoped it would bring him some money along the way.

One thing the reluctant barrister had plenty of was opinions. Black quickly grew frustrated with the ham-fisted way the Pierce administration handled domestic policy. Pierce seemed too confounded willing to compromise with the Abolitionists. He cleanly broke with Pierce after a man from his home state, James Buchanan, came out unequivocally in favor of the popular sovereignty doctrine in the Kansas-Nebraska Act. He joined the plurality in the Democratic Party in their all but official slogan, "Anyone but Pierce!"

Black liked the way Buchanan minced no words being pro-state rights and pro-popular sovereignty. Both Pennsylvanians did not necessarily support the southern institution of slavery but felt northern meddling in Dixie prerogatives would lead to no good result. While he believed that southern succession from the union would be illegal he thought much could be done to avoid such a catastrophe.

All these political considerations were swimming about in Black's head as he watched two slightly inebriated Pierce delegates argue over billiards. The thick haze of tobacco hung at eye level and he finally leapt to his feet with an ability that proved the walking cane as nothing but a prop.

"Richardson! Richardson, you dog-eared roust about! Come here and tell me what on god's green earth could be taking those lackeys."

William Richardson staggered his way over to the impatient man with a tumbler in his hand and put his hand on Black's shoulder, more to steady himself than to put the exasperated delegate to ease.

"Relax, Sam." Richardson pleaded with a slight slur. "Didn't I tell you that Buchanan needs all the delegates he can scrape together? Nothing is amiss. You should have stifled your enthusiasm a bit longer; however, your cow-towing in the foyer this afternoon was a bit much." William Richardson was a man hoping to ride Buchanan's coattails in his own political campaign. A large back slapping windbag when sober he had the talent to became a boor even among fellow drunks. He had enthusiastically thrown his name up for contention in the Illinois gubernatorial campaign but his enthusiasm did not catch spark with the electorate. He was expected to receive a sound drubbing.

Black shoved the robust Richardson off his shoulder in disgust. The inebriated man stood back as if offended and said, "Samuel, I am merely suggesting that you should have held onto to your vote for a longer time like I did. I obtained a fabulous endorsement before I bolted from the Pierce camp. Why so glum, Samuel? I have never known you to refuse such fine Ohio gin."

Sam returned to his table and finished off his glass with a mighty swig. "A lot of good that endorsement will do you," Black began to reconsider his remark and decided that he needed a friend at that moment, even one as loutish as Richardson.

"I want you to know I intend to be the next Illinois governor, Samuel!" Richardson barked with surprising clarity. "I intend to win!"

"I'm sorry, Will." Black said, "I guess that I'm just nervous the boat will leave without me again. I grabbed onto Buchanan both as a fellow Pennsylvanian and as a man who is sick of Pierce's yellow streak. To tell you the truth, Will, I hope I chose well. I could use an appointment because money has been tight. Eliza was never comfortable with me leaving the army. She hates the idea of me in the military but the pay is steady, and she frets so. I am beginning to wonder myself if I should have put in for another promotion. I'm worried I let go of the only thing I was competent at doing. I've never understood the law that well."

Black ordered another drink and offered Richardson the chair beside him. William gratefully accepted the seat as he had begun to grow dizzy, and Black continued the conversation.

"So if you fail to win the governorship will you look for an appointment in the territories? Are you considering Kansas with all of these other vagabonds? I hope not Kansas. Hear that godforsaken desert is a real powder keg."

Richardson regained his bearing once he was seated and stated, "Oh my word no. Nebraska Territory is looking far more promising. I hear there is a fortune to make in their river towns!"

"Nebraska?" Samuel Black said. "There is an idea, wonder if I could convince Eliza to move out of Pennsylvania?"

The conversation came to an abrupt end with a blare of the brass horns and a party herald announced at the top of aching lungs, "Hear ye, Hear ye! Make way for the savior of our magnificent Democratic Party! The next president of these United States—Our own Old Buck! James Buchanan!"

Chapter 2

September 1, 1857 Omaha City, Nebraska Territory

The small but distinguished delegation of notables stood along the strand of river grass just above the back of the landing dock. They looked on as the steamer was guided into its corral for the passengers to disembark. It was early in the morning and the party was grateful for the changing season and dry weather. It cut down on the humidity leaving the grass, and their shoes, dry. The dignitaries were composed of the city's leading men and they knew the President's Indian Commissioner was sure to travel with a large coterie. Most had high hopes for federal appointments and were eager to make an impression with one of President Buchanan's inner circle.

Thomas Cuming looked out at the bustling and prosperous waterfront with its steamers and ferries partaking in energetic commerce. The former territorial governor felt tremendous satisfaction knowing it had been his financial reforms that had regulated the wildcat banks making investment in Nebraska trade possible. He was indifferent as to how he would appear in the eyes of the Commissioner of Indian Affairs, James Denver. He figured that J. S. Morgan had already bent the commissioner's ear with his personal verbal poison and his only hope was to impress the man by taking the high road.

Commissioner of Indian Affairs James Denver was a powerful Democratic Party operative who served as the president's eyes and ears west of the Missouri. He was sent to Nebraska Territory to deal with the Indians and, more importantly, damper down support among local Democratic politicians for a federal homestead land grant act. The idea of free land had energized some Whigs and was popular with the new Republican Party. The Democratic Party was opposed to what they saw as a federally subsidized land grab by the nation's railroads that would use wide-eyed immigrants as middlemen. The railroad would simply snatch up the land as these poor farmers were killed off by Indians or driven to bankruptcy by draught. Few immigrants had the experience or resources to successfully manage a farm even when the land was provided free. The political force behind federal homestead legislation centered on speculators, railroad interests and naïve immigrant groups. Additionally, the administration felt a homestead act would be an unnecessary point of contention with the western tribes. It was an enormous task but the commissioner was up to the challenge; Denver's political reach extended far beyond regulating federal treaties with the American Indian tribes.

At last the steamboat appeared around the southern bend and the dock's horns began to blast out a welcome. The steamer *Great Western* blared out a response and the crowd began to buzz with excitement.

"We should have brought a band, Thomas." General Thayer whispered nervously. "Old J.S. would have arranged for a band."

Thomas nodded and sighed, "Well that is Governor Izard's prerogative, general. I for one do not imagine our finest local ensemble could serenade such strutting peacocks. The governor may simply have chosen to spare our local talent from embarrassment."

"We should have brought a band." Thayer anxiously repeated.

As the steamer docked and the landings were lowered to the shore it became apparent who was Commissioner Denver. A large heavy-set man descended the planking followed by half-dozen dapper gentlemen and a few military officers. Commissioner Denver was a clean-shaven but hard drinking party bulldog that was often sent by the president to assert political intimidation. The man had killed a rival in a duel in California and was known as someone who got his way.

"Good morning gentlemen, President Buchanan sends his greetings and thanks you for assisting me in what will prove to be vital and historical negotiations with these wild Pawnee chieftains." Denver removed a new card from his vest and began to read; "President Buchanan wants you to know that that he is following our progress with a keen interest knowing how important this diplomacy is for the western settlements. He would like you to know that the future of Nebraska Territory is something that he takes a personal interest in and he has absolute confidence in our cooperation to resolve all differences with the Pawnee tribes peacefully while assuring the safety of the settlements."

The commissioner replaced the card and began to vigorously shake Governor Izard's hand. His grip was overpowering and the governor tried not to grimace.

"Commissioner, we welcome you to Nebraska." The governor nervously replied; "I trust your journey wasn't too arduous?"

"Certainly not my good man but we have a great deal to discuss." Commissioner Denver grabbed Izard's elbow and pressed him forward to whisper into his ear; "Might we find a room with a little privacy? The president has some personal requests that must be addressed."

"Commissioner I would like to introduce you to my fine cabinet . . . this is General Thayer . . ."

Denver squeezed Izard's elbow with urgency. "Not now you idiot . . ." He whispered out of the side of his mouth . . . "I do not have time for this foolishness . . . Get us a room!"

Izard stood flabbergasted and motioned the gathering to the depot. "Gentlemen this way please."

The Nebraskans literally bounced off one another in their haste to remove themselves from the landing. Thomas had to keep from smiling as he saw Izard and Thayer exchange worried glances. Thayer's lieutenant, O'Kelly, directed the party to a billiards room adjacent to the depot saloon and the governor noticed there were hardly any chairs. Why did he not make better arrangements? He fumed to himself.

"I am sorry, Commissioner Denver. We expected to return to The State House before speaking . . ."

"Pay that no mind, Governor Izard. Once that door is secured I will get right to the point."

Thayer motioned to O'Kelly to shut the door and protect their privacy. The lieutenant glanced at Izard confused as to whether he should remain. Immediately Denver slammed the door.

"Does your territorial administration understand what it is to be a good Democrat governor?" Denver shouted! "I should think not after having heard the reports that reached Washington."

"Commissioner, I do not know what you have heard but I assure you . . ."

"Governor, I hear that there is a bill, supported by your administration I might add, in this territorial assembly advocating homesteader legislation. If that is not outrageous enough I have heard there are members of your cabinet who feel that popular sovereignty is a flawed compromise to the slavery issue. I have even heard that you listen to the advice of an abolitionist!"

Izard gave an angry and slightly desperate glance to Cuming who appeared to have a bemused look. "Sir . . . surely you understand local sentiments must be taken into account on these issues."

"I do not understand, governor! Neither does the president understand!" Denver bellowed. "Do you not understand that the very fabric of our republic is being torn apart by these local sentiments? If we cannot maintain cohesion within our own party how can we hope to keep our nation united? Gentlemen, please remember you are federal appointees serving at the discretion of our president. You will not advocate abolitionist policies that will only antagonize the serenity of the republic. Each one of the persons in this room is an agent of a federal territory and is beholding to this administration. You will not advocate homestead legislation that will enrage the sensibilities of both the savage and civilized tribes. Do I make myself clear? We will not discuss these matters further!"

Denver had grown red in the face with anger and all the men stood silently. It was Cuming who broke the silence by clearing his throat. "Commissioner Denver, I do not mean to be disagreeable, surely I do not sir, but what if these positions are not consistent with our values?"

Denver stood dumbfounded that someone had actually spoken back to the authority of the executive. "Then sir, President Buchannan will find someone who shares his values."

Cuming smiled at Izard and Thayer and proudly announced; "Then sir, as I have already been replaced, my conscience should remain at ease!"

Denver was shocked. He shouted, "Who is this man? Who is this man?"

"This is the former governor, Thomas Cuming, sir. He sometimes does not remember his place!" Izard put his emphasis upon the word "former" and pointed him toward the door. Thayer anxiously hustled a chuckling Thomas out the door.

Once across the threshold the door was unceremonious slammed behind him. Thomas took a moment to straighten his tie but kept his amused look.

"My word," Samuel Black said as he looked on from the position he deliberately chose along the bar rail. "I think that is the quickest time his majesty took to release his ire out on someone. Usually one doesn't receive the "Denver treatment" until one has rubbed him sore for a while."

Thomas looked down and said; "I am sure the good commissioner has had a long trip. The journey must have been taxing on his temperament. Besides, it is clear I failed him in not being a dutiful Democrat."

Black raised the water and whisky to his lips and said; "I am a damn good Democrat and he still rides my ass from time to time. Denver's a pompous blowhard and an ass." Black swallowed what was in the glass in one swig.

"My good man would you say that to his face?" Thomas asked.

Black was quick to answer, "Hell no! I need a job."

Thomas approached and leaned against the rail. The saloon tender knew him and poured the usual—coffee and two spoons of goat milk. "I see . . . what our republic needs more of . . . political courage."

Black looked at the drink Thomas was served and knew whom he was beside. He did not appreciate the irony at his expense. "You're Thomas Cuming aren't you?"

"Ah, I see my reputation precedes me. Should I feel flattered?"

Black shrugged and said; "Only if you enjoy being thought of as a shyster and a knave, a black Republican who would sell his mother for a dollar."

Thomas took a sip to check the temperature of the coffee. He said; "My mother, I see . . . she passed years ago . . . rest her soul . . . so she is not available for commerce. May I guess the reporter of this description was the honorable Mr. Morton?"

"It was indeed. I was impressed Morton considers you such a rascal."

"That means nothing to me, sir." Cuming reported as he swallowed his lukewarm coffee in an instant. "Well my good man, I do hope you enjoy your stay in our fine town. Omaha City will soon be the pearl of the river towns! Arthur, make sure you provide this man with another drink of his choosing. Put it on my tab for I must be on my way."

"Well thank you governor. Would you like to know my name?" Black asked.

"Sir, this has been a delightful conversation but there is no need for further introductions. Either you will be long gone after the cheerful commissioner completes our treaty negotiations; or you stay in which case we will have ample opportunities to be properly introduced."

Black felt himself a bit put off but he quickly shrugged and drank the complimentary beverage. He did not have long to mend his ego as the commissioner and chastised dignitaries had completed their discussion.

"Black!" thundered Denver as he entered the drinking hall, "Make sure my luggage is transported to the hotel. Governor, I shall need a conveyance."

Izard nodded and shouted directions to his underlings. It was clear that federal authorities were once again in charge in Nebraska Territory.

Chapter 3

September 19, 1857
Table Creek west of Nebraska City

The grass lying lazily toward the creek's basin was already beginning to lose its summer color and vibrancy. Much of the undergrowth located some six odd miles west of the Missouri basin was not even grass according to the exacting pronouncement of Julius Sterling Morton. The foliage of the dissected plains surrounding Nebraska City was infant shrubs, thick-set weeds and low creeper. Morton had studied all manner of the grasslands. While politics had always been his deepest passion, agronomy ran a close second and native grasses fascinated him. He concluded that the prairie carpet was impervious to hail, hard frosts, and floods. The herbs and thatches lying underneath the creek banks would even survive the occasional prairie fire. The grasslands could withstand all of the terrors of nature but it was not eternal. He knew an iron plow would be its demise.

In a meadow four miles north of the town hall, the Pawnee had begun to gather. Six months prior, the tribe had been called in to account for its supposed refusal to comply with the Treaty of Fort Childs signed years before by tribal elders and the Angry Chief. *Petalasharo* had tried to arrive early. He was anxious to meet the clan leaders and bands but he had not gotten to Table Creek soon enough. *Petalasharo* saw a couple of hundred Pawnee had arrived already and set up a large camp of thatched wickiups. Seldom had they gathered in this number so close to one of the permanent towns of the whites. Setting up the encampment had gone peacefully, a source of water had been found and a perimeter had been determined. The town marshal with a few deputies had visited and exchange pleasantries with the Horse Chief whom had been the first chief to arrive. The white diplomats had seemed surprisingly accommodating to the Pawnee requests and Horse Chief speculated the marshal was not the man with whom the Pawnee would be dealing.

"That is true, Horse. We are to speak with one of the Great Father's men called Denver. Have you ever attended one of these treaty ceremonies my friend?"

"No *Petalasharo* I have not. I am afraid of what will happen. I am afraid for the Pawnee." Horse Chief answered with concern, "We have heard the Great Chief, *Sharitarish Malan,* wishes to speak through your voice when it is time to put the mark on the white's man paper. Is this true?"

Petalasharo nodded as if agreeing with the man's fear but he smiled and said, "I understand but I do not think we need to fear the whites here so close to their women and homes." He looked up to the cloudless sky and said, "Still we should be watchful. The Pawnee have many enemies, Horse. We need to make sure the people are protected. Let us make sure the night sentinels know the importance of their task. Has Little Anger arrived?"

"No not yet. I received news his band was visited by the Standing Clouds.[10] The priests need to participate in the ceremonies prior to leaving."

Petalasharo nodded and simply stated, "That is as it should be. I am camped with my people. Let me know when the Little Anger arrives so that I can speak with him. We should speak while his women set up the lodging. It is important for us to understand what is about to come."

Petalasharo left Horse Chief and strolled through the new village to his wife's wickiup. He felt strangely at peace despite knowing the magnitude of the decisions that would have to be made.

*　*　*

---

[10]   Standing Clouds were tornadoes. Tornadoes were Pawnee gods. A tornado was a mystical experience for the Pawnee that required the priests to perform ceremonies thanking the gods for all of nature's wonders. If the Standing Clouds were not thanked properly they were more ferocious when they inevitably returned.

"Easy gal . . . We're doing fine . . . Shh." Sam Black patted the horse's barrel chest as he smoothed the hairbrush over her flank. He noted the knots in her coat and surmised that the mare had not been groomed in some time. The horse's fur was mottled and bare in some spots but the coat did not concern the experienced cavalry officer. He knew that the animal had just been fed a consistent diet of stale oats. All she would need was some extra attention and steady dry feed and the horse would become a reliable mount.

Black had been lucky with the horse but, as usual, unlucky with funds. Stuck out in Omaha money that was supposed to have arrived from an old army buddy never appeared. He had been forced to ask the prickly good graces of Commissioner Denver to purchase a horse. The commissioner snorted that the taxpayers could not pick up the tab for a personal mount and the party coffers were dry so he sent his wayward assistant to Secretary Morton, hat in hand. It was the first time the men had met. Black felt that Morton was insufferably smug as he required a signed note and then handed over enough carrying cash to purchase the horse and three or four meals at the Doutcher House.

I am surrounded by pompous popinjays. Black thought to himself as he calculated how many drinks he could purchase if he chose to eat light.

The horse had been a bargain. Black smoothed the animal's coat and took time to pluck burs out of its bobtail. Black always seemed at peace around horses. He preferred their company to even his favorite barkeeps. He took a quick sip out of his midnight flask and whispered soothingly to the animal, "Judging by your fetters you were racing stock . . . Weren't you . . . just got a bit old . . . I know how that feels."

Black knew he was not all that old, just turned forty-one, but you are as old as you feel and he felt all of his years. Financial problems had followed Sam Black like a lonesome dog his entire life and those problems wore on him. He remembered high hopes returning from the Mexican War and how each of those hopes had been dashed; his failed run for congress, his business fiascoes, his desperate cow towing to braggarts like Denver and this money bags Morton all made him feel less than he should. His one bright spot was his darling Eliza who he had married prior to the war. Unfortunately, their marriage had seen cloudy days. Their first few years together had been good. After some bad investments the coffers ran dry and things grew rocky. Black knew that he had been a disappointment to her, although she seldom spoke of it. He could tell what a disappointment whenever he had to ask her to call on one of his former officers for a loan; or the time they had to cash in their veteran's allowance to pay a creditor. It was the look of sadness in her eyes as she struggled to provide for the children while her Samuel was chasing another dream.

He wished he had a head for business or even lawyering. He could not get a firm grasp on either pursuit, although he felt he studied on them enough. His greatest fear was he would have to go back to soldiering. Black supposed that he was a competent officer. He had a head for the military. He had been given accolades after the war but even there he had his doubts. When he was with the dashing officer corps, at times, he felt as an imposter. They were all so confident knowing they had easy lives and homes to return to after battle. It even caused him to second-guess himself on the field. Not often but more than most knew.

Black knew he had courage. At least brave enough to get him through the Mexican War, but he knew better than anyone he was also a coward. He remembered moments of hesitation and hurried retreats that, if they become public, would certainly tarnish his war medallions. Still, he had been steady under fire at Cerro Gordo and that was the story told and retold.

"Cerro Gordo," he said to himself out loud. "Got a medal for that fracas, didn't you. What a pitiful joke?"

While friends said Black had brains for the army he figured following orders never seemed too complicated. He had an awful fear that following orders and soldiering was the only thing he could do to make a living. Samuel knew his wife and urchins deserved better than an officer's pension and it saddened him to his marrow.

"Well now you do look fine." Black muttered after he stepped back, took a quick sip and admired his grooming. "You and I will put on a fine show at that treaty signing ceremony. We will be the finest pair of lapdogs those injuns will have ever beheld!"

Chapter 4

Sharitarish Tiki rode ahead of his band making haste to arrive at the Pawnee treaty gathering as soon as possible. The tornado that had struck his village was an unfortunate delay as the Little Angry Chief was under orders from his father to appear before the other chiefs had time to consult and conspire. The Great Chief wanted this matter concluded quickly. Little Anger was pleased his father had sent word *Petalasharo* would be the chief negotiator with the whites and the son was once again impressed with his father's foresight. It would cut down on factions conspiring. Both the Big Anger and Little Anger knew *Petalasharo* was a measured and thoughtful man. Thoughtful but not one to upset a simmering stew. He was also popular with the all of the Pawnee bands and sufficiently dignified to be given the great honor. The man was perfect for his father's purpose. Little Anger understood that in keeping their family distant from the treaty and its consequences they could avoid future backlash. It would be to their benefit.

At one time, Little Anger had been a disappointment to his father. It was hard to be the eldest son of the Great Chief. He wasted much of his young apprentice years finding excuses to roam about the countryside, skipping from village to village depending on which maiden had caught his eye for the moment. His father worried he lacked the discipline to become a raider or a priest and Little Anger would soon lose the respect of the elders. His son wanted to follow his father's footsteps into diplomacy but they both knew he had much to learn. Little Anger had lived a trite life and it hurt him in the eyes of others. It was the Big Angry Chief's mysterious reputation that had convinced the whites he was the man to deal with in matters involving the Pawnee. The Angry Chief had been a boyhood friend of the first *Petalasharo* and became the Great Chief when that man had died at an early age. It seemed as if he had lasted through the ages.

Like all fathers in his later years, the Great Chief *Sharitarish Malan* worried his son would never find his purpose in life. With age, however, Little Anger ceased his wandering ways and set about making himself his reclusive father's indispensable right arm. His relieved father felt his son simply matured a bit late. Little Anger knew, however, he was running out of maiden's lodges where their mothers continued to be welcoming. The last blow was when the mother of *Eerit Ta* began to refuse him meals. *Eerit Ta*, or Seeing Deer, was a quiet Pawnee maiden of middling beauty who had always pined for the Little Anger. She loved him despite his dalliances and wandering ways. He was so handsome and proud. Perhaps he was not a skilled hunter or a fierce warrior but she knew he was the man for her. She thought of the day when she would have her own lodge and *Sharitarish Tiki* would eat at her fire. Their children would play at their feet. That day seemed too far off as she and her mother followed Little Anger's band toward the meeting of the great council with the whites.

The second *Petalasharo* was about ten years older than Little Anger. They both thought well enough on one another, or at least Little Anger thought that *Petalasharo* liked him. For his part, *Petalasharo* did not quite know what to think of him. He knew that Little Anger was only listened to because of his father's authority, but he seemed harmless enough. Mostly *Petalasharo* was thankful that *Sharitarish Tiki* left his daughters and his wives alone.

Petalasharo was surprised when the Little Anger showed up within his lodge. It had been his understanding Little Anger's band was at least a day's journey west due to the delay with the tornado. He quickly set his wives to task preparing a meal and *Pahaat Icas* gave the young man a freshly drawn pottage of water. *Petalasharo* was always eager to play the host and he offered a pipe with his best tobacco. The two began to discuss Little Anger's trip and how much damage the tornado had caused. Little Anger was dismissive of the event stating that equipment had been strewn about as the band was readying for the journey but no one was injured. Thankfully, the pony herd was not scattered so they were not terribly detained. It may have been possible, Little Anger, insisted to have arrived here as scheduled but the priest would not be deterred from offering thanks to the Standing Cloud gods.

"It was a waste of time." Little Anger declared.

Petalasharo bristled as he realized Little Anger had inherited his father dismissive attitude toward the spirit world. Many Pawnee had turned away from the faith of their forefathers after the diseases had ravaged their families and their enemies had triumphed in battle, and many turned to the white man's god. *Sharitarish Malan* often seemed even more heretical. *Petalasharo* felt he believed in no god whatsoever.

"Your delay was no great matter." *Petalasharo* stated evenly. "The whites have not interfered with the setting up of the camp. The marshal has even been welcoming to our people. Horse Chief feels he is a man we can trust."

Little Chief nodded and smoked deeply of the tobacco. "That is the not the man who speaks for the Great Father. Have you met this man, Denver?"

Petalasharo shook his head. "No, he has not come into our camp. We have not even spoken with his messenger boys to tell us when we shall meet."

Little Anger felt some relief he had not missed any of the negotiations. He continued to listen.

"We were in no great hurry to begin since *Sharitarish's* eyes and ears had not arrived. We did not expect you for a few more days."

Little Anger smiled at this consideration. It stoked his ego.

"I am glad you have arrived Little Anger. It is good for us to discuss our people's requests before we go before this man Denver. If I am to sign a new treaty we must look after the needs of the people."

"There will be no requests to put before the white men."

Petalasharo was shocked. "No requests? But our people need for traders and deliverymen to be fair. Our people need weapons to fight our enemies. We need to insure that we will not be harassed on our hunts. It would be right if we asked for blue coats to protect our villages.[11] How can we help our people with making no requests?"

"Our people will not be helped trading more with the whites. Do you not see that is what leads to the diseases and death? Our people are plenty strong to fight our enemies. We need no involvement with the whites for our protection. We certainly do not need more involvement with blue coats. No, we are to meet with them and sign their foolish paper. It makes no difference what is on the paper or what will be said. The people will continue on as before."

---

[11]   U.S. Federal Cavalry

Petalasharo sat in stunned silence for a long moment. "The whites will remember what is on the paper. The Great Father feels the paper is sacred."

"The paper has no meaning, especially to the whites."

"The paper should mean something to the Pawnee. It will mean something to our elders. Does your father fear what will be decided?"

Little Anger scoffed and knocked the ashes from his pipe. They sat in silence for a moment. Finally, *Petalasharo* asked, "Why does the Great Chief fear the white man?"

"Fear? My father fears no man, least of all the white man."

Petalasharo asked, "Why does he not want us to deal with the whites?"

"We do not need the whites." Little Anger insisted. "We will sign their paper then go."

Petalasharo stated he had seen what they have done to other tribes. "Do you not remember when the Squaw Killer crossed through our land? We thought that he marched to his destruction leading so few blue coats into the land of the throat-cutters. It was the throat-cutters who were driven into the mountains."[12]

Petalasharo continued, "My father was once a boy who had not seen many moons. He had gone to the white man's town of St. Louis to meet with their chiefs. During the night a bell was rung and all of the whites ran towards the center of town. My father was curious as all boys are and followed to see what the white men would do. One of the white men's buildings was on fire and the whites had stood in a long line like blue coats on parade. They lifted buckets of water out of a hole and passed the bucket among themselves to pour upon the fire. He watched in wonder as the many tongues of the whites found unison. Many of the whites in that line owned many ponies and many of the whites slept in the gutters. Many of the whites were very old and must have seen many fires. Many were young and may never have seen a fire; but all knew what to do. It was as if they had known what to do from their cradleboard. The whites had one purpose; one thought and the fire did not last long. My father knew that the Pawnee must never become one thought to the whites. The Pawnee must never become a fire."

---

[12]   Lt. William Harney marched an army detachment across the land of the Pawnee and defeated *Lakota* Sioux at The Battle of the Blue Water in 1855.

Little Anger shrugged indifferent to the story.

"Does your father believe that signing this paper tomorrow will make the Pawnee invisible?"

"No." Little Anger stated. "But they will not bother us. The whites only want to cross the land to the mountains. They will be content to fight our enemies. Our enemies will be pleased to fight with them as well."

Petalasharo breathed deep and said, "Your father is wrong. If he would leave his lodge he would see many whites continue towards the mountains but many whites stay. More and more white men come and they bring their women and children. They bother our game trying to grow their scraggly crops. They kill the buffalo. I fear our people have not seen the end of this."

Little Anger said with a simple finality, "My father has spoken."

"This should be discussed with all of the chiefs. I will send the messenger boys to gather those that have arrived."

Little Anger answered icily, "You may gather the chiefs as you wish but the Great Chief has made his decision."

The two sat in formal silence for the rest of the afternoon. That evening a hasty conclave of the chiefs was held and the consensus was as Little Anger suggested. No one wished to defy the Great Chief. Little Anger assured the chiefs that the treaty was no great matter as the whites seldom paid attention to their words. Even the fact that this treaty gathering was called for suggested that the treaty passed on the Grand Island was being ignored.[13]

Petalasharo felt a darkness descend upon the lodge. He could not believe that the Angry Chiefs had turned the Pawnee people as cynical and deceitful as they were themselves. He was also concerned the whites would not ignore this treaty as they had ignored treaties in the past. However, he was the chosen diplomat for the confederate Pawnee people and they had spoken. The Pawnee people, or at least their chiefs, were firmly in agreement with *Sharitarish Malan*. He would do what was expected of him. As he sat smoking and thinking he had an idea. He would call for the Old Knife Chief. He only hoped the old man could arrive in time.

---

[13]   Fort Childs Treaty of 1848

Chapter 5

September 24, 1857
Nebraska City, Nebraska Territory

The arrival of dignitaries and tradesmen to the treaty negotiations nearly doubled the population of Nebraska City. J. S. Morton was now the secretary of the territory and he was determined to ingratiate himself with the Commissioner. While Morton and Commissioner Denver entertained the local and federal politicians and bureaucrats on Morton's estate; the fur traders, prostitutes, and whisky peddlers holed up in shadier boarding houses and saloons located by the river. It was here Black decided to spend his time using the excuse to look after his and the delegation's recently purchased animals. He chose to drink with company that asked few questions. The clatter and shouting of the frontier town is what he would awake to and this morning he suffered through an unusually severe headache.

Skimming the thin crust off his morning buttermilk with his thumb, he surveyed the handful of whiskey bottles arrayed about the room. They were unfortunately and inexplicably empty.

Damn it. He thought to himself as he rubbed his temple. That's why the headache. No matter. He would simply have to get through the morning without a jolt of elixir. He felt reassured he had coins for a small bottle at lunch. The evening would take care of itself. He dug out his timepiece and was shocked at the late hour. Almost immediately there was a knock on the door.

"Mr. Black. Are you in there? Mr. Black?"

Damn, thought Black, "Who is it? What do you want?"

"Commissioner Denver sent me, sir." A young-sounding voice answered through the door. "He wants to know where you are keeping yourself. He and Secretary Morton were expecting you an hour ago."

"Damn it today is the day!" He whispered. Black was desperately trying to get his clothing smoothed over and his hair parted correctly. Sam did not want to appear as if he had just leapt out of bed.

"Give me a moment, lad." Black found his boots and danced into them. Patting some dry cologne on his cheeks he took a quick glance into his shaving mirror and decided he could probably get by with the stubble. He only prayed his eyes were not overly blood-shot. Black opened the door and found Lieutenant O'Kelly about to knock a second time.

"I beg your pardon sir . . . Commissioner Denver wanted me to fetch you as soon as possible. They have gathered at Secretary Morton's home and are expecting you take notes of their meeting."

"I understand, lieutenant. I must have lost track of time after my morning paper." Black fibbed. "Can you show me the way?"

"Certainly sir, I have taken the liberty of having your mount saddled. Our horses should be tied just outside the door. I would suggest a riding coat, sir. We may get some rain."

Black was horrified with the thought of a horseback ride with his throbbing head but he tried not to show his angst. Despite his pounding head Black was impressed with the officer's efficiency and would have complimented him but the morning glare, even through the clouds, was merciless on his headache.

"Sir, are you ok?" Lieutenant O'Kelly inquired noticing Samuel falter.

Black took a deep breath and with iron determination stood straight and tall. "It is nothing my boy, simply composing myself for the rigors of the day." He slapped O'Kelly on the back and muttered a silent curse to himself . . . "No need for a rain coat either. Once those blowhards from Washington City get to talking those clouds will be swept form the sky!" Black put on his pleasant politician's face to mask his hangover. He thought, dear God, if I get through this day I shan't touch whisky again . . . . or at least I shan't touch it on a weeknight.

The two climbed upon the horses and set off to the Morton estate, known to the locals as Arbor Lodge.

*　　*　　*

Nebraska City sat on the eastern end of a flat, diamond shaped rise perched above the Missouri River. North Table Creek and the South Table Creek bordered the points of the diamond and it was along the southern brook that the Pawnee had their encampment. *Petalasharo* felt uneasy since his discussion with Little Anger and the chiefs the night before. Not even speaking with his wife or chanting his sunrise prayers had returned balance to his thoughts.

The sky was covered with high clouds that portended rain. A pink veil of sunlight hung down in the eastern sky in the distance. *Petalasharo* noticed a stirring in the white's village and realized the treaty ceremonies would soon begin.

Perhaps Little Anger is correct and the whites do not intend to follow today's treaty. He thought. What is the meaning of this foolishness then? Does a fox chase a rabbit he does not intend to catch? Why did the whites call the Pawnee here? Why do they themselves gather? *Petalasharo* shook his head and decided if his father had never understood the whites he should never hope to. His thoughts went back to his father and his memory was pleasant. Father joined our ancestors many years ago and yet I still feel his medicine. *Petalasharo* whispered to himself almost in prayer, "Help my medicine be strong today Father. I must speak wise words at the council fire for the good of our people."

*   *   *

"Gentleman, gentleman, could I ride with you for a moment?"

Black glanced over his shoulder and saw Thomas Cuming snapping his buggy and horse forward to come up beside the pair. The street was crowded and the governor's buggy horse seemed miffed and restless with the unanticipated hurry.

"Governor?" Black stopped his horse despite the lieutenant's obvious wish to continue. "I did not expect to see you in Nebraska City." Black wondered if it was actually the surprise Cuming was in town, or the delight that the controversial but popular former governor deign to speak with him that placed the smile upon his face.

"Might I impose upon you, gentlemen? Mr. Black, if I could have a momentary word?"

"Certainly governor, but we are in a passel of a hurry. We are expected at Secretary Morton's home to prepare for the proceedings today. I am certain such a distinguished gentleman as you would be more than welcome to join us."

As the carriage drew up, Thomas spoke with a wry smile, "Your invitation is most kind Mr. Black, but alas, it is not yours to give. I am afraid that our most honorable Secretary Morton would prefer Mephistopheles himself at his doorstep. He has made it clear on more than one occasion. The majority of these occasions occurred prior to your arrival on our fair soil."

Black patted the shoulder of his horse and returned the smile. "If you do not mind me asking, how did you put that bee in old J.S.'s bonnet? He does seem to speak unkindly toward you."

Lieutenant O'Kelly rode back and spoke directly to Samuel. "Sir . . . we really need to be on our way. General Thayer ordered me to bring you directly and I am sure they are waiting."

Cuming snapped the buggy whip and proceeded forward. "Quite right lieutenant, they must not be kept in high expectation. We can speak as we ride." He continued. "I assure you, Mr. Black, I hold no ill will towards J.S. Morton, but I know him for what he is and he despises me for that awareness. Granted he is not an evil man. No, no . . . quite to the contrary. He is a man of the earth and, as such, he is a man perfectly suited to our present time and our present place. He loves the soil and he loves its bounty. So much so he can see the spark of humanity only within someone who is, or desires to be, connected to land. He may be pretending to be in lock stock with the party on the controversial homestead issue but that is only while Commissioner Denver is here."

"This is powerful interesting governor but I do not believe you rode us down to discuss Mr. Morton's nature," replied Black. "If we are going to chew the fat I'd also be obliged to ask you to call me Sam."

"Splendid! You are quite right. As always, you must forgive my digression, Samuel. It is one of my unforgivable defects." Cuming continued, "Secretary Morton, however, does lend himself to a convenient gateway towards our topic. He is, despite what I am sure would be vigorous denials, far more similar to the noble redman's character than he would care to admit. Both the good secretary and the red savage are emotionally connected with the earth. Of course it is primitive and absurd, whether in a white man or savage, but there you have it. Old J.S. sees the connection as his individual worth, the Indian sees the connection as his collective worth."

"Governor, mind me if I interrupt, but I still do not understand you."

"One of my greatest regrets as governor was not laying a better foundation for future dialogue with the tribes. There always seemed so many pressing matters at the time. I do not have faith that Commissioner Denver will take this opportunity to discuss with Pawnee's leadership how best to address the issues that will surely arise. In my last year in office, I sent General Thayer to the Pawnee to discuss frictions that had arisen. Thayer was furious with the Pawnee at the time because he felt that some of the braves stole his lunch! Isn't that absurd? I said to him myself that he should have packed more than a couple of baked ham sandwiches . . . it was nothing more than a couple of pranksters, and he could do with shedding a few pounds, but he heard none of it. He was positively beside himself. I have always had a particular aversion to soldiers as diplomats."

Black interrupted expecting by now the need to keep Cuming on point. "Do forgive me sir . . . but we have almost arrived. What do you need to tell me?"

"Quite, quite . . . General Thayer did have the opportunity to discuss the situation with a tribal dignitary by the Anglicized name of Man Chief. Even he was quite impressed with the Pawnee chieftain. He is indeed a man who can be negotiated with. Man Chief let it slip to General Thayer there was dissention within the Pawnee and their leadership. Man Chief does not believe the current principal headman, a surly gentleman according to his name, Black Angry Chief, is a wise man. Thayer actually gave me the impression that Man Chief, and a number of Pawnee feel this Black Angry Chief is quite mad. The concern is their people have scattered and wandered off. That was not much of a concern twenty, ten, or even five years ago, but now their numbers have dwindled. The numbers of bands, clans, even lodges and families have reduced so that Man Chief fears for their future. We are in a stronger position for negotiating with them than we realize."

"Well that is interesting but surely Denver knows all of this."

Cuming shrugged, "Perhaps . . . but perhaps not."

"Surely Thayer has told him, or he has spoken to Morton."

"Psshaw . . . Thayer blows with the wind. He was my right hand as governor, but with Morton's rise he has scurried off to greener pastures."

"What would you like me to do?" Black asked.

"Right now, just mention the Pawnee are not trying to negotiate for more land, quite the opposite, their chiefs, or at least the faction led by Man Chief would prefer less land or at least all of the Pawnee on agency land. He feels consolidating the bands could preserve their cultural identity. This would serve both our peoples. With them in one place they will be easier to watch and bring along in the path toward civilization. What issues are important to Man Chief are his savages' hunting rights and a guarantee of protection from their enemies. Give them that but they should be forced to comply with the past treaty. They may howl, children often do. Give them a firm deadline. The military . . ."

"Sir, we really must get into the drawing room. They are waiting." Lieutenant O'Kelly interjected.

Cuming nodded to the young officer and put out his hand to Black. Sam leaned down across his horse and shook the ex-governor's hand. Black said he was most obliged as Cuming waived and snapped his carriage forward. Sam Black did not know it then but it was the last time he would see or speak with Governor Thomas Cuming.

$$* \quad * \quad *$$

Samuel Black never got the opportunity to speak with Commissioner Denver. He actually got the impression he was not needed at all. In some ways, he was thankful for this, giving him time to drink some coffee and ease his pounding head. He hoped the entire conference would go like this and it wouldn't be necessary for him to even open his mouth.

Chapter 6

Following the gathering of the dignitaries and the chiefs along the rise, Denver opened with a lengthy speech welcoming the Pawnee to this historic gathering. His opening address lasted nearly three hours. It included lengthy pronouncements of what benefits would come to the Pawnee upon another successful negotiation with the new Great White Father, James Buchanan. *Petalasharo* listened carefully to the hurried words of the translator trying to pick up what the whites wanted. Finally, Denver got to the gist of the conference. The Pawnee must cease wandering. The Great White Father wanted them to return to the preserve generously given to them in 1848. They would be guaranteed a perpetual right to continue to hunt the buffalo but they must settle upon the land that had been given to them along the Loup Rivers. Denver droned on about the rights of ingress and egress that would be followed by the Pawnee and overseen by the agents. He spoke of a schedule for the delivery of goods and equipment for farming. The commissioner promised trips to Washington City and foretold of delegations of diplomats and dignitaries that would visit the tribes with gifts. He held up the official treaty document in one hand and offered the pen to the chiefs.

"Now my good fellows," Denver announced. "Who will be the first to touch the pen and secure our eternal friendship?"

The chiefs looked toward the delegation impassively. It was as if they had not understood a word said although many had been speaking English for years. They were all waiting for *Petalasharo* to begin.

Petalasharo stood and looked over the chiefs. All looked up to him except for Little Anger who continued to puff at his pipe. *Petalasharo* lifted his hand toward Denver and smiled. He then nodded to the translator and began, "I see many great men before me this day. These men I know are great because they speak the words of the Great Father in Washington. They come before us and we are humble by their greatness. Denver does not need to ask that we touch his pen because we will do so. He does need to know that his Pawnee children are no longer safe on the land along the northern rivers. The throat-cutters have visited this land too often and many of the Pawnee weep after their visits. The Pawnee will need land south of the flat water.[14] We will be safe in the land of the *Kitakahaki*."

At these words both Morton and Little Anger looked at *Petalasharo* in surprise. *Petalasharo* sat back upon the ground and awaited Denver's response. Little Anger gave a fuming look and brushed the bottom of his chin giving the sign for "what is this?"

Denver sighed and spoke. "Man Chief, the Great Father understands your historical disagreements with the *Lakota* Sioux. We have heard happy reports the Sioux and the Pawnee are no longer at war and that is good."

All the Pawnee chiefs including Little Anger looked up as this statement was translated.

Denver continued. "Since the agreement was entered at Horse Creek[15] peace has been insured between all of the tribes. I myself have received assurances from the Sioux headmen of their friendly intentions."

The Pawnee chiefs began to look at one another uncomfortably. Horse Chief started to laugh and even Little Anger's face betrayed a disbelieving smile.

Petalasharo stated, "The Great White Father can listen to the *Lakota* words but he does not live near them as do the Pawnee. We hear their words and feel their hatred. The peace that was promised by the *Lakota*, Arapaho, and Cheyenne has not been delivered. Surely the white men know this."

Denver leaned over and conferred with Thayer. The two shared whispers that seemed to confirm the Pawnee's accounts of recent trouble. The white men gathered were starting to grow restless with the realization this was not entirely a ceremonial exercise.

Denver spoke up once again, "Man Chief surely you are not saying that the Pawnee are completely innocent in these affairs. It is my

---

14   The Platte River
15   Fort Laramie Treaty of 1857

understanding the Sioux claim to have been incited to violence by your braves."

This remark stirred the Pawnee chiefs as it was translated. *Petalasharo* spoke quietly, "The Pawnee have lived in this land now claimed by the whites far longer than the *Lakota*. We greeted the *Omahaw* into this land. We greeted the *Lakota* into this land; we greeted the French, Spaniards, and Americans into this land. We do not incite anyone into violence on this land. We simply live here along the rivers. Now the time has come and the Pawnee are humble. We do not claim the land to ourselves. You must give us our due. We have always shared what we had with the whites. We shared it with the whites when we were many and the whites few. Now we are few and the whites many. We will continue to share the land but we wish to have our villages south of the flat water."

Morton hurried over to Denver and began whispering into Denver's ear. Land south of the Platte was in his political domain. He would not allow Denver to even consider bargaining it away. Little Anger stood beside *Petalasharo* and made it clear this was not a question the Great Chief would wish for negotiations to stall upon. *Petalasharo* nodded to the Little Anger he understood but "he" was negotiating for the Pawnee.

"That request cannot be granted I'm afraid." Denver stated. "The Pawnee have good agricultural land along the Loups. I understand this is the land of your ancestors. Will you not defend this land from the Sioux?"

Denver's last question ignited the passions of several of the Pawnee who stood and shouted at the white delegation.

"Who are you to tell us how to defend our land!" was the only translation that made it through the cacophony of voices.

Morton took a step backwards as he was amazed how quickly the stern men became angry and vocal. Morton whispered to Denver that this was not a good thing. Black's face grew anxious as he thought of the Pawnee warriors turning on violent on the fearful whites. Why didn't he bring his gun?

An aged warrior lifted his hand into the air and asked to speak. It was Old Knife Chief, *Lechelasharo*, an elder who carried great weight with the Pawnee. The Knife Chief seemed as old as the rocks and rivers. His face had the textured wrinkles of hackberry bark. The Pawnee grew silent and *Lechelasharo* began to speak.

"If the whites demand the Pawnee live along the Loups, the Pawnee will do so. That is our ground and many of our ancestors are buried within its hills. But it is only the ancestral land of the *Skidi* Pawnee. The lands of the *Kitakahaki* and the *Chaui* are south of the flat water. These lands we will give to you, but to give up our sacred village of *Pah-Huku* is a grave thing. The Pawnee cannot do it without having our hearts made heavy. The Pawnee have many sacred sites that must be remembered and kept for our people to visit. There is *Pah-Hur* and *Pahowa*.[16]

Petalasharo began to speak after the Knife Chief and it began to appear to Little Anger the two had planned their statements in advance. "We will move the tribe if that is the will of the Great White Father, but give us time." He paused for the translators to catch up and then continued. "The village of *Pah-Huku* must be transported over many moons. Our people have many food stores and furs located there. We will need to have time, perhaps a few seasons. Many of our old ones cannot travel easily. Will the whites provide us with wagons and food to ease our passage? Will the whites insure foodstuffs for the old while the young are transporting the bands?"

Denver looked over towards Morton who nodded anxiously. It appeared that Morton was willing to move mountains to keep the Pawnee from acquiring land south of the Platte.

"If there is anything that the local authorities can provide I am sure they are willing to do so." Denver said. "You can see that as the Commissioner of Indian Affairs my hands would be tied with many of your immediate requests."

Petalasharo responded, "We have faith a great man such has yourself speaks powerful words with his people and the Great White Father. But many of the things I will speak of for the good of my people are not so immediate. Let us continue to speak after we share the tobacco of the Calumet."

Indeed, Knife Chief and *Petalasharo* had prearranged the opening remarks. The two chiefs had spoken and each felt the Pawnee should not meekly succumb to every demand of the whites. *Petalasharo* felt strongly the Pawnee should at least attempt to be granted some concessions. He learned through his dealings with other headmen whites were especially touchy in negotiations concerning land titles. He was well aware the Pawnee had nearly as many enemies south of the Platte as to the north,

---

16   A natural artesian spring considered sacred by the Pawnee. It was inundated with the construction of the Glen Elder Reservoir in Mitchell County, Kansas.

but the demand worked to perfection. Now the real negotiations could begin.

As the treaty ceremony continued, Black was impressed with the quiet and thoughtful dignity of the chief negotiator for the Pawnee. This must have been the Man Chief whom Thayer had recently met.

He leaned over to Lieutenant O'Kelly and asked him if he recognized the noble Pawnee. O'Kelly nodded and Black whispered. "Remember his face well. We must be able to recall this Man Chief if our paths cross in the future."

Little Anger looked down for the remaining three days of the negotiations. He felt that *Petalasharo* usurped his authority. It was a slight that he would not soon forget.

Chapter 7

Nebraska City, Nebraska Territory April 1, 1857

"Judge not lest ye be judged! Pray for their soul for Damnation is Eternal!"

John Brown seemed oblivious to the crowd gathered around the freight wagon in which he stood. He shouted his words up to the placid white clouds in the sky. This made his speech even more foreboding to the citizens gathered round. It was if he were speaking with the Divinity himself. John Brown was, by anyone's account, an abolitionist firebrand. A large man with a dark complexion his snow white beard set his fiery face in a perfect framework for piercing gray eyes. His voice sounded like thunder and caused crows to fly from the trees each time he began a harangue.

"Lord, our God, grant upon the righteous your unbound mercies! Tear from the eyes of the slavers, the foul Pharisees of our Republic, the unholy blindfold that allows them to hold the colored man in bondage! We do not ask for mercy for the wicked but your own terrible justice. Do upon them what is only right if they fail to see the error in their godless prideful ways! Sweep them from our Republic with a blast of your nostrils so that the righteous are spared!"

"The man is insane," whispered J.S. Morton as he and Sam Black stood toward the back of the gathering. "I knew the abolitionists were smuggling slaves up through my town but I doubted they would send this lunatic our way."

Black nodded in reluctant agreement. He was against slavery in principal. Surely he would never own a slave but it was not an issue for the federal government to meddle. He agreed with most of his fellow

Democrats; it was a local issue and religion had nothing to do with the problem.

"The Lord God Almighty has purged the earth before when it saw his creation succumb to sin and vice! Our fair land must repent! Repent I say for His judgment shall be terrible! Fire burning the flesh! Brother raising his hand against brother! Son shall murder father! Repent, for he who embraces gluttony, sloth, and pride shall have his soul judged for eternity!"

Morton shook his head and said, "That rouser should be arrested for disturbing these good folk. You see to it he is put away should he appear in your court Black."

Samuel looked at Morton sideways. He had seen Morton himself make some borderline brimstone speeches. He wondered how Morton could be so hypocritical.

Morton continued, "By the way . . . congratulations on your federal judgeship appointment. I must admit I did not think you had so many friends in Washington."

Black answered, "I am sure it is Will Richardson's idea. I knew the man in Pennsylvania and he is a friend of the President."

"This nation must choose whether it will embrace the pride of man's written laws or see His judgment thrust upon it by a higher court! Slavery is an evil and vengeance is mine sayeth the Lord! My blood will count for nothing in the eyes of God if I speak a falsehood. However, if I am to die to end a terrible wrong, my soul has already been purified by His grace! Repent or this republic will not escape His wrath!"

Black began to shiver at the man's intensity and several of the women in the audience began to back away. A man standing off along the boardwalk raised his arm as if he were at a revival and shouted "Amen!" Even the small children were spellbound.

J.S. Morton, however, was not fazed. His mind was still on Black's judgeship. "However it came about Black good show! Perhaps now you can start paying me back some of the coin that is due."

Samuel suddenly stiffened and grew uncomfortable. "I have been meaning to discuss that with you J.S., I would like to ask . . ."

Morton laughed out loud and slapped Black on the back. "Samuel, I am not asking to be repaid now. You take me wrong old boy!"

John Brown seemed to hear Morton laugh even at a distance. He laid his head back and screamed to the heavens, "God save our American Republic! God save it from these slavers! These Babylonian whores!"

With that vile word of indiscretion ladies covered the ears of their children. Respectable men once again hurried about their business and a few of the rougher teamsters began to shout even lewder remarks. A few wagon loaders even asked for the Babylonian ladies' addresses to go a calling. The ribald remarks seemed to break the spell John Brown had cast and the crowd quickly thinned.

"Well you see that, Black. The show is over!" Morton began to walk away still conversing. "No no . . . you do not need to mind our accounting. Besides Samuel, there are many ways to pay back a debt . . ."

Samuel smiled at Morton but he began to feel uneasy. He looked back at John Brown. He was no longer looking at the sky. The madman seemed to be looking straight at him and the look was frightening. Samuel thought he was looking into the face of a prophet.

"Why do you dawdle, Black? That mindless minister is not worth our time. You must be about other business. But first you should know that your wife has arrived."

"Eliza's here, in Nebraska City?" Samuel looked suspicious.

"Black, why should you doubt me? Do you believe some of that rubbish that tee totaling swindler Cuming fills your ears with? It is so blasted astounding that man feels so highly of himself. He has a wife who cares more about making money than she does about him. Cannot blame his poor suffering wife much, if I had to listen to philosophy according to Socrates all day I would find alternative amusements." Morton laughed. "Here, take a few dollars and do not worry about the accounting. Mrs. Black is at the Bletchly House. Arrived here on a steamboat and my docking boy sent word to me. She asked for you but he told me first and I wanted to deliver the happy news myself. Take her to a good eatery and see a performance. I will call upon you in the morning to be about business."

*   *   *

Samuel looked about the street awkwardly. He was dumbfounded that Eliza had found her way to Nebraska. Must be Morton's doing . . . . maybe . . . he wondered. What game is he playing now? Had Eliza run out of money? Were the children fine?

Dust was blowing down the pounded clay of the main street sandwiched between the clapboard storefronts and proprietors were gamely trying to sweep their boardwalks clean. It was a losing cause.

Samuel knew where the Bletchly House was located. He had often had a drink or two within its confines. He wondered if Morton had told Eliza her husband would call on her today. He pulled his timepiece out of his pocket and saw it was nearing noon. Bit early for a serious drink he thought . . . . had not even had lunch yet. Perhaps he could get a sandwich and put some whisky in his milk. No, he should have a beer. If he limited himself to one he knew it would fortify him against whatever argument she wanted to have. He hurried down the street trying to stick close to the storefronts, as he wanted to remain inconspicuous. It would be like her to be silently prowling about town and he needed to wait to see her when he was good and ready. He figured in his mind how much lunch and a beer would run and knew he still would have enough to show Eliza a fine time, if she chose to be civil. He even thought it might be a magnanimous gesture to pay a little forward on her room and board. Surely she would not being moving into his back room.

Black found himself in the billiard house catty corner with the Bletchly House and took a table. He was somewhat more at ease in these confines knowing Eliza never entered gaming halls. He ordered his beer and pork garnished with onions and had his fill. Seeing little time had lapsed he ordered another beer and then, using the same logic, he asked for milk and one finger of whiskey. Thoughts ran through his head how to approach Eliza. He knew he had not sent money back since . . . When? He could not recall. But he was a federal judge now, all that was in the past. He wondered whether the children were with her. He doubted it as he felt Morton would have mentioned that detail. He got up, left a small tip and purchased a peppermint on the way out the door. Sufficiently fortified, he made his way to the Bletchly House with a newfound confidence.

Eliza

Chapter 1

Black found Eliza in the sitting room by a window reading a book. Her face seemed to glow softly in the daylight. He approached quietly as he had forgotten how pretty she could make herself. He took off his hat and was speechless, but only for a moment.

"Hello, Eliza." He said. "I heard you had arrived."

"Hello, Samuel." She said without looking up. "I knew you would come."

"Hell, Eliza." Sam spat. "Of course I came to see you." He looked around for a chair to pull up but could only see a large settee against the far wall. He looked back at his wife and saw she was looking straight at him. He asked if she would join him for conversation. He saw her look away and out the window. She had a far off and lonely look about her. Maybe she was simply tired from the journey.

"Surely Samuel, but first I want to apologize for my last letter. I have thought about what I had written to you and it was unfair." Her gaze returned to him. "Oh come here and take off your coat. I have never seen it so badly in need of mending."

Samuel wanted to take her by the hand but he only said, "Let's go over there. We will both be more comfortable." He looked back at the others gathered in the foyer and motioned to the settee hoping to keep their conversation private.

Eliza rose and walked across the room with dignity. Black realized at that moment how he had missed her. He took off his jacket and she produced a needle and thread from the pocket of her dress and began to patch a seam. Once they were situated he asked after their children.

"They are all well. Julia and Robert in are looking after them in Pittsburgh. I feared taking the young ones on such an arduous journey.

The trip was long and hot but I feel all but the Thomas would have managed. I miss him frightfully. He does want to see you again."

"I could not have asked for a finer son." Sam could only mumble embarrassed by his neglect. "Eliza why are you here? I am happy to see you, of course . . . but where did you get the money?"

"I raised it Samuel . . . or at least most of it . . . Father paid for the rest . . . or at least what we thought was the rest. The steamboat purser wanted an additional luggage fee and I have to admit without that nice Julius Morton I fear they would not have let me disembark." She finished his patch and handed him back the jacket.

"Morton helped you out did he?" Black asked her. "Believe me he is taking an accounting."

"I told you Samuel, I raised most of it! A seamstress is always in demand."

Black admired her quick handiwork and nodded. He wanted to get the topic off the subject of money quickly. "It is no matter Eliza I am now a federal judge! Isn't that remarkable? Out here for this short of time . . . I did not even have to hang up a shingle and my appointment came through. Nebraska is a splendid territory for Democrats!"

Eliza nodded and her eyes sparkled like Black had remembered. "I was surprised when Mr. Morton told me of your good luck. So it is true. I had thought all good fortune was behind us." She looked down when she said this. "Still I am afraid for us. I did not think you enjoyed the law. I thought a law practice would make you begin drinking again."

Sam suddenly became quiet and looked down. "It is true that I found practicing law difficult . . . such pompous show and pretenses . . . but the judiciary should be easier; no scratching other lawyer's eyes out for clients, no more chasing down flea ridden no-accounts for the fees. I will make close to $2.00 per day! Paid for by the Federal Territory! Imagine how well we shall live!"

Suddenly Eliza began to cry and hide her face. Samuel grew concerned and laid his hand on her shoulder. "What is it my dear? What have I said?"

"Oh Samuel, I should not carry on so . . .," Eliza sobbed, "It has been hard . . . the collectors have been after us . . . they are like wolves! I called upon General Mitchell's widow but she can barely feed her own family. Senator Johnson would not return my letters. I tried to bring in what I could as a seamstress but it was never enough."

The guilt rushed in upon Black and he placed his hand upon her knee. "Like I said Eliza that is behind us; see I have some coin now." He showed her the money Morton had lent him. "I will put some toward your board and, in time, we can send for the children."

Eliza's face grew pale and she nearly shouted at him, "We will send for them now Samuel!"

"In time Eliza, we surely shall . . . I need to get set in my position and then . . ."

"No Samuel, we must have them here! Do you think that my sister can care for another three young ones so easily with her own children underfoot and Robert so ill?"

Black tried to sound comforting, "It will take some time, Eliza. We will need to find suitable accommodations surely . . ."

"But Julius Morton will lend us the money surely that nice man will . . ." Eliza's voice was growing desperate.

"No he will not lend us more money . . . I owe that "nice" man enough as is!" Black was growing angrier. "I can send Julia money if need be!"

"Like you sent us money, Samuel? How much did you send us, Samuel? I can see you cannot even tell how much you sent to me but I can! Do you want to know how much you sent in two and a half years?"

"Enough, Eliza! You know the reasons . . ."

"Eight dollars and ninety-five cents! That is how much it cost you to support your wife and children!"

For a second Samuel was angry enough to strike her but he realized the couple in the foyer was looking in on them. He glared back at her angrily and then slowly got to his feet. "Enough Eliza, I will do what I can for your boarding bill but we will talk no more today." He turned and walked away pausing before he crossed the threshold. "I do not know why you mock me. I did not come here for this."

"You are still a good-for-nothing scamp, Samuel! You left us to starve!"

Samuel stood trying to subdue his anger. He backed away and could hear her quiet sobs behind the door as it was closed. He calmly approached the housemistress and handed her a dollar, enough to keep Eliza in her room for a little more than a week. The man proceeded directly to his favorite watering hole and asked for a whisky.

*　　*　　*

The Omaha Bee reported that the former territorial governor, Thomas Cuming, after a brief but devastating illness, died surrounded by the family and the books he so loved. He was buried at Prospect Hill Cemetery in the wooded bluffs north of The State House. The man was thirty years old. Omaha City turned out in force for the funeral conducted at the Methodist Church. Even Bradigan O'Kelly attended the service having received a dispensation from a Council Bluff's bishop. Margaret Cuming, normally so poised, was momentarily devastated and nearly broke down as she placed the two Indian head dollars over her husband's eyes. An eloquent funeral oration spoke of his life's loves and pursuits. A poem was drafted in his eternal memory:

> Light be the turf of thy tomb;
> May its verdure like emeralds be;
> There should not be the shadow of gloom;
> In aught that reminds us of thee.
> Young flowers and an evergreen tree
> May spring from the spot of thy rest,
> But no cypress or yew let us see,
> For why should we mourn for the blest?[17]

The Omaha newspapers were full of praise for the man who had united the factious frontier communities into a recognized federal territory and kept it from descending into the violence of Bleeding Kansas. Would there be any doubt Nebraska would be elevated to statehood? Thanks to Governor Cuming, *The Omaha Bee* reported, it seems a sure thing. His friends spoke highly of Cuming's ambition and drive. Even his enemies gave him a degree of respect, which had been noticeably absent during his lifetime. One influential Nebraska voice refused to comment in any way towards the former governor, however, Julius Sterling Morton declined to speak further upon his old nemesis. Within the Secretary's mind, silence was to be considered as much praise as he could muster for Governor Cuming.

---

[17]   Funeral Oration by James M. Woolworth; April 17, 1857

The Black Administration

Chapter 1

November 2, 1857
Omaha City, Nebraska Territory

As soon as Commissioner Denver was out of Nebraska Territory, J.S. Morton distanced himself from administration policy on the proposed homestead act. He was never a political fool and he knew the sentiment within the territory was strongly in favor of sweeping homestead legislation regardless of the future impact it may have upon naïve immigrants or the American Indian tribes. His demands for a homestead act won him no support in Washington and he grew more dependent upon his influence with the locals.

The Honorable Samuel W. Black was appointed the federal judge in Omaha. He had never experienced professional success as he had throughout the last six months. Black began to earn enough money to purchase a home for his family and even began to make payments on the loan owed to Morton. The old political curmudgeon reluctantly accepted the monthly payments; although he made it clear he would have preferred the loan paid back by favorable judicial decisions for his landowning cronies. Black was not above weighing the scales of justices from time to time but he could not bring himself to be outright bought and paid for. For the most part, he ignored the intricacies of the law and relied upon a sense of fundamental fairness. It was a form of jurisprudence that could only exist on the western frontier where appellate practice was nearly unheard of and unimaginably expensive, even for the Morton and Cuming families of Nebraska. Indeed, Thomas Cuming's widow invested prudently in freighting manufactured goods across the Missouri and was soon the wealthiest woman in the territory.

Samuel's old friend William Richardson had even been appointed
as the territorial governor after Denver had returned to Washington.
This was due in part to negative reports on Izard's commitment to the
Democratic Party. Richardson knew enough to keep his mouth shut on
issues regarding federal homestead legislation and slavery so he had a fair
shot at completing a full term. He decided it was best to tow the party
line when possible. The man needed the job after being soundly defeated
in the Illinois governor's race. Richardson's time in Illinois was not a
complete waste, however. He lugged an outdated version of the Illinois
State Statutes and black letter law across the Iowa prairie and arranged for
a ferry to haul all the codices across the Missouri to the Nebraska State
House. A minor disaster was averted when the ferry hit an ice flow and
nearly capsized. Much cargo spilled into the water but the books were
only slightly worse for wear. The legislative clerks dried the books as best
they could and physically cut and pasted all references from the State of
Illinois to the Territory of Nebraska. Nebraska had an instant criminal
and civil code ready for consideration. Under Richardson's guidance the
territorial assembly put their stamp of approval on the legislation and he
became the father of Nebraska law.

Samuel's court inherited the original codicils and he displayed them
proudly in his federal courtroom. Black joked that the books were too
waterlogged to actually use but then he found reading the law was often a
hindrance to effectively seeing justice done.

Eliza and Sam purchased a home that was modest but firmly
constructed. They were finally able to send for their children. On the
day the couple picked up the children along the docks Eliza placed an
affectionate kiss on his cheek. Black felt so good he retired to celebrate
with a drink or two, or twelve.

Chapter 2

Pah-Huku Village
December 12, 1857

The great Pawnee village of *Pah-Huku* lay on the southern bank near the northern bend of the Platte River. It rested nearly fifty miles from the town of Omaha City but whites were continuously settling near the village and wandering into the Elkhorn River Valley. The village had been what the whites would consider the "capitol" of the Pawnee Confederation during its hey-day at the dawn of the nineteenth century. Situated close to one of the most sacred sites of the Pawnee religion, the point where the proud Platte River wandered closest to the pole star, many older Pawnee traveled to *Pah-Huku* on spiritual pilgrimages. It was the oldest of the Pawnee settlements and had significance to the tribe beyond the number of lodges and carefully kept food caches.[18] An enormous grand earth lodge sitting in the middle of the village was all that remained of the majesty of the great Pawnee chiefs who had driven the Spanish out of the northern plains.

The population of *Pah-Huku* had been first decimated by disease, and then many of the Pawnee wandered south of the Platte seeking refuge from the sickness and respite from the constant harassment of the Sioux. Finally, many Pawnee listened to the promises of the white man and many of the chiefs to come settle at the Pawnee Agency. Here they would

---

[18] George Hyde estimates *Skidi* Pawnee first settled the village around the time Hernando Cortes landed in Mexico at the beginning of the 16th century. The village was then conquered by the Southern or Black Pawnee during their migration to the Platte River. In the 1850s it was a *Chaui* Pawnee village.

be safe. At least that was the promise of the white man. The land would be theirs for eternity.

Even the most stubborn ruler must eventually meet his end and as the winter of 1857 descended upon the prairie, the Great Chief closed his eyes for the last time. Surrounded by his many wives and most loyal followers he quietly passed away to the soft cadence of an olive tree rattle. The death of *Sharitarish Malan* came as a shock to the tribe, for many Pawnee felt the man would live forever. With his passing it seemed as if the entire world was placed on its head. In one generation, and largely under his leadership, the Pawnee had gone from being lords of the Platte River to unwanted intruders along its banks. White men ruled the river valley and had taken the flat plains for their wagon train road. The Sioux, Cheyenne, and Arapaho pressed upon them from the north and west.

Criers were sent out to each of the Pawnee villages to stand atop the earth lodges and sing the chief's death song. *Petalasharo* had thought the man was insane but he kept his tongue until after the Great Chief's passing. He could barely remember a time when the formidable old man had not exerted influence among the tribe. With the Big Anger's passing he knew the Pawnee would have one final opportunity to stand as men and protect their land and property as they had once done.

"What will the Pawnee do my husband?" asked *Pahaat Icas* as she rested her head against her husband's shoulder. "I know that I should be fearful for the future but for some reason I am not. Can the Pawnee survive without a strong leader?"

Petalasharo stroked her long black hair as he considered her question. He learned a trick from his father never to answer a question before two breaths had escaped from his lips. He found this rule was especially useful answering questions from wives. "The Pawnee will do what the Pawnee have always done woman. They will survive on this land."

Petalasharo adored Red Turtle since they first met the year after he had joined the *Chaui* in the *Pah-Huku* village. She listened to his words and he always found her companionship reassuring.

His wife continued, "But the whites will want a chief to negotiate with. The Pawnee are so scattered right now, who could bring them together? They listened to no one but old *Sharitarish*."

"The chiefs never listened to that man either which is why the Pawnee remain so scattered. Only the braves who continued to raid our neighbors listened to that old man's ranting and that is why we have lost such good will from the other tribes. The old *Sharitarish's* death is a gift from the stars. They see how the Pawnee have suffered and we must come together with our friends to rebuild our unity. The Great Chief would have never allowed this. The whites mistook decisiveness for wisdom and courage for honor. He did their bidding and warred upon our neighbors . . . we must walk another path."

"Soon the *Chaui* elders will have to decide upon a new great chief my husband." *Pahaat Icas* looked at him coyly. "If they are as wise as their grandfathers they will choose another *Petalasharo*."

Petalasharo looked at his wife with a glimmer. "You flatter your husband."

"It is true there are others and you are only half *Chaui* but you still would make a wise great chief."

"Ah my dear, *Pahaat* . . . you forget the Big Anger had a son . . . if I had to gamble many horses upon the question I would bet the next great chief will be *Sharitarish Tiki*."

Chapter 3

The year 1858 should have been the happiest period of Samuel Black's life. The man enjoyed his work, he had reestablished his social standing, and financial security, once unheard of for him, was nearly within his grasp. But a demon had gotten in him. He knew that he was drinking too much. He may have been able to disguise it from the uninterested public, but to those who had a passing familiarity with him, his drinking was impossible to hide. Many suspected it for some time.

Black's life had settled into a routine. He would arise hung over at six a.m. and try to ingest some crème and toast. He would usually make it to The State House by seven, hear cases and arguments until three and then work in his chambers until five or six in the evening. He would then travel to the Herndon House or another dignified establishment for dinner, drinks and often billiards. Most nights he made it back home for a nightcap or two. He rarely saw Eliza as he would sleep in his study on the davenport. Eliza knew enough not to disturb the routine. She cherished the time with her children and was grateful to her husband for turning their finances around. Still, when they did interact, arguing inevitably followed.

Samuel spent most of his free time with Governor Richardson and his political cronies. All of the men drank more than their share, and Black felt everyone tipped a glass or two, but Samuel was growing more and more concerned about his own drinking. It seemed he was the only one among them that drank alone. He began to hide his imbibing from even his boon companions. Samuel Black knew this was not normal.

William Richardson seemed to tire quickly under the strain of his governorship. He was always at odds with representatives of the federal administration and the various factions of local interests. He would no more than get an issue resolved in one arena than a new problem would develop in another. Two problems seemed terribly vexing; the local demand for the territory to make a permanent decision on the slave issue and political pressure to push for a homestead act. While each issue needed to be resolved at the federal level, local politicians screamed angrily for Nebraska Territory to take a stand and let their voices be heard. It was with relief Richardson took the opportunity to escape territorial politics and return to an appointed seat in his home state of Illinois.

Snow had fallen in a thick cold blanket when word came to Judge Black's chambers by one of the dock's messenger boys. His carefully crafted routine of dispensing law during the day and drinking to oblivion at night was about to be upset. President James Buchanan, quickly running out of reliable Democrats willing to travel to Nebraska, appointed him as the next territorial governor.

Samuel Black had become the fifth executive in less than five years. Nebraska Territory covered a vast swath of North America. Running from its southern border with Kansas and eastern border with Iowa, it followed the Missouri and Big Sioux Rivers north to the Canadian border and west to the continental divide. Administratively, the territorial government responsibilities were far less impressive. Its' influence remained largely limited to the population in southeast Nebraska and the settlements hugging the northern bank of Platte River Valley west to the hamlet of Lone Tree. The Great Overland Road and the vast Indian hunting preserves were nominally the responsibility of the federal garrisons of the U. S. Army and the string of forts stretching across the continent. Still administering Nebraska Territory was an enormous challenge. Black undertook it with a whiskey bottle tucked under his jacket.

Chapter 4

April 3, 1859
Lancaster, Nebraska Territory

"The Pawnee are camped over by Yankee Hill," blustered Patrick Davis in his heavy Welsh brogue. "What are ya planning on doin' about it, Donovan?"

"Why are you asking me, Davis?" Joseph Donovan replied with consternation evident in his voice. "I am not the law in these parts." Mr. Donovan had just stopped in the general store to pick up some nails to work on his shed, and cheese for his wife's dinner preparations. He was taken off guard by the three concerned citizens who immediately approached him.

"You were in the army, weren't ya? Fought with our dearly departed Governor Cuming against the Mexicans, didn't ya? Taking care of these injun rascals should not be too much strain for a war hero? Two steers were taken from the Davis place jus' last week. It won't be long my pigs will disappear and maybe my milking cow as well. I'll be in one hell of a fix. Jeremiah Garret lost his pigs last week!" The three men nodded in agreement and the storekeeper looked on sympathetically.

"Patrick, you know Garret only lost himself one pig!" interrupted Petr Kolchak the local Polish tack handler. "Knowin' Garret, he probably got drunk and lost it himself!"

"That's not the point," added Jim Goodrich, the local banker. "My wife was followed by two of those Injun beggars coming up to our very door! Nearly scared poor Lulu to death! Would of walked right in if she hadn't screamed."

Joe Donovan looked down at his well-worn boots in consternation. He had retired from the military and felt that he had earned a respite from these types of difficulties but the Pawnee were becoming a problem. It had been over a year since the Treaty of Table Creek had been signed and the settlers had been informed that all Pawnee were to move north of the Platte River, and yet they were still here! Donovan could not understand it. They wandered about, rarely setting up camp for more than a few days, never establishing a village or planting crops. They seemed to know they were not welcome yet they continued to loiter. He knew the Indians stole, although, he noticed, it was far less than rumored. Rarely did they take much what mattered but being a god-fearing man it was the principal of the thing!

Donovan shook his head looking downward and softly said, "Really not my concern . . . No Pawnee has bothered my family. You should take your worries to the sheriff."

"Now Joe," the banker's voice became slippery and motioned him off to one side. "You know this involves us all. We can't wait until these savages hurt someone. Might be you can keep one of these Indians from getting hurt with people being as edgy as they are. The authorities need to know and you're the only man fit enough without children who can get the word out. I will look in on Angela while you're gone . . ."

Joe continued to give Goodrich a quiet stare until the banker spoke up again. "You have a note coming due this harvest. The bank would consider rolling it over again . . . Matter of fact I could just about guarantee it if you could help us out on this."

Joe looked up. The additional time would be helpful. He started to nod and began to work it over in his mind how he would explain it to Angela. As man of conscience he couldn't in turn ignore his neighbors.

Joe nodded and everyone gathered around to slap him on his back. Goodrich even decided to take care of his cheese purchase. The banker noted in the back of his mind that nothing was mentioned suspending the interest on the Donovan loan.

Joe asked the men to write down their concerns and he would see what could be done. The nearest sheriff was more than thirty miles away, but Joe knew that there was little a sheriff could or would do. Donovan needed to travel to Omaha City.

That afternoon, Joseph Donovan filled his satchel with jerky and hardtack and his wife packed a couple of boiled eggs and bedding. Word of Donovan's trip on behalf of the town had gotten around and few neighbors stopped by to relate their own encounters with wandering Pawnee. They gave him a list of allegedly stolen items, mostly missing eggs and chickens. After he had heard the stories, Joe gave Angela a tired hug and set out, hoping to make it to the Platte by nightfall. Donovan had indeed been a quartermaster sergeant of Thomas Cuming's in the Mexican War and he had been one of Lieutenant O'Kelly's instructors at Jefferson Barracks. He rode out of Lancaster toward Platte Crossing hoping to make it across the river before nightfall. He felt the militia needed to be informed of what was going on and he figured he might as well be the person to carry that word.

Chapter 5

Omaha City, Nebraska Territory

"My dear General Thayer," the famous newspaper editor extolled, "Military men will always be welcome within the new Republican Party. A Republican leader such as you might find himself in some powerful and lucrative positions when Nebraska becomes a state."

"If" Nebraska becomes a state, Mr. Greeley," Thayer corrected the visitor. "That is a mighty big "if". Right now we don't have near the necessary population, besides southern politicians do not think highly of adding more "free" states. And with J. Sterling and his companions, Nebraska will always be a Democratic state. If an educated man like Thomas Cuming didn't see much advantage in switching parties, I don't reckon there would be much advantage to me becoming a Republican."

Greeley continued his sales job; "You have heard of Robert Furnas I presume."

Thayer laughed, "Sure, he was in the General Assembly during that squatter's fiasco, made a name for himself up in Florence during that charade. He became quite an agriculturalist I hear, so I'm sure that he an' Morton will be like peas in a pod."

"Don't be so sure about that, my good man. Morton will drift with the winds of advantage but Mr. Furnas is strongly considering Republican principals. I have invited the man to the Republican Territorial Convention in Bellevue this August. It would behoove you to join us."

Horace Greeley was the powerful editor of the New York Tribune, what many considered the closest thing to a national newspaper in the country. An invitation by a man such as Greeley was seldom turned down. As a philosopher and enthusiastic advocate of the conquest of the American West, he had become a friend of Thomas Cuming five years prior during the former governor's visit to the nation's capital. He was as surprised as anyone of Cuming's untimely demise. The rich and brilliant editor was on his way to tour the gold fields north of Pikes Peak when he stopped to visit his friend's grave and recruit promising men to his newest pet project, the infantile Republican Party.

"You do not think that Republicanism has much of a future?" Greeley took a heavy drag off of his Dominican Cigar and blew it quickly into the air of the Herndon House's drawing room. "I will tell you that this beloved republic of ours will see a change of biblical proportions before the next decade is out. We will see a final sweeping away of vested generational privilege and that slave-holding aristocracy. Soon land ownership will be the true measure of worth rather than gold. That sickly-colored metal's only practical application is to be an anchor to men's dreams. That is the reason I am traveling to Pikes Peak, to expose the degeneracy and poverty brought about by the misguided quest for gold. If a fraction of those misguided fools could be convinced to set up legitimate land claims, Nebraska would be populated enough to become a state in no time. Republicanism shall lead the way."

"Well, I know Thomas did not have much use for land claims, land barons or slave holders. You bring in more of those people waving deeds, pretty soon they will be trying to tote in slaves. Nebraska will become another Kansas. I could not agree to that madness. I agree with Cuming, God rest the man's soul, Nebraska was and always will be a pathway to the west. He wanted the continental railroad to follow the Platte Valley and I think that is more likely. It is best if our merchants made their money through commerce and trade rather than the production of commodities or land ownership. It is true that the fur trade has died down a bit, but that's only because our Indian friends have grown less cooperative. A sickness has affected them—hard of late, but that is sure to pass."

Horace Greeley puffed even more eagerly upon his cigar. He had little use for Indians or their welfare. He hoped that sickness would be the destruction of their race. "Their internal traits have simply made them unfit for modernity." He stated, "Haven't you read Darwin my good man? Could anything be clearer? The most cooperative red man could only be a burden to our nation's destiny. We will not need to kill them off . . . they will simply disappear with the mighty bustle of a new continent."

General Thayer looked down into his whisky glass and considered the newsman's words. "Sir, I don't know how I can argue against that right now—but I don't agree. I haven't studied much Darwin, I'll admit, but I have dealt with Indians my whole life. These Indians will not simply disappear. They are a thieving lot and survivors to boot. They may put up one hell of a fight. Indians may be worthy adversaries for a man with steel in his gut."

"Perhaps. Killing Indians will undeniably be less controversial than killing whites—even ones as ignorant as southerners." Greeley smiled and picked up a glass sitting on the end table. "You have become quite a philosopher yourself, so it can be said Thomas did not die in vain. He was a man of passion. Here is to the former governor. He was always an excellent conversationalist during the evening hours. You do him proud!"

"Thank you sir, I apologized that I cannot escort you myself but word has come in that the Pawnee and Otoe are growing restless. I need to stay with the militia."

"Understood my good man, but please read up on Republicanism. Our nation will soon need men of humble yet iron clad principals. If you play your cards right, I am sure that our government could find a more suitable service for you than remaining a prairie policeman!"

Greeley looked hard up and down his Dominican cigar and took two quick drags; "But I do agree with you on the railroad prospect. With all of the fuss that the southerners are kicking up right now the country will need a northern route for its railroad. That means the Platte River Valley and that means settlements all along its route."

Thayer considered this and said; "Buchanan favors the southern route, weather would make laying tracks easier and cheaper. It's also closer to the mountain passes, but if there is a war, and Missouri and Kansas aren't friendly to Washington . . . Nebraska might be chosen. But an American civil war? God forbid the thought."

"My good man," Greeley boasted; "it would not be a war. Don't you study politics and what they gripe about? The southerners, by their own intellectual reasoning, could never field a national army with all of their crowing over state's rights. They can barely stand one another let alone cooperate. The southern states would be destroyed piecemeal. You should be cheering the southern politicians on even with this disagreeable bloodshed in Kansas. I applaud each bullet shot in Kansas because it guarantees a rail spike driven in Nebraska!"

Colonel Thayer looked down because he doubted Horace Greeley had ever even heard a bullet shot in anger.

The man continued; "The southerners' ranting is far more useful to you and Nebraska's aspirations than you realize. And be not further troubled about a civil war, at least not much of a war. Only two brigades for each rebellious state would be required to bring them to heel. Become a Republican I tell you again! We will sweep this land of slavery and polygamy—southerners and Mormons be damned! Unfortunately, I do not see many opportunities for a soldier to show his grit against such adversaries."

Thayer poured himself another two fingers of whiskey. He leaned forward and said, "There's always Indians to fight."

Greeley laughed in agreement. Too true, too true! A future Republican politician would find a few military victories very useful . . . look how far that rail-splitting Abe Lincoln got from the Black Hawk War . . . truth be told I doubt that man ever fired a musket with an impolite intent in his life! Find yourself some Indians to fight Thayer and Washington D.C. will be your oyster!"

Chapter 6

April 5, 1859
Omaha City, Nebraska Territory

Joe Donovan had finally made his way into Omaha City despite the Platte River's worst flooding in anyone's memory. He and Lieutenant O'Kelly were discussing whether the water was bound to rise or fall in the next month. "Cannot imagine there is that much snow up in those Rocky Mountains," Donovan speculated. "Do you suppose it may be due to all that gold digging the miners are doing by Pikes Peak?"

The two men were setting at the Tralee Saloon, a local establishment that was friendly to Catholics and understanding Anglicans. It was located on Harney Street and benefited from being near the docks.

O'Kelly answered, "Doubt it, even if the miners are digging twenty four hours a day they cannot cause that much wash-off."

Joe shook his head and said, "I don't know . . . suppose the gold is underneath the snow and they are dumping it into the river. That could cause a lot of damage. Don't know how many miners that would take though . . . probably a lot more than they have around the gold fields."

"That is rather far-fetched. I would say." O'Kelly offered. "They do not have that many miners and besides, the gold is inside the mountains, not in the snow."

Donovan wasn't all that convinced but he was mighty proud of Cadet O'Kelly. He had blossomed into a fine officer. "You don't know how many miners they have up by Pikes Peak; could be more than we reckon."

"I agree with you there." O'Kelly nodded. "I saw a wagon train pass through last month that had three hundred wagons in it. Those trains are becoming common."

"You know Brady . . . not even all the miners are coming through Nebraska. I here they are traveling through Kansas and Texas. I even heard shiploads of Chinamen are coming in through San Francisco. That many miners could be causing these floods."

O'Kelly had enough of his nonsensical conversation. He had never had the old sergeant's engineering mind. He finally told Joe neither of them was smart enough to figure the flooding out. They just had to deal with it. "Maybe Governor Cuming could have thought on this flood water for a while and come up with a solution, but the man had long since passed"

"What'd he die from anyway, Brady? He wasn't that old. Shoot, he was the youngest officer in our regiment. He seemed like just a kid when he was my lieutenant in Mexico."

O'Kelly nodded his head in agreement. "He was 30 or 31. Can't exactly remember what folks said about how he died but apparently it took him hard. He just seemed wise beyond his years with the way he spoke, what with mentioning all those old Roman generals and Caesars and such."

That brought a smile to Donovan's face as a flood of memories came back. He slapped the table and said, "You bet . . . I remember him saying things like Pompey did this or Cicero said that . . . half the time we had no idea what the man was trying to tell us through those Latin references."

Both men laughed and Bradigan O'Kelly raised his glass. "Here's to Governor Cuming!"

Donovan picked up his glass but the said, "Sorry Brady, I just can't drink with a Crucifix hanging over me."

O'Kelly laughed and looked back at the four foot wooden wall hanging, "I can tell you're not Catholic! I should explain the Tralee doubles as our Parish on Sundays and Holy Days of Obligation. We even had a Council Bluff's bishop or monsignor or something here to consecrate the bar. It functions well as our altar. Now this is only a temporary dispensation mind you. We've already started construction of our own church out on Farnham Street."

"You Catholics," Donovan sighed as he looked warily up at the cross and took a swig of beer. "Can't imagine that thing does any good with the sale of devil's brew in a river town."

"Joe you would be surprised, although, things do slow down a mite during Lent!" O'Kelly said with a twinkle in his eye. "The only entertainments they can't allow are ladies of the evening. But enough about the Tralee," he slapped Donovan on the boot. "It is good seeing you but why are you here? You did not come to drink with me, talk about floods and your old lieutenant."

"That's true, Brady. I came to talk about all the Indians roaming around Lancaster. Folks are getting nervous."

"Indians are everywhere in Nebraska Joe, you know that."

"I know, but why are they still wandering about? Remember that big fuss Morton and the Indian Commissioner made about the Table Creek Treaty. The Pawnee were supposed to move up north like they agreed. Why aren't they there? This is going to lead to trouble."

"Are they causing any trouble?" O'Kelly asked.

"Some neighbors say they stole pigs or eggs and the townsfolk don't like them lingering about the barns and buildings. The farmers say they hear natives moving about at night."

"Can you give me specifics, Joe?"

"Not really." Donovan looked back at the barkeep and motioned for another brew suddenly forgetting his concern with the cross. He really began to wonder what his neighbors were making such a fuss about.

"Then what do you expect me to do about it? Sounds like you need to take it to the sheriff."

"Brady, you know just as well as I do that no sheriff wants to tangle with Indians. If we had a sheriff who would, we wouldn't want that either." Donovan thanked the bartender who brought the beer and dropped a nickel into his hand. "Some publicity seeking tin badge would get a bunch of his buddies together, call them a posse, and who knows where it would lead?"

O'Kelly nodded. He knew hastily deputized frontier possess, and even bona fide elected sheriffs, could quickly turn into overzealous vigilantes.

Donovan continued, "I'd like to talk with General Thayer. He could control the militia."

O'Kelly still seemed skeptical. "We can speak with the general, but I still do not know what the Pawnee have done. Believe me, I know what happened at Spirit Lake, but those were Sioux, not Pawnee.[19] I think the

---

19   In early March 1857, a small band of Santee Sioux revolted against food shortages on their Minnesota Reservation. Dozens of settlers were killed near Spirit Lake, Iowa.

reason people are so jumpy has little to do with Indians. Those thieves your neighbors fear could be escaped slaves. Those natives moving about at night could be Pawnee, or brigands, or Negroes. They could be, God forbid, free-staters or border ruffians. You know about Bleeding Kansas. You're probably right, the general should hear about this but not because of Indians. The war drums I hear right now are not from Pawnee. The drum I hear is being beat by southern slavers."

The men made their way up from the Tralee to the parade field on the far side of The State House. They found General Thayer overseeing a newly formed squad attempting to line up in a basic drill formation.

"My God O'Kelly, would you look at this?" Thayer said with dumbfounded exasperation pointed to the vaguely structured men. "I swear for the life of me I do not know who is more incompetent, our new recruits or that sorry excuse for a sergeant?"

"Sir, this is an old instructor of mine from my plebian days, Joe Donovan. He served under Governor Cuming during the Mexican War as a sergeant. He'd like to report some concerns he has about the Pawnee down by Lancaster."

Thayer's interest was piqued when he heard about the Indians.

"Certainly, I would like to meet a proud veteran of that grand and glorious campaign." Thayer shook Donovan's hand eagerly and led the two on a walk. "What is it you have to say? You know if it was up to me it is about time we gave those Pawnee a handsome licking!"

O'Kelly discretely shook his head but did not say much. Donovan reported as was his agreement and the wheels began to turn in Thayer's head. This may be the opportunity he was looking for.

Chapter 7

April 27, 1859
Pah-Huku Village

Tahirusawichi raised the pipe towards heavens, turned a full circle, and dipped it reverently in each of the four cardinal directions. The tribal headmen were arranged in a circle just below the crest of the hill. To the north flowed the broad Platte River swollen by the spring runoff from the far away Rocky Mountains. The village hugged its southern banks bustling with rare activity. The Pawnee chiefs had gathered in *Pah-Huku*. The elders had chosen a warm sunny afternoon to name their new tribal Great Chief, something that not happened within the memory of most of the men gathered. A great brown eagle floated gently above the gathering as the medicine man sang:

> "Oh, Eagle, come with wings outspread in sunny skies. Oh, Eagle, come and bring us peace, thy gentle peace. Oh, Eagle, come and give new life to us who pray.
>
> Remember the circle of the sky, the stars, and the brown eagle, the great life of the Sun, the young within the nest. Remember the sacredness of things." [20]

As *Tahirusawichi* allowed his words to lift with the prairie wind and as the breeze softened, *Petalasharo* stood and began to speak. "The

---

[20] Pawnee Prayer, Literature of Indigenous Peoples, researched and organized by Glenn Welker.

Great Vault of Heavens cradles the earth and its people in its embrace. The universe is a circle, for do you not have to gaze along in a circle to view the horizon? Are not his arms strong enough to encompass us all? The Pawnee are the most blessed upon this earth for have not the star gods favored our people? As the universe is a circle, as are our lodges. No one side is stronger or weaker than the other. Our families and our clans are a circle. No man is closer to the gods than of any other man. If my words carry greater weight than any other man's I ask you for what cause? We are all Pawnee, the *Akitaru* as well as the chiefs. We all wish for our people to survive. I have asked the gods to guide my words so that I will speak with wisdom. If our people do not fade as the cottonwood leaves when the chill falls upon the land it is not because of words that I have spoken, it is because of the gods continuing to bless us."

Petalasharo continued, "Thank you my brothers for considering me worthy as your head chief. I have dreamed of this moment wondering what I could say to show my gratitude. I do not know what should be said. I am humble. A great chief should never lack for words or sayings of comfort and yet here I am without a tongue. I can only say that I love you. I love my people. I love this land that we dwell upon, raise our children upon, and bury our ancestors within. I . . . I will never forget this moment."

Petalasharo sat and the pipe was lit. *Tahirusawichi* stood to offer the pipe to each of the headmen gathered along the crest. A number of the medicine men began a ceremonial chant and each Pawnee leader forgot the people's problems for the time. They had chosen another Great Chief and it was possible to imagine the Pawnee with a future once more. It was possible to look forward to big harvests and successful hunts. It was possible to look forward to children who played in the water and boys who would hunt in the sun. It was possible to see girls looking forward to weddings and old ones enjoying a gathering to gossip. It was possible to smile and vision a rising sun on the morrow.

The new Great Chief had not predicted how the chiefs would cease to support Little Anger after his father had died. The conservative chiefs remembered Little Anger's wayward earlier years and they did not trust him. The more progressive chief's saw *Petalasharo's* ideas as something that could help the people and needed to be tried before the Pawnee lost too much. It was easy to convince the elders *Petalasharo* was the best choice.

Petalasharo knew his first big task would be to arrange for the summer buffalo hunt. Typically, the Pawnee would travel west to the Platte and Republican River Valley, but there had been trouble this year. Scouts reported the Sioux and Cheyenne were hunting in the area. They were always a menace to the Pawnee people. It was vital for the Pawnee to have a successful hunt without complications. Even getting a sufficient hunting party across the Platte and back loaded with meat and fur would be challenging if the water did not go down. *Petalasharo* had been discussing with the chiefs going up north to the Elkhorn River Valley. Large herds had been reported in the region and *Petalasharo* wanted to reestablish friendships with the Ponca and *Omahaw* tribes. Many of the Pawnee chiefs were impressed and open to their Great Chief's new ideas.

Little Anger witnessed the new Great Chief's favor and seethed with resentment. He chose to bide his time. He knew his time to regain influence would again arrive.

The Burning of the Village at Pah-Huku

Chapter 1

June 12, 1859
Pah-Huku Village

It was a perfect summer day with a gentle breeze out of the northwest. The sky was a deep blue and was dappled with lazy white clouds. *Petalasharo* was sunning himself with his pipe atop *Pahaat Icas's* earth lodge watching his daughters tend a fire. His wife was off tanning deer hides while the Great Chief smoked. The village was abuzz with activity with bands gathering for the great summer hunt.

"*Nawa Petalasharo!*" shouted the Knife Chief as he rode up on his spotted bay pony.[21]

"*Nawa,* my good friend!" answered the Great Chief. "It is good you have come. I have some fresh tobacco for us to share."

Lechelasharo swung down from his horse and climbed atop the lodge. The Knife Chief had traveled to the *Omahaw* to discuss the possibility of hunting together along the northern Elkhorn River. It had been a lengthy and tiring journey for a man his age. With the eagerness of a child, however, he welcomed his friend's offer to smoke. Once he had situated himself, he took up the pipe with great dignity and began to fill the bowl with the rich tobacco.

"How are our friends, the *Omahaw*? Will they join us on the hunt?" *Petalasharo* asked.

"Some *Omahaw* hearts are bad toward the Pawnee. They are angry about the raiding of the past." Knife Chief replied.

---

[21] *Nawa* is a Pawnee greeting.

The Great Chief nodded sadly. It would be difficult to convince other tribes the raids the Angry Chief had encouraged would not continue. *Petalasharo* had sent out criers to each of the bands trying to discourage their braves from raiding the *Omahaw* and Ponca Tribes. He was determined to develop friendly alliances with these tribes.

"But the *Omahaw* remain as fearful of the *Lakota* as we are. They are wary having the *Santee* so close and the *Ogalala* are always too near.[22] The chiefs see wisdom in hunting together."

"Good, Good. The people need a successful hunt. The rains have been too frequent for our crops." *Petalasharo* stated taking a deep draw from his pipe. "I worry the whites will still want the people to move to the agency. We are not ready to move our village."

Knife Chief got his pipe ignited and thought long before the next words were spoken. "Perhaps our white friends have forgotten about our village. They did not send the wagons as promised."

The Great Chief laughed quietly and said, "*Lechelasharo* my old friend, you know the whites have long memories. They remember what they want to remember."

"Ahh . . . Great Chief, yes, they remember when they want to remember such things."

"Yes," *Petalasharo* muttered, "when they want to remember such things. I fear this will be a long difficult summer for our people."

---

[22]   The Santee were in the process of being removed from their ancestral lands in Minnesota. Congress was considering moving the tribe further west in Nebraska Territory along the Missouri and Niobrara Rivers.

Chapter 2

Omaha City, Nebraska Territory

"Are you telling me the bridge at Platte Crossing is out, General Thayer?" Samuel Black looked dumbfounded after having had one too many brews at the Herndon House's newest addition. The owners of the boarding house had fenced off the back plot and planted a number of imported Japanese blossom trees to provide a more sophisticated ambiance. Despite the determined attention of the yardmaster, the trees seemed stubborn to die. The men sat imbibing and enjoying the evening air. The view from the plot was a fine one with the lower terrace of Omaha and the docks spread before them. The evening glow shown on a faint mist on the river and the hills of Iowa lay beyond.

"No Governor." Thayer answered as he nursed his stein while Black and his drinking cronies looked on. "The bridge and its footings are sound, but nothing is going to get across the Platte. The river has swallowed it up. There are two twelve-foot channels that have broken through the eastern causeway. The western causeway is underwater too; although no channels have cut through. I sent O'Kelly over to inspect it and we figured it is only a matter of time."

Black looked over at O'Kelly with curiosity and asked, "Well lieutenant, what did you see?"

"The general's right sir, no wagon could get across over that northern causeway. My horse got up onto the bridge but I had to take his saddle off and he is a good swimmer." O'Kelly reported with a hint of pride in his mount. "I took a few men across. The south side is in better shape but not by much. It has no channels cut yet but that's sure to change with time. I met a delegation from Nebraska City. They were mad as hops. Seems the freighters are backed up all of the way to Lancaster. Morton's man says that the territory or the army needs to get the crossing passable again."

Fenner Ferguson sat at the table paying more attention to his whisky mix than he did the conversation. "Morton can fix that damn bridge himself. He was against putting the thing up in the first place."

Black laughed, "Those squabbles predate my administration. I'm sure this flooding has put a crimp in his pocketbook and now the secretary has changed his mind."

Thayer piped in, "It is an economic issue and a tough one at that. Governor we have one ferry going across but it is too small for buggies let alone wagons. Those freighters need something that can carry Conestogas. The army won't lift a finger. They say this is our problem."

The governor was more than irritated as the conversation was severely cutting into his drinking time. Thayer continued when Black did not respond. "We need to fix it obviously and that's going to take funding. I left a good man in charge down there to start on the sandbagging, Joe Donovan. He knows some men in those parts . . . but they will need to be paid."

Black looked at the general and scowled. "The territory has no money Thayer. If Morton wants that crossing fixed he can pour his own coin into it."

"Governor you do not understand. The territory needs the bridge passable more than the South Platters. Without that crossing Morton can do whatever he pleases—secede if he wants, he has threatened it before; or maybe convince enough fools they would be better off throwing in their lot with Kansas." Thayer looked at his lieutenant to make sure he had the engineering report right. "The entrance of the south side needs shored up with sandbanks and a dyke. We need to be doing some channeling on our side to get the river back within its banks. Governor you need to go down and inspect our operation."

Black grew even more annoyed, "Why me, Thayer?"

"Governor, I can't offer federal voucher script. Only you or the treasurer can do that what with the assembly reforms. You know Wyman's in Washington City."[23]

---

[23] W.W. Wyman, Nebraska Territorial Treasurer

"Damnation, Thayer! This sounds like another of your Indian scares! You better not be crying wolf on this one too. Why is everything a confounded emergency?"

Thayer sat up looking as if he had been insulted. He pressed his hand over his heart and said, "Governor, I have never cried wolf when the citizens of our territory did not need our protection!"

"Bah . . . tell that one to your underlings, Thayer." Black took a shot and ordered a repeater. "I'll go but I want an escort. I will take your aid de camp."

"Thank you sir, I am sure it will be Lieutenant O'Kelly's privilege!"

Black looked deep into his whiskey glass and took a quick sip. "Damn it," he muttered. "We will need to get an early start, lieutenant. I trust you know my mount and can have it saddled at dawn. If I am not there I trust you will come get me." Black reached for the bottle to pour himself another drink as O'Kelly and Thayer looked at one another.

Thayer's eyes rolled. "Hope Black is fit in the morning." the general whispered to O'Kelly. "You make sure he gets started and makes that trip, even if you have to pour him in the saddle.

"Yes, sir." Bradigan sighed. "I'll sure do my best."

Chapter 3

June 13, 1859
Platte Bridge Crossing

Much to O'Kelly's astonishment and relief, Governor Black emerged from his front door as dawn was breaking. His wife accompanied him. She wanted to make sure her Samuel got up upon his horse safely. Eliza's puffy eyes betrayed that she had been crying and she turned her husband toward her and gave the man a sorrowful hug. O'Kelly diplomatically turned the horses away to pretend not to be interested in their conversation.

"I do not know why you do this to us Samuel, drinking like you do. You remind me of a dumb animal insisting upon putting his head in the trap time and time again to get a morsel. I know you are determined to kill yourself this way. There is nothing I can do about that, but don't you see how this hurts me and the children?"

Samuel looked eager to be on his way and O'Kelly heard him say he was alright and he only hurt himself. He teetered down the front steps and with a determined effort swung himself into the saddle. O'Kelly gave Mrs. Black a short and respectful tip of the hat and the two rode off in silence.

After they had gone a distance the governor asked that they slow their horses' trot.

"Certainly, sir."

"Was Eliza awake when I arrived home last night?" Black quietly asked recalling vaguely the lieutenant dragging him into the house. "I must admit, I do not rightly recall."

"Yes, governor she was and she seemed none too pleased." O'Kelly answered. "I must admit this morning you seem not much worse for wear."

Black smiled a bit to himself and then leaned over and with a chuckle said, "Lieutenant can't you tell I am still feeling the whisky. Give it an hour and then I am in for a harsh spell."

Sure enough, an hour into the ride, with the sun now fully over the horizon, the governor stopped his horse, got onto the ground on hands and knees and vomited. He then found a scrub brush and relieved himself of other fluids. Presently, returning to the horse, Sam rested his head upon the saddlebag for a moment and then practically drug himself up onto the mount. That was the last indication he continued to feel poorly.

The day drew warm and muggy but they made good time. The only words spoken by Black the rest of the trip were "I am getting too old for this." O'Kelly heard him utter that observation a few times before late afternoon and, just before dinner time, the two rode down the bluffs along the northern table into the Platte River Valley. Black saw that Thayer had not been exaggerating. The bridge looked more like a lonely barge adrift in a wide long lake.

He gazed over to the far side and saw a dozen men gamely trying to sand bag the southern bank and return the river to its regular channel.

"Damnation," the governor swore. "This will be a chore!" His hand slipped into his front pocket and took a quick drink of warm spirits. "I am getting too old for this!"

Chapter 4

June 20, 1859
Pah-Huku Village

The entire village had expected a large influx of bands for the summer hunt. This year it was even more exciting with all Pawnee interested in seeing the new Great Chief. The turnout was even more than expected. The usually sedate village was quickly transformed to a thriving and bustling staging area. The women and boys gathered the food, mules and horses and prepared the travoises for what everyone hoped would be loads of fresh buffalo meat and skins. The village was heady with anticipation and anxious to be off. Few noticed the concern hidden in *Petalasharo's* mind.

A group of *Skidi* braves had reported that several settlers had taken rifle shots at them last week and small groups of whites had been seen lurking in the area for the last few full moons. Little Anger had spoken big words at the last council fire. He had stated that it was because the white men now saw the Pawnee as weak since they no longer raided the tribes to the east.

"Why would the whites not see the Pawnee as women since they heard *Petalasharo's* words at the treaty talk?" Little Anger began to sing in a high woman's voice mocking the Great Chief. "We Pawnee need help from our enemies! Our people need food! Our people need blankets! We are no longer men and need the blue coats to protect us!"

The lesser chiefs forgot their dignity for a moment and began to laugh. The Great Chief himself looked amused, as he had never seen such a performance. Only the Knife Chief, *Lechelasharo* sat quietly smoking.

"*Sharitarish Tiki* should stop now," roared Horse Chief with laughter. "The white men will think he IS a woman. They will put him in a dress, and make him till the fields!"

Little Anger now grew frustrated seeing that his joke had gone too well. He spoke now in his regular voice shouting that if the *Omahaw* and the Ponca no longer feared the Pawnee, how would the whites or the *Lakota* respect them?

Petalasharo decided to speak. "I agree with *Sharitarish*. This is a heavy matter. It is even more important than whether he or I could fit in a dress."

The chiefs and elders chuckled.

The Great Chief continued to make his point. "It is important to maintain the dignity of our people. I do not agree with him that refusing to raid against our brothers makes us weak. I am grateful the *Omahaw* will hunt with us."

Little Anger quickly spoke up. "While my father was Great Chief the Pawnee did not need to hunt with the *Omahaw*!"

Petalasharo quickly answered. "The Pawnee do not need to hunt with the *Omahaw* now but we choose to do so." He looked about the lodge at the faces wondering what other words would be spoken. He lit his pipe to increase the drama of the moment and then spoke in the middle of a puff. "We choose to do so because we are wiser men."

Little Anger rose to his feet and shouted. "You dare to speak bad words at my father!"

The Great Chief looked up and said nothing. Knife Chief began to speak and all eyes turned toward the man. "*Sharitarish Malan* was a wise man while he was Great Chief. *Petalasharo* did not say he was unwise. Big Anger had words of wisdom because the gods are wise. Now we have a new Great Chief and the gods are no less wise. He now has the words of wisdom and, it is true, our hunts have not been good lately. While we hunt with our brothers the *Omahaw* we will be in new land and away from the whites and our enemies. This is wise."

Horse Chief pulled Little Anger to the ground once again and jokingly asked for some more "*Petalasharo* woman talk." Little Anger began to rub his hands together and began shriek another loud voice asking for wagons. The lodge's mood once more lightened as the Great Chief began to grin and look down. He said a silent prayer for the safety of his people and the success of his hunters. He was glad the chiefs were laughing again. It had been a long time since the tribe had much to celebrate.

Chapter 5

June 21, 1859

Crossing a swollen river was always more challenging for white men than it was the agile natives of the plains. The whites relied upon heavy plow horses to haul questionably buoyant wagons. The inevitably overloaded boxes were constantly bogging down or tipping midstream while the Indians were content to haul smaller loads with their supple little ponies.

Black had now been helping the workers rechannel the river for close to a week with limited success. He was now fuming as howls from merchants and freighters both north and south of the Platte were ringing in his ears. Typically, the workers found him genial. At least in the first week but with the demands of others Black grew testy. The man had nearly had enough and was close to abandoning the project. The one bright spot was the remarkable effort put forward by Joe Donovan. Having learned his organizational skills from Cuming, the man had developed a system relying upon shifting work details that alternated between digging and bagging and operating a system of two ferry convoys. The governor was sore with many of the politician's expectations but he was always satisfied with Donovan's work.

The two men rode along the south bank trying to determine the best spot to begin work on another levee. It was close to dusk and Donovan found the lowering sunlight made it easier to pick out subtle eddies and changes in flow that reflected the river bottom. The river seemed to glow a hazy orange as it reflected the evening sky.

"You know when I first heard Thayer had promised you and your men payment to work on this endeavor I was none too happy." Black admitted. "But you have proven your worth especially with those ferries."

134

"Well," Donovan answered, "I had to learn something in the Mexican War. Cuming and I may have not seen much combat but the quartermaster general sure kept us busy. I always feel bad when someone points out that I did not do my share of fighting."

Black pulled his horse up short and reached for his liquor vial. "You listen to none of those chicken louts. You think any of those garden generals ever handled a quarterlies task? Hear you and Cuming were posted in Galveston."

"Yes sir. We were indeed."

"My God man, I went through that bloody swamp on my way back. You had one hell of a backbone to listen to those wounded soldiers cry night and day." Black took a sip of his whiskey. "Our transport was docked in the bay. Thought the worst screaming I heard was on a battlefield, but the moaning and crying you put up with . . . didn't matter whether it was English or Spanish . . . Don't take much of a scholar to make out a boy crying for his mother."

Donovan thought he saw the governor shudder a little but he righted himself and offered him a swig. Donovan took the vile and noticed how light it was. He took a small sip and returned it to its owner. Black took it back and immediately drained the contents.

"My good fellow, I will say again how pleased I am at the work you've done. Can't say I thought you had the grit to even sleep out under the stars after I heard Thayer go on about your report of those Pawnee near Lancaster. Thayer made it out you were a real chicken little."

Donovan's ears picked up. "He did sir? Now what exactly did he say?"

"Oh . . . how you and your neighbor folk were all riled up about the Pawnee wandering around their farmsteads swiping chickens and young-uns from their cradle."

Donovan looked a bit concerned, "Brady . . . or I'm sorry, Lieutenant O'Kelly and I discussed it beforehand. I hope the general understood I tried to make my report accurate. Sure do not recall saying any children were taken."

"Oh relax Donovan, I know how Thayer is itching to get into the field and knock heads with someone. I know how he exaggerates such matters."

"Yes, sir." Donovan said.

"You have more than proven your worth to me. We should get back to the camp now our light has left us. We can do more accurate fieldwork at dawn."

Joe nodded in agreement and escorted the governor to his tent. Once inside Black began looking for his hidden stash of spirits for his nightcap. Not where he typically the stored the jug . . . He felt a momentary panic. He began tearing apart his travel gear growing more and more desperate as he could not find what he would need to get a decent night sleep. His mind began to race. It must have been stolen. He could bring the men together and have them fined and sent home if they would not return the booze. But how would that look? How could he make them fess up? Could he have the camp searched? Should he? He thought and pondered. Could he have gone through his stash already? He had been drinking a little. Surely not enough . . . what with the nightmares?

Black stood up decisively. He knew what he was going to do. Retrieving his last letter to Eliza he wrote a quick salutation on the bottom and folded it into an envelope. Leaving his tent he marched over to the campfire and found Joe Donovan enjoying a cheroot with some of the men.

"Gentlemen, I have decided to head for Nebraska City tonight. There is no point in dawdling. We need supplies that should have my authorization and personal attention so I will be off."

Black took all of the men by surprise. Donovan looked up and said, "Sir, I thought we were going to ponder on that upstream levee tomorrow?"

The governor raised his hat and replied, "No need for me to be there. I trust your judgment. Naturally, you will be in charge here and Reuters will continue to watch over the northern works."

Donovan looked at each man still beside himself. One of the men took a small drink from his own bottle noticed the governor was watching him suspiciously.

Donovan continued, "Least you could head out in the morning. No need taking chances."

"No Joseph. I do not need such concern. Have someone saddle my mount."

Donovan gave in and offered to have one of the men ride with him on the full day's journey. "Never hurts to have an extra gun hand. We can send McGuire. He is not much help with the work scheduled for tomorrow."

Black thought about it and nodded, "Fine, fine."

"Doxy, see to the governor's horse and rile McGuire." A small lad leapt up and ran out to the rope corral. Donovan got up and walked over to Black.

"See to it that this letter gets on the packet for my wife in Omaha City in the morning." Black handed Donovan the letter.

"Are you sure about this sir? Those bushwhackers have been mite good about getting our vouchers and orders to Nebraska City. It is nothing that cannot wait."

"Enough Joe, I will head through Weeping Willow and then on to the Missouri. I'll be back before you know it."

It was close to midnight before the governor and his companion rode off to the southeast. Donovan saw the two disappear into the darkness. Strange, he thought to himself. He began to worry . . . Hope nothing goes wrong. My wife always says I am losing things. How could I report I lost a governor?

Chapter 6

June 24, 1859
North of *Pah-Huku* Village

Most of the Pawnee had swum or rode the breadth of the swollen Platte River and were gathering along its northern bank. Many of the tribe, mostly the elders and the children, had wandered off to the south or set off on their own—back to the agency. The village would be deserted for the next month or so while the tribe was off collecting the meat, robes, and sinews from the shaggy buffalo. These items would be necessary for the Pawnee to survive the cold months of winter. Teepees would now be the shelter of choice, as the Pawnee would follow the well-known and oft-beaten paths to the northern hunting grounds.

The hunting party was composed of the fittest members of the tribe. The hunters were all warriors and the younger women who accompanied the party to help butcher the bison were hard workers and brave beyond belief. There were also older boys who would tend the horse herd. These lads were anxious to make names for themselves. The tribe had completed making preparations for the final send off and now it was time to enjoy one last night in the Platte River Valley.

The Great Chief was pleased with the preparations that had been made. Perhaps his anxiety had been unnecessary; for now it seemed as if all was right in the world. It was a magical evening as the Pawnee danced and feasted in the quiet muggy air. Miles to the west magnificent thunderheads piled upon one another laying streams of lightning to the earth. It was the type of summer evening the Pawnee had looked forward to and celebrated for centuries

Petalasharo stood with his wife before their teepee and watched the tribe sing and dance and parade. He paid particular attention to the boys run back and forth from the fires to the horse herd. The Great Chief remembered many summer hunts from his past. Those hunts were always so full of excitement for a boy and he thought back to the first time he was allowed to follow and help with the horses. It was a warm and gratifying memory. He hugged his wife and could not help but feel a tremendous amount of contentment and joy.

Pahaat Icas patted her husband's arms and kissed him on the cheek. "Go now my husband." She said. "It would not do for the Great Chief to miss the evening prayers." Reluctantly *Petalasharo* smiled and agreed. He then quickly strode off in the direction of a thumping drum. He looked up at the sky and then to the clouds that had devoured the setting sun. He thought to himself that it would be a good night for prayers although the clouds would soon be upon them. The singers may not be able to enjoy the stars for very long but we will see a splendid sunset.

Chapter 7

June 25, 1859
Omaha City, Nebraska Territory

Eliza Black received her husband's dispatch a few hours after the supper meal. The mail carrier had been assuring her that letters originating from south of the Platte were long delayed due to the flooding but that did not mean no letters were coming. She had waited nervously and now it arrived. Eliza held it carefully before opening the letter wondering what type of a mood he had been in at the time it was written. She saw the writing was firm and legible. The woman knew from the penmanship her husband's hand had been steady indicating he had had a few spirits. She withdrew to the drawing room and found a comfortable seat. Opening the letter she began to read.

> *Dearest Eliza,*
>
> *You were quite right, as I am sure that you know. The damnable ride down to the river nearly did this old man in. I would have you know that, at least thus far, I have refrained from so much as a sip. I fear your temper woman! There was no need for the children to be awakened that last morning. I was well on my way although I quite agree I should not imbibe so freely when duty shall call early in the morning.*
>
> *My God Eliza! If you had my problems you would drink as well. I look out for both you and the children or do you disagree with that assertion? Money shall no longer be a concern of yours and yet you begrudge me relief. Perhaps I have not done so in the past but that is truly behind us. Have I not told you so?*

I look out for you, and before I did so, your father looked out for you. Have you not relied upon your sister as well? Who is there to look out for me? Who can I turn to with questions of propriety and correctness? I have only my mind and strength to rely upon and it has gotten us this far. I do not know why I put up with your damnable preaching when your mouth contorts with shrieking it reminds me too much of your disagreeable father.

I do not know where I shall gain the courage to return to you but, of course, I will do so. We are two rudderless ships lashed port to stern for fear the waves will prove too temptuous to sail alone.

The river has proven even more swollen than reported. It is remarkable Thayer spoke true on this one occasion. I do hope the man keeps this reliability up but I fear accuracy will prove too much of a burden to bear. You should see the loggerheads pounding the sand and running the ferries we have down here. The Territory will end up paying these vagrants a fine penny. My God . . . what else is there to do?

There is one chap who seems capable. Perhaps the first South Platter I have met who actually thinks about his words prior to spewing forth. Donovan is his name and, right as I can tell, he served under Cuming in the infirmary post of Galveston. Perhaps he knew Kellogg? Do not get me started on that witless knave?

I must leave so I will see this missive off on the next post. Obligations require my attention in Nebr. City. Pat the small ones on their heads for me and give them my kindest regards. They should not worry so much for me. Perhaps you flap your gums at them too often?

> *My dearest sweet Eliza,*
> *Truly my heart is yours, Samuel*

Eliza put the letter down and looked around for the children, seeing that none were about she put her head down and began to weep.

Chapter 8

Along Maple Creek

Nearly four hundred Pawnee crossed the Maple Creek and began to make their first nightly encampment along the far butte just north and outside of the Platte River Valley. They had already covered ten miles and none of their enthusiasm for the hunt had dimmed with the trek. The boys had been catching prairie hens and rabbits for the stews during the march and the women began to set up the evening cook fires and the teepees.

It was one of the younger boys who first noticed the gray smear along the southern horizon. Perhaps he was homesick, or perhaps, he was just trying to determine how far the tribe had traveled. For some reason his eyes were sharp and he knew something was wrong. He pointed out the oily strand of smoke to one of his friends and word quickly spread. The tribesmen knew the land and looked upon the curves and swells of the distant hills as familiarly as they admired their wives. They knew their village was on fire. *Petalasharo* looked out warily. He instantly thought it could have been lit by accident, perhaps a forgotten lodge fire. But no; the smoke grew blacker and he knew someone was in the village burning their old lodges and food caches.

The chiefs gathered the men. They would need to protect the tribe and caution was always called for. After a defensive perimeter was organized, and the horse herd was secured within the draw of the creek, two groups of scouts were sent back to investigate the fire. They were instructed to ride five miles and then approach the camp on foot. A young warrior named Sky Chief was to lead the scouts. *Petalasharo* gathered the medicine men and priests about him to pray. It had been a terribly tiring day and despite the anxiety for their village, most of the

Pawnee succumbed to sleep amid the gentle chants and songs of their leaders.

The Great Chief knew how vital the food stores of *Pah-Huku* were to the immediate future of his people. They would insure food, medicines, and material for the long winter ahead. The caches were fallback provisions that would keep starvation at bay regardless how successful was the summer hunt. He was determined to keep the vigil until the scouts would return.

It was long after the sun had set and the worrisome smoke was no longer visible when Sky Chief returned to the encampment. He leapt off the horse and immediately made his way through the curious people to the Great Chief. *Petalasharo* and Little Anger were waiting by the fire, with the Great Chief doing much better to hide his concern than the younger chief.

Sky Chief bent down by the fire and began to rub his hands. He muttered a quick prayer, which the chiefs recognized as being an incantation uttered prior to a momentous announcement.

"The village has been burned. *Pah-Huku* is no more." Sky Chief said in a near whisper.

The chiefs began to look to one another and then to their Great Chief. *Petalasharo* simply nodded. It was Little Anger who spoke up. "This is because the Pawnee are no longer feared!" He shouted. "Who could dare do such a thing?"

Sky Chief nodded to the brave who had traveled with him. The brave handed Sky Chief a broken arrow and Sky Chief handed it to Little Anger. Little Anger took but a moment to examine the arrow and handed it to *Petalasharo*. Both chiefs knew at once that it had the etchings of the *Lakota*.

"I do not think the throat-cutters burned the village."[24] Sky Chief announced. "My braves saw from a distance riders and horses leaving. We saw one horse had the markings of an Otoe, the other horses were unmarked but their tracks were shod in the white man's way. One of the riders wore a ceremonial Comanche head dress."

"It was the white man!" Little Anger announced. "They only pretended to be Indians. The shod ponies show their deceit!"

---

[24]   Throat-cutters was a term the Pawnee used for *Lakota* or Teton Sioux due to the intense warfare between the tribes.

Petalasharo held up his hand to redirect the questions, "We need to know of the village. What has become of the food stores?"

"The stores are no more. All of the caches were burned outside of the Great Lodge. The meat was burned quickly. The maize and nuts took longer. Perhaps some of the hides can be saved. My braves reported the smell of the white man's lanterns on the ashes."[25]

"Is the encampment in danger?" Horse Chief asked. *Petalasharo* nodded at the wise question.

Sky Chief was ready with an answer. "No, we saw only a handful of tracks. Our braves will deal with whatever comes."

Horse Chief looked anxiously and said, "that does not mean no enemies are about. There could be many warriors hidden within the valley, or even in the hills where the people will head."

Petalasharo nodded and said, "It is wise to remain on guard."

Little Anger once again spoke up. "So we are no longer Pawnee but mice hiding from our enemies? We must ride back and strike those who have done this especially since they were white men!"

Petalasharo asked Sky Chief, "What is it you wish to do?"

"I wish to ride back and drive these raiders from their land. If they are whites they will be easy to track and punish. I also fear for our people who left *Pah-Huku* and remain south of the flat water."

The Great Chief nodded but added, "If they are white?"

"What can you mean?" Little Anger shouted, "If they are white? Have the whites not bothered our people? We know they are out there! I am ashamed to be Pawnee if we continue to hide as women!"

Finally Knife Chief spoke up. "We must be wise my brothers. If the food stores are gone then we need to hunt. We cannot hunt and chase raiders through the hills. Our women and children would curse our bravery in the winter when their bellies are empty and the children have no hides."

Little Anger answered back, "We need to kill the men who burned our sacred village! Did *Pah-Huku* mean nothing to you? My father was a man and if he were here he would strike our enemies."

"Your father wanted to give the whites the village. That is what he wanted us to say at Table Creek or have you forgotten!" *Petalasharo* spoke up with a tinge of mirth in his voice now as he looked directly at Little Anger.

---

25 Spermaceti oil or possibly kerosene.

"*Sharitarish Malan* said words to the white man but words mean nothing; especially words to the white man! He would have ground them into the sand had they tried to burn *Pah-Huku*! We have become women!"

Many of the braves were now gathering and began to listen to the talk of Little Anger. Their anxiety was growing and morphing into a thirst for vengeance.

Petalasharo spat back, "Were the Pawnee women when the Delaware burned our village the year of the bad drought?[26] Were the Pawnee women when the *Lakota* burned the Old Village when I was a boy?"[27] What did *Sharitarish Malan* do to avenge those attacks except collect more ponies for his herds?"

"You speak badly of my father?" Little Anger stared in disbelief.

Petalasharo sat back and thought. He did not regret his words but he realized that he had not spoken, as a chief should. He had not spoken with dignity. He held his thoughts and waited for two breaths to talk again. "Little Anger is right. The Angry Chief did as he should have done. He made sure the people had food and horses to trade. That is an example we should follow now. The Pawnee must outlast our enemies whether they are white are red. For our people to last we must have food and continue on the hunt. I tell no warrior what he should do but to be a man for our people, we need hunters. Our brothers, the *Omahaw* wait for us along the Elkhorn. We should join them. Our hunt needs to be successful."

Knife Chief spoke up before anyone else and stated *Petalasharo's* good judgment should be followed and the matter seemed to have been decided for the majority of the tribe. The Great Chief rose with dignity and retired to his teepee. Sky Chief announced that he would continue to track the raiders and give fight if the opportunity arose. He asked for braves to join him and thirty warriors were chosen. Little Anger was not

---

[26] The summer of 1832 Delaware and Osage warriors sacked a *Chaui* Pawnee village.

[27] The Sioux attacked and burned the *Skidi* Villages the summers of 1843-1846. The attack that was the most devastating occurred June 27, 1843. Hyde relates that 120-150 Pawnee were killed and 41 lodges burned. It is referred to as the Battle of the Lodges.

one of them. He felt accompanying the tribe on the hunt would provide more opportunities to undermine the Great Chief's leadership.

Petalasharo could not sleep that night. He knew that the men of the tribe would burn for revenge and who could blame them? The great village of *Pah-Huku* was lost. He felt like crying for his people, but he decided that his harsh words had already shown too many of his emotions this evening. He could no longer afford emotions, for as the Pawnee Great Chief, his emotions were no longer his alone.

Depredations Along
the Elkhorn

Chapter 1

June 26, 1859
2 miles south of Fontanelle, Nebraska Territory

Francis Depuy was terribly proud of his farmstead. His property featured two wood frame buildings, a vegetable cellar, sod barn, and a fenced corral. His wife, Sarah, had long dreamed of a wooden floor that would not get muddy in the drizzle and pasty with snow frost. She dreamed of a polished floor that could be properly swept in the summer and covered with fine rugs in the winter. Francis had been saving money for the boarding in an old jar in the cellar and he had nearly secured the twenty-five dollars to purchase the supplies. The family was nearing their goal and only waited for the next weekend to travel to town to speak with the hardware merchant.

Indians had often visited their home; usually small groups of no more than a half dozen or so as they wandered from village to village. *Omahaw,* Pawnee and Ponca were the most common but the Depuy's had even been visited by Sioux and Cheyenne. The Depuy's took their religion seriously and unlike most settlers in the Elkhorn River Valley, they had not imported their faith from Europe. Francis Depuy had grown up in Boston and was baptized on the bank of the Charles River within sight of the Anglican bastion of the Old North Church. He believed that faith without works was dead and required his family to follow the tenants of the New Testament in their interactions with others; all others whether they be white, red, black, or yellow. The Depuys seldom had a great deal, but they shared what they had with their occasional visitors. The Indians, for their part, respected the gentle couple and were never as much as a nuisance.

Depuy had just begun weeding his sweet corn with his five year old daughter when the pair picked up a sound they had never heard before. It was Indian voices crying out in an unearthly crescendo. Looking about Francis did not seeing anyone, nothing but his growing crop and the grasslands beyond. He did not know what to do. He seldom carried his old Kentucky rifle and that was only when he was concerned coyotes or wolves were nearby. Cautiously, he reached for his daughter and pulled her close. She did not know enough to be frightened.

The cries seemed to multiply but still he could not see any Indians about. Quickly he got down on one knee and told his daughter to run for the house and to have her mother send her and her brother down the vegetable cellar. The girl ran for all she was worth although Francis doubted she was the least bit frightened. The small child ran to the far side of the farmhouse where her mother was holding her older brother anxiously.

"Papa wants us to go to the cellar, but I don't want to go."

Sarah looked down at the children with the angry war cries ringing in her ears. Visiting Indians had never screamed before and the sound was so unearthly and terrifying. Sarah thought the worst.

"Come now you two. Jimmy, take your little sister to the cellar like your pa says." She hurried them off in the right direction. "I have to fetch something."

Sarah ran into the house and grabbed the single shot rifle off the wall. She checked and made sure that it was primed and loaded and made off for the cellar. A moment of panic set in as she returned to the outside and heard the Indian screams had grown louder and seemed even more fierce. Bursting into the vegetable cellar she found Jimmy holding his sister closely who had by now sensed the fear in those around her and had begun to cry.

"Take this Jimmy and don't let anyone get through that door. No one Jimmy! And don't leave no matter what you hear! Your pa and I will be back for you. Don't you or your sister make a sound, you hear me! I need to go find your pa now. We will be back for you soon as things are safe." Sarah Depuy hugged the children and paused. She began a fearful cry and Jimmy began to cry. "Don't make a sound!"

"Yes ma."

"Stay here and don't you leave." Sarah got up and left the two sobbing children. She saw her husband standing in the yard talking with the fiercest looking Indian she ever seen. The Indian had his hair roached up and back in the Pawnee fashion, but this one seemed different from any Pawnee they had met before. The man was a warrior. He was heavily armed with both a bow and a battle-ax and his face was painted half red and half blue. The screaming had subsided but she heard crashing sounds coming from her home. She ran to her husband who quickly gathered his wife in his arms.

"What is it Frances? What do they want?"

"Shhh . . . Sarah. I don't rightly know but I don't want them to hurt us."

A terrible crash was heard and Sarah recognized the sound of her fine dinnerware being broken upon the ground. She bit her lip to keep a sob in her throat and hugged her husband tighter. Two braves emerged from the home with links of sausage wrapped around their necks and their mouths stuffed with boiled eggs. They carried pillows and quilts under their arms and began tossing the items upon their horses. The warriors were painted as fiercely as the first Pawnee but loaded down with their spoils they seemed far less dangerous.

The first Pawnee said something unintelligible to Francis and made motions with his arm that Depuy instantly recognized as Indian sign for horse.

"No." Depuy answered. "We have no horses here. I raise crops."

The Pawnee said something again to his companions and they walked toward the stable. In a moment, they were leading Depuy's plow oxen with halters and tack draped over their backs.

"No" Depuy said as he walked toward the animals and grabbed for one of the halters. "I need these animals. Please take something else!"

The fierce Pawnee screamed a cry and frightened Sarah into a cry as well. Francis turned around and saw the warrior had a pistol pointing at his head. Depuy folded his hands to imitate prayer and pointed to the prairie. "Please go now . . . take what you want but please go now. Please."

The fierce warrior appeared somewhat mollified and then one of the braves holding one of oxen by the ear said something. The Pawnee began to argue and Francis began to think that they were debating whether to take the oxen with them. Finally the fierce warrior rode up to the cattle and shot both through the flat part of their skulls. Lightning could not have killed the animals quicker and one of the braves had to jump away from the falling carcass. Sarah screamed again and Depuy continued to make the feeble gestures with his hands. "Please go . . . Please just go."

The fierce Pawnee looked about and saw the vegetable shed. He pointed it out to the braves and they began to move toward the sod structure. Sarah saw where they intended to go and screamed. She had to get there first. They could not find her children. She would not let them. She flung her body against the door to bar the Pawnee's way and the door slammed against its frame. A sharp rifle report sounded from inside the shelter and a bullet tore through the door into Sarah's back.

Francis Depuy stared in horror at his wife. She was still clinging to the door frame with a bullet wound in her heart. He ran to her immediately realizing that one of the children must have mistakenly shot their mother. Drawing her into his arms he helped her lie down against the cellar's walls. He cried and screamed in anger as he felt his wife's life drain from her body. Sarah felt a great relief in her final moment. With her dimming vision she saw the shocked Indians mount their horses and ride away.

Chapter 2

June 27, 1859
6 miles west of Fontanelle, Nebraska Territory

Uriah Thomas had always been a bachelor and the man was happy with his lot in life. He had a nice spread of 10 acres stretching across rolling hills and three acres of good bottomland along the banks of the Elkhorn River. Uriah felt he had earned himself a good life, one he was more than happy to share with his seven dogs. He ran a hog operation and his pigs loved to wallow in the mud along the river. Uriah would take his dozen sows and boars down to the river where they could roll and play. His dogs helped look after the lot and seemed to enjoy watching the hogs bury their snouts deep in the smooth sandy loam. Uriah liked raising hogs. It was far less effort than farming. His dogs did most of the difficult work keeping them rounded up and the pigs were allowed to feed themselves eating turnips, mushrooms, prairie grass, dead mice, whatever they could sink their teeth into. Uriah felt it was a good life, he would never grow rich but then again, he was not an ambitious man.

Thomas liked to take a bottle of whisky down to the riverbank while the hogs wallowed. He would lie in the shade with his lazier dogs and sip some of the bitter liquid. At times he even would rest his eyes and nap some. He was never afraid of having a pig run off on him. He understood they were as content with their life as Uriah was with his. Indians had visited the hog farmer before but he was never as charitable as the Depuys. He never had much that they wanted, pork was never a favored dish with Indians of any tribe, but what he did have he refused to share, especially his liquor.

The fierce Pawnee knew Thomas, having been turned away by him at the end of a shotgun a few years back. They did not intend to give him the opportunity to collect a firearm this time and Uriah obliged them by drinking more than he had intended. This time the Pawnee did not cry out. The two braves crawled down the banks of the river keeping their scent up wind. It was not until they were nearly upon Uriah and his hogs that the first dog barked a warning. An arrow quickly silenced the cur and then the next hound was killed. The fierce Pawnee brought his moccasin down upon Uriah's throat and bludgeoned the next dog trying to protect her master. The remaining dogs were now barking up a storm and the two Pawnee braves had to shoot them down in a hail of arrows.

The fierce Pawnee looked down at the fat bachelor and saw nothing more than anger. Why is this man not afraid? He must be out of head from drink. The Pawnee reached down to grab the bottle and took a generous swig. Uriah was screaming like the devil and struggling to get free but years of soft living had made him helpless. The braves shared the bottle and then began to club the hogs. Five died before the rest scattered and ran onto the prairie.

Uriah was shoved into his soddie while the Indians took their time ransacking the outer buildings. They found little of value but did take his shotgun and deer jerky and three bottles of cheap local whisky. The fierce Pawnee would have killed Uriah but he remembered the words of *Sharitarish Tiki*. "Kill no whites. Only make them fear the wrath of the Pawnee."

Thomas was too inebriated to understand how close he was to being killed. He was struck on the side of his head and locked in the old soddie. He spent the rest of the day half knocked out and half passed out. It was only toward the following dawn he was able to gain his release and stagger toward Fontanelle.

Chapter 3

June 28, 1859

Little Anger had indeed met with the warrior Yellow Sun the night of the burning of the *Pah-Huku* village and had instructed him to punish the whites. Yellow Sun had been a competent warrior in his day but the man had long since reached his prime. Yellow Sun could still strike fear in many enemies, however, with a large battle worn body and a fierce face that had been exposed to the harshest extremes of weather. He had two devoted and eager sons and he long professed a deep resentment of the whites because his sister had been killed by one. Little Anger also found in Yellow Sun a useful trait. The weathered warrior was smart enough to accomplish his tasks and too stupid to receive acclaim. The man was also too lazy to go on a killing spree. He would do what he was told to do and stay quiet about it. In addition, Yellow Sun would never compete with Little Anger for leadership. Yellow Sun was not only an *Akitaru*, or commoner; he was perfectly satisfied to remain so.

Little Anger wished to send a message to the whites that the Pawnee needed to be feared and respected. If the settlements along the Elkhorn were cleared out of these meddlesome trespassers, Little Anger could present it as a *fait accompli* and take immediate credit. The elders would then recognize him for his cunning and wisdom and bestow upon him the prestige that was rightfully his. Little Anger knew timing was everything and so far so good.

Unfortunately, Yellow Sun's boys were not as discreet as Little Anger would have wished. They began to brag to their fellow tribesman about their exploits. The two spoke of how they ate hearty of the white man's porridge and drank Uriah Thomas's whisky. They laughed at killing those fat pigs and wished they could find more to kill. The Pawnee were, as a whole, not hateful of the white man but anger at the burning of *Pah-Huku* burned in their hearts. Many heard this talk and rejoiced.

Soon many of the hunters were sneaking off one by one looking for opportunities to wreak havoc. They ran off a shepherd boy along Maple Creek and slaughtered the lambs. They burned a wheat field north at the terminus of Looking Glass Creek and butchered the heifer belonging to Jonathan Clemens. Most of the tribe, however, continued following their leaders to the hunting grounds. Most saw wisdom in ignoring the wild talk and understood the need to stay to their tasks.

Old Uriah Thomas had freed himself from the wrecked soddie the Pawnee had locked him into and ran off to the nearest town to warn the populace and scare them with a colorful accounting of his ordeal. Settlers in the area were terrified and flocked en masse eastward. The massacre at Spirit Lake was still a fresh memory as were the near constant reports of bloodshed and violence in Kansas. They found comfort in numbers and tiny groups gathered to make their way to Dead Timbers.

The settlers moved along in silence petrified their horse's neighs and wagon creaks would betray them to savages who would sweep down and take their scalps. Regardless of the strength and numbers in their groups they were terrified the Indians would attack out of the hills in countless waves. The prairie had never seemed so terrifying and mistakes occurred due to sheer anxiety. Two horses were ran to death, a tiny child broke her arm when a buggy overturned attempting to cross a washout, and numbers of livestock were either abandoned or lost out on the grasslands. The miseries mounted as the exhausted and frightened exiles swarmed into Dead Timbers.

The settlement at Dead Timbers was the largest town on the Elkhorn. It had a well-trod main street that featured a clapboard dry goods store, livery stable, land office, smithy and bank, and even a boardinghouse with attached saloon. Trading occurred there frequently and the town often entertained Pawnee, Ponca, and *Omahaw* Indians. The smithy and the bank were both brick structures and the stable was sod. The settlers quickly decided if they were to fort up against the natives these buildings would provide the most protection. Wagons and barrels were tipped over and soon the town had a defensive perimeter and resembled a crude fortress. The women and children began cutting up linens for bandages and the men stockpiled arms and ammunition.

It was soon decided the fort was secure enough to send out riders for help. Two young men and a boy were chosen and instructed to take separate routes to notify the authorities in Omaha of their plight. The scene of their departure was heart rendering because no one knew where the Indians were. Could the entire territory have been overrun? Was Omaha City burned to the ground? The wildest theories were given credence by the settler's ignorance of the situation.

Chapter 4

June 29, 1859
Along the Elkhorn River

The Pawnee were in fact moving further away from Dead Timbers and the majority of the tribe knew nothing of the terror a dozen or two warriors had inspired. The tribe was still following the river as it wound northwest. Antelope were plentiful with the waters running so high that summer and the hunters were able to quickly gather meat for the trip. The game was so plentiful many of the hunters were hopeful the buffalo would prove just as numerous. However, most of the Pawnee still had heavy hearts from the destruction of the village. They knew they could never go back and things would never be the same.

Petalasharo never spoke of *Pah-Huku* since that night they saw the flames. He simply repeated that they needed to concentrate on the tribe's business at hand. The old, the young, the sick, all depended on the success of the hunt. Lodges and food stores could be rebuilt. However this summer, and the opportunity to gather hides and meat with their brothers, the *Omahaw,* may never come again.

There had been much bad blood between his people and the *Omahaw.* It was time to soothe those wounds and heal the bad feeling with their brothers. The white men were coming upon them and no one could trust what they would say or do. The *Lakota* were always near and ready to descend upon either tribe lusting for their game and scalps. Could anyone defeat the *Lakota*? Perhaps the whites could but the Lakota would not die easily. He had seen that too often in the past. There were enemies all around. What could the Pawnee do? He thought. What should the Pawnee do?

Chapter 5

South of Fontanelle, Nebraska Territory

Depuy and the children tried desperately to understand what tragedy had just befallen them. Nothing was done rest of the day after the Pawnee left. They simply huddled together around the dining table reciting prayers on and off while Sarah's body lay in the cellar. Finally, Frances decided they needed to leave, but first Sarah needed to be buried. He waited until the sunrise. It took all of the next day to dig a grave deep enough to keep coyotes out. Frances went about the work with a small potato shovel and the labor was hard. The man had not eaten a morsel and he was exhausted having not slept. He required frequent pauses and progress was slow. Darkness had fallen and a thin sickle golden moon rose over the southeastern horizon. Depuy did not have the time to construct a coffin and so Sarah was wrapped in two heavy winter quilts she had stitched with her own hands. The feel of her in his arms, cold and stiff, made him shudder as he gently lowered her downward.

The night was a sullen and sad as the moon reluctantly lifted itself into the sky. Frances Depuy had buried his wife in a field just to the south of his family's house. His two children offered what help they could although his son sobbed quietly until his mother was placed into the ground. He was old enough to understand the enormity of what had happened. Frances was able to keep his composure but only because of the two children. Without a saddle horse Depuy led his family to town. Luckily there were a lot of settlers rushing downstream with the same idea and it was not too long before they were able to catch a ride in the back of a bushwhacker's wagon. They made it to Fontanelle the next morning.

Word had already reached the settlement and most locals believed the worst. Stories of bloody massacres and a widespread Indian uprising

chilled spines and boiled blood. Sheriff J. W. Pattison of Fontanelle
organized twenty men to form a county posse and ride out onto the
prairie. He was a hard man who had moved up from Kansas with a
price on his head for siding with the abolitionists in the wrong town.
Six years before he had shot to death two border ruffians who had
vengeful kinfolk. Rather than kill all of his neighbors the man packed up
his family and did not stop at the Nebraska border. The town council
noticed that here was man with backbone and bestowed him with a star.

Pattison formed up the posse leaving a few older deputies to manage
the refugees. He then sent word of the outrages to Omaha City. The
intent of the posse was simply to gather survivors as they scouted the way
to Dead Timbers. Pattison and his men did not lack courage, for no one
knew how many Indians were out there.

Chapter 6

June 30, 1859

The residents and refugees of Dead Timber spent a long terrifying night holed up peering over their makeshift walls thrown together from barrels, wagons and sidewalk planking. The moon cast a glow over the landscape that seemed to reveal thousands of hiding places along the outlying grasses and shrubs. A sentry thought he saw eyes peering from a copse of trees. He consulted with his companions. The nervous sentries decided it would be wise to conduct a raconteur. Unfortunately, no one had a stout enough heart and it was decided to wait for sunrise.

Dawn broke warm and slow upon the land. It seemed even the morning sun was nervous to peep over the horizon. Still, with the sun's light came an uptick in town's morale, yet anxiety lingered. No one knew whether word had reached other settlements of their plight. Some sentries thought they had heard rifle shots to the south, but no one could have been sure.

* * *

A mile and half to the south, two of the sheriff's men came across a half dozen Pawnee trying to light a deserted cabin on fire. They fired on the group and the Indians retreated into the cabin. The shots drew more Indians who begin shouting and firing arrows from an arroyo running along north of the spread. Now it was the turn of the whites to take cover leaping behind some fencing. They returned fire but began to pick their targets with more deliberation knowing they had limited ammunition. The noise attracted the rest of the posse who came charging over a hillock. The cabin and the arroyo were now under a constant stream of fire with only a few sporadic shots coming from the Pawnee. Pattison no more than ordered the men to stop firing and began to look over the situation when Indians burst through the window and made a rush for the ditch. At first, the posse was taken by surprise and in the process of reloading, but a hasty burst of gunfire killed one Indian through the door and another fell just before he reached the arroyo. The posse felt that a few others had been hit and one man began to chase the braves. An arrow shot into his shoulder caused the man to drop and crawl back to the others.

The gunfire fire lasted longer than the sheriff thought prudent. It appeared no one knew who they were shooting at any longer and he shouted for it to stop. Once again Pattison ordered a ceasefire. The firing reluctantly subsided. He knew he had to put an end to this. The sheriff sent six men to go the right and six to the left. He spoke to the men who had originally driven the Pawnee into the cabin and tried to determine how many Indians could remain inside. The sheriff saw that the grass was thick along the ditch and only the good Lord would know how many natives could be hiding in the brush. He wanted to encircle as many as he could and wait them out.

Pattison had been a sheriff for many years now and he took his oath seriously. He had a burning sense of justice. It may have been frontier justice, but it was justice just the same. He had never been a soldier. To him these Indians needed to be arrested and brought before the law, not killed in a gunfight. Many of the posse did not share his reluctance for immediate bloodshed, they wanted to ignite the cabin and let it burn.

Around noon his men reported the encirclement had been completed. Not a shot had been fired for four or five hours and there had been no signs of life. Pattison ordered the circle of men to move forward slowly and within an hour the cabin and arroyo were secured. Three Indian bodies were found. The one brave shot inside the cabin remained where he fell, and the one who had nearly made it to the arroyo crawled only a few feet further before dying. There was a dead Pawnee shot in the back lying inside the arroyo. Blood poured into the broken ground and ran down toward the river. The Indian had a bow strung over his back and so the posse assumed he was the one who had shot the arrow. Before Pattison could order otherwise the dead Indian's body was thrown unceremoniously into the river.

Pattison now had a decision to make. Blood had been shed. His men had put a stop to an act of arson but the owners of the cabin were nowhere to be found. Had the settlers been captured and taken hostage by the Indians who had escaped? His deputy wanted to cross the Elkhorn and follow the Indians who had escaped. He pondered for a moment trying to decide what he and his men should do. He knew Dead Timbers was just a few miles upriver. Suddenly, he and his men heard war whoops from north of the Elkhorn and they all quickly gathered. The sheriff knew his men were edgy and tired. He was himself shaken by the Indian cries he had heard. The decision was made. The party would make haste toward Dead Timbers hoping that the town still stood. No one protested as the screams had persuaded all to avoid further conflict. The posse followed the river northeast.

Late that evening, Sheriff Pattison and his posse were welcomed into Dead Timbers like titans of battle. The settlers cheered the men and were truly grateful for this first sign that the outside world knew of their troubles. Pattison told the story of the skirmish they had had at the cabin the day before and the mystery surrounding the rifle fire had been solved.

"That was Moore's cabin!" A settler shouted. "He and his family are in Dead Timbers with us."

The cabin's owner was found and he was thankful Pattison and his posse was able to prevent the burning of his home. No one mentioned they had considered burning the structure, Indians and all. Everyone agreed the Indians who had been killed in the firefight brought the deaths on themselves. The men were served a hearty meal and the beer began to flow freely. It was not too long before the atmosphere turned nearly festive, far different from the fearful silence that had reigned the previous night.

"Those thieving and murdering savages!" The citizens of Dead Timber shouted despite the fact that no one from their community had been killed and the loss of their property was unknown. It was enough for them to have allowed fear to drive them from their homes.

As the evening wore on, guards were posted and it was agreed that Pattison and his men should sleep in Dead Timbers prior to continuing the reconnaissance in the morning. Prior to nightfall a thick black smoke was seen rolling over the hills north of the town site. It was clear to everyone the fires had been intentionally lit. Sheriff Pattison felt with nightfall it would be too dangerous to investigate and the matter was left until morning.

The Pawnee War

Chapter 1

July 1, 1859
Omaha City, Nebraska Territory

"Where is the governor?" Thayer shouted once again.

Lieutenant O'Kelly looked straight ahead and began to repeat his report. "Sir, we don't know . . . according to Mr. Donovan's report the governor . . ."

"I know . . . I know! The governor went to Nebraska City to sign requisitions or some sort of nonsense and has not been seen since. That is the gist of what you are telling me right, lieutenant?" Thayer repeated the information for his own sake as he sat down heavily in his office chair.

"Yes general."

Thayer looked out The State House's window as he glared down onto the bustle of the city alive with rumors and refugees. Omaha was abuzz with news of the "Great Indian Uprising." The general shook his head with the scarcity of reliable information and the governor's disappearance. "Can you tell me something I do not know? When did the man leave for these damned necessary supplies?"

"Well according to the report . . ." O'Kelly read from his hastily scribbled notes. "Donovan saw him off the night of the twenty first. A local laborer accompanied Governor Black to gather these planking, sand bags, nails, coffee . . . ."

"Get to the point! O'Kelly."

"Yes, sir. Donovan ascertained they would follow the path through Weeping Willow. When he had heard nothing for four days he left the outfit to track the two down." O'Kelly looked down understanding the idiocy of the governor's actions. He reluctantly continued. "I know

Joseph Donovan, sir. You met him yourself and know his caliber. He is a good man and he will find our governor."

"Did Donovan have an accompaniment with him, a squad or armed men or something?"

O'Kelly gulped and said he was not certain. His report did not mention a search party at all. It only stated Donovan ventured out and left the Platte Crossing Ferries under the charge of the chief longshoreman.

Thayer nodded and said, "Well he may be a good man but he is a fool. Out on the prairie alone? How is he going to find Black and get word back to us? As you can see I am surrounded by fools and idiots."

O'Kelly said, "Yes, sir."

Thayer looked up realizing what he had just said. "Present company excluded of course."

O'Kelly nodded, "Of course, sir."

Thayer started to ponder the situation out loud. "I feel we could be on the verge of a great catastrophe, lieutenant. This could be the worst Indian uprising since Spirit Lake. Possibly worse-who knows how many have been killed? Black could have been killed, Mr. Donovan too." Thayer drummed his fingers, mulling over those thoughts. He shook his head. "No, my feeling is our governor may just be on one of his drinking benders. Damn irresponsible if you ask me."

"I agree sir . . . but?"

"But what? Speak up!"

O'Kelly continued. "We do not know, sir. On the one hand it is true we have not heard of depredations that far south recently; but that's not to say there are not hostiles in the locality.

"No reported depredations south of the Platte correct?"

"That is correct."

"Have we heard anything from the army?"

"A courier came in from Fort Kearny yesterday. Nothing unusual except a thunderstorm rolled through last few days, overland traffic was mild and the river was running mighty high. No Indian activity reported at all."

"So what is your sense of it, lieutenant?"

"I would prefer not to say, sir. It is not my place."

"Damn it man! I am the one who has to make decisions here. I understand this is between friends."

"Off the record, sir?"

"Off the record, lieutenant."

"The Pawnee seem belligerent but no one has been reported killed. Mass thievery seems to be the purpose. It is too soon to say they want war. The governor . . ."

"Yes. Speak up man!"

"The only reason I say what I am about to say is I fear for the safety of the settlers. I do not say this against Governor Black as I do not have anything against the man, however, he drinks too much too often. I have seen him on occasion unfit for the office that he holds. Whether that is the present situation I do not know—but it is mysterious."

Thayer thought about it staring out the window. "I agree, lieutenant. It is mysterious. Now I do not begrudge a man his spirits, I trust you don't either. On holidays there is nothing more natural but to cut loose a bit, but Black has a too common taste for it."

O'Kelly nodded in agreement as Thayer asked, "do you know where Secretary Morton is right now?"

"Yes, sir. The territorial secretary is at the land office."

"Will you accompany me lieutenant?"

O'Kelly knew the general's question was in fact a command. "Yes sir!"

The two soldiers made their way out of The State House and made their way quickly down Capitol Hill. As they walked O'Kelly was thinking on what he had just said. It was true Governor Black's drinking bothered him but he was concerned more this so called Indian uprising could turn tragic. He knew his immediate superior was itching for a fight. O'Kelly did not trust him to measure his response to any misdeeds the Indians had done. He tried to take it all in and balance his thoughts . . . He did not know what was going on. How bad was it out there?

The street teemed with rumors of the violence on the frontier and the pair did not get far before they were accosted with well-meaning citizens with anxious questions. The citizenry was brushed off. Thayer did not spend any time dawdling and quickly made his way over to Farnham Street. Turning the corner he nearly ran into J.S. Morton making his way to the State House. The three retreated into the nearest place of business, a hardware store, and the secretary locked the door behind them.

"Hey what is the meaning of this?" shouted the proprietor. "Oh, I'm sorry Secretary Morton. I did not see it was you and the general there. I am just concerned that I am trying to run a business here."

"Sorry about this, Jim." Morton shouted back. "It will only be just a moment . . . official business of the territory you understand. I need a bit of privacy with the general and his man, won't be long."

"Sure thing Mr. Morton, have you heard about the damn Injuns? They are burning everything up north."

"Jim, sorry about the intrusion but we need to discuss the situation if you don't mind."

"Oh . . . alright." Jim looked down at his feet and then sought out something to do. Since no customers were about he found a feather duster and began cleaning the merchandise trying nonchalantly to stay within earshot.

Morton turned back to Thayer and demanded to know what was going on.

Thayer said, "Mr. Secretary, we don't rightly just now but we believe it is serious."

"Damn it man. Course it is serious." J.S. spat back. "I hear that all the Indians on the prairie are thirsting for blood and heading this way. One woman has already been killed and how many more have we not heard about?"

Thayer and O'Kelly looked at one another in confusion.

"Sir? We had not heard. Who was killed?" O'Kelly asked.

"How the devil would I know? I just heard it was a farmer's wife up by Fontanelle."

Thayer spoke, "Sir, we have not heard about a woman dying but we do have it confirmed there has been an uprising of Pawnee near Fontanelle."

"Where is the army? Are they sending us soldiers? Has the governor asked for support yet?"

Thayer looked down and then looked directly at Secretary Morton. "We have sent riders to Fort Kearny but our last reports indicate they have no idea what is happening. As far as the governor goes . . . well . . . we think he is in Nebraska City."

"Why is he not here and why do you not know whether he is in Nebraska City?"

O'Kelly piped in. "As you know sir, he was down overseeing the work on the Platte Crossing Bridge. He had to go to Nebraska City to sign requisitions. A friend of mine has been set off to fetch him."

Thayer looked hard at O'Kelly. "We're concerned that Black will not be found quickly . . . I fear he is drinking. Time is of the essence, Secretary Morton. I need authorization to muster the militia and protect the settlements. Every second we delay gives those devils more time to rampage." Morton smiled a bit when he heard that inebriation might be involved. He knew Black liked to visit with Mr. Barleycorn. His wheels were in motion to try to turn this to his advantage.

Morton bit his lip and took time to consider the dilemma. He turned his back to the men and caught the shopkeeper eavesdropping. "Jim, would you mind?"

Jim continued to look on . . . "Don't mind a bit, Mr. Morton."

J.S. Morton shook his head and turned back.

Thayer appeared to grow anxious. "Sir, I need that authority!"

"Well lieutenant, do you agree with the general's assessment?" Morton asked earnestly.

O'Kelly was suddenly very uncomfortable. He shuffled on his feet and looked at his superior. "Mr. Secretary, any answer would be above my grade . . . but I share the general's concern. There is simply much we do not know." His answer seemed to satisfy both men.

"I cannot give you authorization, general. The territorial attorney has that power. You must get him to agree."

"Secretary Morton, you know what a yellow-spined coward that man is . . . besides which he is one of Black's drinking buddies."

O'Kelly did not know what relevance with whom Black drank was to the conversation but to Morton it seemed to make sense. The secretary nodded.

"Fine general, you and your men must march out as soon as you judge necessary. I will prepare the papers."

"Thank you sir, the citizens of the territory thank you!" Thayer stated melodramatically as he made his way to the door.

"General, the citizens will thank me if you win this war. You have your war now. You make sure we win."

Both O'Kelly and Thayer saluted the secretary and hurried off. The men needed to be gathered and provisions collected. Both Thayer and O'Kelly knew the dozens of tasks that needed to be completed before nightfall.

Chapter 2

Nebraska City, Nebraska Territory

Joseph Donovan looked down at the two men crumpled in the corner of Lovely Nelly's Saloon. He could tell right away, practically from the first glance, one of the passed out drunkards was the governor of the territory. He had seen sots before. It would have been hard living the existence he had; freighter, soldier, and settler, without coming across the sight of men who chose to escape reality with a bottle. He had seen men too passionate about leaving behind their trouble, at least for a moment, through liquor. Perhaps he had been such a man himself a time or two. No. He shook his head sadly and thought to himself, even on his worst day, he had not been this bad.

"Would they be friends of yours?" asked Lovely Nelly, the owner and operator of the establishment. Nelly also made some money on the side entertaining the men less than virtuously. She actually made a fair profit on her time. Lovely Nelly had her charms despite a physique that could have confused the non-regulars with the establishment's bouncer.

"Yes sir . . . or sorry ma'am." Jim blushed at his mistake. "At least one is . . . I am sorry ma'am, it is just I was deep in thought and the light is dark. I just saw . . ."

Nelly scowled quickly. "No need to apologize, just get your pals out of here. I don't mind them stinking up the place but they haven't spent a dime for a half dozen hours."

"Yes ma'am," Jim nodded and realized that the two men did, somewhat surprisingly given their present location, indeed emit an odor. He knelt down by the Black and awkwardly shook the man's shoulder. "Sir . . . Wake up . . . Wake up, governor." Donovan looked up nervous and anxious he had been overheard. He wisely thought it best to keep Black's lofty title a secret." Everyone was looking upon him intently

172

but no one seemed to have cared who was sprawled on the floor. "Mr. Black . . . Sir . . . Samuel . . . Sam! Wake up Sam!" He began to push on the governor's shoulder looking for a dry spot. Both men's clothing was soaked from either booze or piss. Donovan thought it was best he did not know which. He began to shake more forcefully but only succeeded in rousing Black's inebriated companion.

"Sam! Sam! We are being put upon by a brigand!" The drunk hollered.

"You're not bein' robbed, Charlie!" One of the patrons bellied up to the bar shouted in reassurance. "This man is Sam's friend."

"Here you go, darling. This might revive him!" Lovely Nelly said as she handed Joe a shaker of water. "Pour it on em' and get their smelly hides out of here!"

Donovan looked dubious but he obliged and drenched both of the sots. Black came up sputtering.

"My God! Where am I? Joe! Where am I? Did Eliza send you? Tell her I am not here."

"No sir, it's just me, Joe Donovan. Eliza didn't send for you. Lieutenant O'Kelly sent me. I need to get you to Omaha City."

"Omaha?"

"Yes, sir."

Samuel rubbed his puffy face and felt the throbbing of his head. He began to grow more aware of his surroundings but that clarity only made his stomach turn. He wanted to crawl back into his inebriation. "You sure Eliza didn't send you? Be just like her you know."

"No sir. O'Kelly did. Can we get up and out of here?"

"He looks like a brigand, Sam. Let me kick his ass!" The skinny drunk hollered as he kicked his feet.

Joe did not even look at the man, which was just as well. He passed out again in another moment. Samuel looked at his pathetic friend curled up on the spittle-covered floor and thought to himself how jealous he was that he could not drift off too.

"Let's get up, sir." Joe repeated with more emphasis.

Black very reluctantly rose to wobbly feet and stood partially supported by Donovan. His head was killing him and he began to turn thirty shades of purple.

"Darlin'! If he pukes once more on this floor I'm making you clean it up!" Shouted Nelly.

Joe took the hint and hustled Samuel to the door. The pair made it into the alley where Black vomited two days of booze and bile and gut.

He leaned against the building and dry-heaved for ten solid minutes before he was able to stand up straight.

Joe stood there showing remarkable patience, inside proud of himself for tracking down the man.

"We're not going to Omaha, are we Joe?" the governor asked as his color partially returned.

"Yes sir and we head out right now." Joe said with an absolute determination.

The governor leaned back against the wood of the wall and looked up toward the sky. His eyes were closed and Donovan actually saw a tear stream down his cheek. He felt like he had woken up into a nightmare but then he had felt this way waking up many mornings before.

"I will never make it Joe. Just let me go back."

"No sir. I can't let you. There is trouble up in Omaha City with Indians and we need to get back."

Black was confused and in physical torment with a burning ache deep in his head and guts that seemed twisted all over. "Trouble? Indians? Omaha?"

Donovan looked up at the sky and said, "Yes sir, we are going to catch the next steamer so you have some time to clean up . . . but we need to get moving."

"My God, no." Black covered his eyes with his hands and scraped crust out of the corners. He had woken up to nightmares before but this was the first time he woke up to responsibility like this. No . . . he remembered . . . He was a governor. And he had been doing well . . . or relatively well . . . or at least well enough . . . well enough for everyone except Eliza. He felt the shame . . . Shame he could not even describe it was so powerful. But no, he had felt that before too. Too powerful was the shame to describe but not powerful enough to keep coming back to . . . it was familiar . . . coming back to the drink . . . again . . . and again . . . and again.

This nightmare was the same as the past but somehow different. Eliza wasn't here. Joe was here and he could not be put off. Indian troubles? Omaha? A war? It was too much. He hurt too badly. It was too much. Another war? It was overwhelming . . . but it wasn't. It was the same thing again and again. Suddenly he became very angry at Joe.

Black had an edge to his voice, "I ain't got a thing against whatever Indians you're concerned about. I'm sure as hell not up for another war! I've seen more war than you!"

Black surprised himself with the bitterness in him. He was just painfully wrung out and still a tad dizzy.

Joe was quiet for a moment. He said, "I 'spose that's true, governor. Thing about war is it comes upon us from time to time."

Both men were quiet. Black took a deep breath and said, "Nothing is so cruel as to keep a man from his sipping whiskey."

Donovan looked at Black and smiled. He produced a whisky bottle and handed it to Black. "Governor, you've been doing more than just sippin'. And I'm not as cruel as all that, but we share this bottle and you only drink after I take a shot. We share this. You hear me? All you are going to do is sip 'cause that is all we have. We have to make it last."

Black reached for the vile thankfully . . . . trying not to reach for it desperately but thankfully. "You do have a streak of compassion in you, Joe! Maybe I was wrong. I am starting to believe Eliza did not send you after all!"

He took a healthy swig but Joe grabbed it away. "Now we have to do something." No sooner had Joe placed the bottle a safe distance away he reached up and grabbed Black by the collar and hauled him backwards into the horse trough. "Sorry about this sir. No time for a proper scrubbing," Donovan said as he gave the governor a few hefty dunks despite his sputtering. "Now get up. You can dry walking to the steamboat." He picked up the bottle and took a nip.

Black struggled out of the murky water and coughed a bit but, remarkably, he felt better. "You're a hard man, Joseph Donovan. I'd have had you whipped in Mexico."

Donovan chose not to say anything and offered the bottle back. Black took it but this time took a smaller sip. The governor returned it and laughed. "Let's get back to Omaha."

Chapter 3

July 3, 1859 Fontanelle, Nebraska Territory

General Thayer impressed himself with the force that had been put together as they rode to Fontanelle. He had a full company of Organized Territorial Militia composed of one hundred sixty-eight troopers. The Omaha City Self-Protection League had a dozen volunteer representatives and O'Kelly had gotten the local sheriff to lend the militia six deputies and a dozen trail horses. The fire squad had also been persuaded to pitch in two large freight wagons and thirty-two powerful draft horses although O'Kelly had been forced to sign off an insurance receipt for the wagons. Thayer told the men to be extra careful with the freighters.

The men were in good spirits marching northwest and they continued to run into settler's fleeing eastward. Every soldier, militia or volunteer, was fired up with patriotic fervor and looking to avenge wrongs real or imagined.

The militia arrived in Fontanelle by nightfall. The townsfolk had largely forted up in the Methodist Church where a small force of volunteers under the guidance of Sheriff Pattison's geriatric deputy. The deputy at least provided some semblance of order.

Thayer and O'Kelly walked into the church foyer and immediately asked to speak with the man whose wife had been murdered. Francis Depuy was reluctant to leave his children but he was convinced to at least meet with the general by the persistence of the old deputy. He was led to the sitting room where Thayer and O'Kelly waited to interview the man. Thayer sat at a writing desk and O'Kelly stood beside him with a note pad and pencil. Francis was offered a seat on the far side of the desk.

General Thayer began, "Sir, I want to begin by expressing the deepest condolences to you. Your family has suffered a terrible loss. We cannot hope to compensate you and your children for the loss of this woman. However, the highest authorities of our territory have been notified and we want to assure you this cowardly act of savagery will be avenged."

Depuy remained silent. He rubbed his large calloused hands together as if he wanted the interview over. Thayer asked if he needed a glass of beer or a refreshment. Depuy did not seem to listen and stared at the general with a vacant look in his eyes.

O'Kelly noticed that Depuy seemed to still be in a haze and lifted up a finger trying to get the man's attention. "Sir, Mr. Depuy, we know this is difficult but we ask you to bear with us. We have some questions about who killed your wife. We want to make sure the proper man is brought to justice. Could you describe him? How many were with him? How well armed were the Indians?"

Depuy remained sitting silent in his chair.

Thayer spoke up a bit anxious, "I understand you are a religious man. Perhaps a pacifist or a Quaker of sorts?" Still the man did not speak. Thayer continued. "We assure you the savage who murdered you wife will be apprehended and brought before the law—if possible."

Depuy sighed deep and an uncomfortable silence passed. O'Kelly was about to give up with the questions but then Frances began to talk. "Gentleman, it does pain me to say this . . . but my son shot my wife. The boy was scared and confused. It was not murder but a horrible accident. The Indians did not shoot my wife."

O'Kelly and Thayer looked at one another in confusion. O'Kelly spoke, "We understood your family was attacked by the Pawnee renegades?"

Depuy nodded, "The Pawnee did come to my place . . . They were thieving . . . I think . . . The Indians meant my family no good, that is true, but I feel their hearts were set upon theft and destruction of property, not killing. I cannot say they meant to physically harm us." He paused before he continued, "Jimmy is just a child; it was Sarah's foolishness that left my rifle in his hands. She must have been too scared to think clearly."

O'Kelly asked because he was not following, "Could you tell us again? Might it be possible to identify the Indian who shot Sarah?"

Depuy looked straight at O'Kelly and life came to his eyes, "My Jimmy shot his mama. Wasn't no Indian."

Thayer spoke up. "Mr. Depuy, am I understanding you correctly? Your son killed your wife?"

Depuy nodded sadly and looked down. "How many times do I have to tell you? Yes, the bullet came from our own rifle. I expect Jimmy was defending his baby sister."

Thayer and O'Kelly once again glanced at one another and Thayer stood up in consternation. He felt that his great cause had just been robbed of some of its righteousness. O'Kelly was embarrassed by his superior's behavior and continued with the interview. "Mr. Depuy, did the Indians take anything you are aware of?"

The interview continued but Thayer paid no further attention. He slowly walked out onto the front door and down the church steps. He glanced over the men bedding down their animals. The general shook his head and resolved the Indians still needed to be brought to justice. Thievery was still crime and the woman had been killed in the commission of that crime. Yes sir. Thayer thought. These Indians still need to see a reckoning!

*   *   *

Little Anger was concerned. Not only had too many warriors been disappearing over the last few days but there were rumors several bands had actually been in fire fights with the whites. He had tried to keep this raiding quiet, preferably involving only Yellow Sun and his sons. He had wanted Yellow Sun to have a few bloodless profitable raids, which is why he had sent the band first to Depuy's. Frances Depuy was noted among the Indians to be a lover of peace and his family charitable beyond reason. Who would have thought Depuy would use a gun?

Little Anger had not expected for them raid drunken Uriah Thomas. Perhaps he and Yellow Sun had some bad blood in the past. The plunder proved better with Thomas but word had gotten around. Why did they not stay quiet? It must have been one of the son's as the father barely spoke to friend or foe.

Yellow Sun, or *Saa Codacot*, was a bull of a man who was never much for socializing with anyone outside of his son's and their wives. With the death of his wife and two daughters from the sickness years ago he withdrew from interactions among the people. It wasn't that he was rude or bitter. He was simply quiet. He would nod rather than answer with a yes. He turned away rather than object. Observers could not tell whether he was filled with joy or terror. His face had the ugly look of a grim buffalo.

Sharitarish had approached him after the discussion involving the burning of the village. He did not recall why it was Yellow Sun he first enlisted. The man had seemed as unmoved as ever, but his sons were distraught over *Pah-Huku*. Little Anger remembered the man's long face and eyes like an ox, expressionless. His son's gathered around and raiding was discussed. The boys had nodded eagerly but Little Anger was not sure whether he had enticed Yellow Sun or not, not until the man blinked and gave a slow nod. Little Anger took that as an assent. He impressed upon the men that *Petalasharo* would put an end to raiding if he heard of it. Yellow Sun nodded again as if he needed not to be told. His sons would be cuffed into obedience for although they had grown large and strong; they followed him in all things. It was even rumored their wives had been chosen by the willingness to accept Yellow Sun's strange ways.

Regardless, Yellow Sun and his sons retired to their own fire that night, leaving Little Anger with his thoughts. *Sharitarish Tiki* had been confident about his scheme that night. Why was his heart beginning to sink?

Chapter 4

The weather was perfect prior to the dawn on Independence Day. What was especially fortunate was the northbound steamboat *Colorado Queen* was docked and loaded as per schedule and had plenty of room for additional passengers. Both men had decided it would be best if the governor's identity remained hidden. Black readily agreed. He continued to feel poorly and tried to maintain the precise nipping schedule that Donovan devised. Black had begun to get the shakes. Within an hour the steamers grinders were fired and the paddles churned the boat northward. Black remained ill but he was grateful to have a place at a galley table complete with a questionable breakfast and hot black coffee. The governor drank the coffee as soon as it was poured.

"Did you see yesterday's paper?" Joe Donovan asked as he dropped the *Nebraska City Press* unto the table.

Black looked up slowly nursing his stubborn hangover. He had barely had time to touch the cold greasy breakfast the galley offered and was looking forlornly into his empty cup of coffee.

"Eat up sir. We won't get much time in Omaha." Donovan was trying to keep the governor's spirits up since the man had realized that Donovan was intent upon sticking to the prearranged rationing of the whisky bottle. Black knew a good soldier always ate what was put before him and forced down the pork-buttered flapjack. He tried to settle his stomach by concentrating on the printed words.

> North Bend, Nebr. Terr.—A party of traveling woodcutters reported that the formidable bastion of Pawnee Indian

power located six miles west of the settlement was reduced to glistening cinders by other marauding red raiders. The onslaught upon the village was reckoned to have taken place within the last month. The Pawnee village, known as Pahucue by the locals, had been deserted by the majority of the villagers when it was set upon by Sioux warriors for whom the Pawnee maintain a tribal blood feud. The Pawnee redoubt had been a renowned village at the time the first white man appeared upon these ancient plains. At the time of the attack, the Sioux found only a few old persons and children who had been deserted by their tribesmen. The wood-cutters report that they could find no evidence of survivors.

"Do you suppose that village burning is what those Indians are riled about?" Donovan asked after he felt Black had sufficient time to read the article.

Black gave a small burp. After he had swallowed down an urge to retch he said, "Hell if I know but it would rile me. Not sure I'd believe that paper regardless. Those boys are nothing but muckrakers, the lot of em! I only take the *Nebraska City Press* to the latrine and it's not for reading!"

Donovan noticed how shaky Black was reaching for the coffee pot. He wondered whether the governor needed another jolt of whiskey. No, wait 'til he asks, Joe thought.

Black began to take an interest in what this all meant. "What did O'Kelly tell you about the Pawnee?"

"No more than what I have already said." Donovan answered as he helped pour a cup. "Apparently you are needed. O'Kelly was upset you weren't at the crossing. I got the impression he expects the militia will need to ride out to protect Omaha. He believes Thayer is chewing for a fight."

Black slurped the coffee fresh from the pot a bit too eagerly and decided it was still too hot. "Thayer is a dumbass." Black whispered but Donovan caught the remark and could not help but smile. Black continued. ". . . still he is general of the militia. I do need to get back to Omaha so that our proud militia is not paraded into a poltroon's fiasco. Not just sure what the Pawnee are sore about but they do not intend to attack the city."

Donovan nodded. Black felt another wave of nausea coming on. "Shall we get some air?"

Donovan readily agreed and the men descended the galley stairs to the deck besides the starboard stack. They stood by the rail and watched the wooded bluffs of river wall float by. It was a quiet morning. A wisp of belch and coal dust lingered by the boat due to the still air. The morning mist, thickened by the paddlewheel, was invigorating. The air was warming as the sun rose and it was going to be a gorgeous summer day.

Black thought he might as well bring up the topic he knew they were both thinking upon. "Joe, what are you going to say about the circumstances that you er . . . found me in back in Nebraska City?"

Joe was quiet. Although he had been pondering that same thing he had not come to a conclusion. "Don't know. What should say? I wasn't planning on bringing it up unless they ask."

"I know that was not one of my most proud moments."

"Governor, that is none of my business. 'Sides I've drank too much before." Joe wanted to move along with the conversation although he knew he had not drunk like that, even in his earlier years. It was easier to stretch the truth a bit. "I would just cut back some."

Black smiled. "Well I've done well today. Still—It will be sometime while we are on this pleasure cruise, Donovan. Might we share a sip and get the morning off correctly?"

Donovan thought for a moment and then he decided it was about time. A nip would probably not do him any harm either. The bottle was slipped out and a toast was shared in the sunrise.

The river pilot bought the steamer into the eastern channel to hug the far side of the river as it neared the mouth of the confluence with the Platte. The meeting of the rivers always brought the dangers of the shifting deltas rarely visible and the crew hurried to the stations with their sounding cords.

It was at the confluence that they heard the first word of the tumult in Omaha City. Dinghies floated aside and news was passed between the crews and passengers. The pilot was informed he needed to soon return to the other shore as a flotilla of steamers were heading south evacuating many of children of Omaha's wealthy to Nebraska City. The crew was also warned to watch for cross traffic nearer to the docks. Ferries were carrying refugees east to Council Bluffs. Most of the information gathered by the passengers was fragmentary. However, the two were informed by the crew Thayer had already marched out with the militia and had headed north. Donovan was a good friend to the first mate and so he considered it as reliable as rumors come. The information was passed onto Black and it was decided that a messenger would be sent on ahead by rider. He drafted a quick note and it read:

Most Honorable Secretary of Nebraska, J.S. Morton:

Greetings, Please see to the gathering of the federal council for frank discussions on the indian troubles. Governor Samuel Black will convene in emergency session at the State House upon his arrival in Omaha City early evening July 5, 1859.

My regards Mr. Secretary,
S. Black, FG Nebr. Terr.

"Perhaps I should have wished the secretary a happy Independence Day?" Black mentioned as they watched the rider carry the dispatch north.

Donovan smiled and said, "No. What you wrote is just fine. Hard telling is if he is not gathering votes to have you impeached as we speak. If it would have been me though, I would have sent off a note to my wife."

Black smiled wryly, "It is apparent you do not know Morton. He would not dare do that, Mr. Donovan. Why cause a fuss when others will do it for him. As for my wife, you certainly underestimate her capabilities. A note from me is unnecessary for her to know my whereabouts. Are you a gambling man?"

"Not really, governor."

Black chuckled. "A pity. I would give you two to one odds that she will be lambasting me as soon as we step onto the docking pier!"

*   *   *

As Donovan and Black floated up against the great current, O'Kelly and Thayer were meeting in their own war council with the dignitaries of Fontanelle. The lieutenant suggested to his superior that scouts should be sent out in three directions. Thayer smoked a morning pipe as he listened to O'Kelly's plan. The first scouts would head due north until they made it to the Missouri, the second scouts would follow the Elkhorn northwest rescuing settlers as needed and informing Dead Timbers relief was on the way. The third and final scout would follow Pebble Creek west looking for Indians and directing additional volunteers to Dead Timbers.

O'Kelly concluded his proposal. "Sir, I think we could all make good time and reconvene in Dead Timbers five days from now, four if we have good weather."

Thayer was concerned about losing the men for the scouting parties and said so.

The lieutenant knew that was a concern. "We need to know where the Pawnee are sir. If we continue just looking for the next burning homestead we could end up being ambushed."

"Quite right. Quiet right." Thayer said as he considered the dryness of his tobacco.

"I thought I would lead the party up to Dead Timbers." O'Kelly stated.

"Absolutely not." Thayer was suddenly drawn into the conversation.

"But sir, that is the only direction we know for sure the Indians have gone."

"I forbid it, lieutenant. Who will take down my orders and make certain they are speedily carried out?" Thayer placed the pipe back into his mouth and puffed out arid grey smoke.

O'Kelly saw the determination in his superior's face and knew he would get nowhere arguing. "Who do you suggest we have lead the scout up the Elkhorn?"

"Deputy Schoer will do."

John Schoer was Sheriff Pattison's deputy only because he had been a constable in Lexington, Kentucky in the 40s. Perhaps he had battled his share of thugs and southern half-wits in years back, but now a stiff breeze looked like it could cause him a tumble. He was a scraggly figure but he happened to be well armed carrying an 1851 Colt Navy revolver. Nevertheless, he looked up with a hint of surprise on his face.

O'Kelly looked even more dumbstruck. "But sir, Deputy Schoer is not with the militia."

"What does that matter, lieutenant? He is a fine man and a patriot. Besides he knows the territory."

"I would be honored, general!" The deputy said as he stood. "Except I do not want any militia soldiers, just my two fellow deputies will do. Our sheriff is out there and we need the satisfaction of riding to his relief."

"Bravo, deputy! We will give those savages a good licking! Now gentleman, if you would allow me to get to my breakfast." Thayer saluted the men and made it clear the war council was over. "Lieutenant, if you will see to the men and their supplies?"

O'Kelly saluted smart, "yes sir." He could not believe his ears. He had seen the caliber of the deputies and he knew there was a reason Sheriff Pattison had left the gentlemen behind to guard Fontanelle. Deputy Schoer certainly did not share O'Kelly's doubts. He guessed the Indians were far off by now and Pattison had them on the run. They would make Dead Timbers by midafternoon with plenty of time to have a hearty meal and a nap.

Chapter 5

Pawnee Hunting Camp
Elkhorn River

The Pawnee hunting teepee was a miniature earth lodge of animal hide. The sacred bundle hung along the west wall and the entrance opened to the east. *Pahaat Icas* played particular attention to her abode. She knew her husband enjoyed entertaining guests so she was always mindful of spontaneous visitors. The Great Chief had much to consider as he sat and ate by his wife's fire. It was a simple meal of pemmican and dried fruit, yet *Petalasharo* always enjoyed his wife's selections. Still his mind was troubled. The food sitting before him was barely touched.

"Why do you ignore your meal, husband? I see something is bothering you. You spent much time at your prayers this morning."

"It is nothing." *Petalasharo* fibbed.

"Do you dare tell *Pahaat Icas* a falsehood? The Great Chief knows me better than that."

"Yes it is true, I have been thinking much. I do not know where our braves have been going. Many have been missing and not eyeing the game. It has been too long. Ever since . . . ever since we saw the village burned."

His wife sighed. "Some young men seem to have more on their minds than the hunt, I agree. It is rumored they have been up to mischief. But no one knows how many or for how long."

"This was a concern of my father and his elders. They worried about the young men and what hot blood ran through their limbs. Our elders have struggled with that problem since the Corn Mother's creation, yet here I am without a solution."

186

Red Turtle sat beside her husband and warmly gave him a hug. Laying her head on his shoulder she said, "You will not find a solution. It is the same with wives and daughters. You cannot solve the troubles brought upon by nature."

The Great Chief nodded thoughtfully.

"Perhaps you can only discover what mischief they have been about. Surely one of the chiefs knows."

"That is why my heart is heavy. What do the chiefs know? Could they be behind it?"

"Have you asked them?"

"No." *Petalasharo* looked down.

His wife scoffed. "That is foolish. For a bear to catch a fish he must go to the river. You meet the chiefs every day to discuss the hunt. Why not ask when you have them near?"

The Great Chief looked up and was struck with the simplicity of her words. He began to chuckle.

Red Turtle continued, "That is not all that distresses my husband. He has been odd all morning."

"That is true. I had a dream last night. I have thought about the meaning of the dream and it troubles me."

"You must speak to one of the medicine men about dreams. Remember your dreams are not your own any longer. You dream for all of us now."

The Great Chief nodded and began to eat his meal. He had heard the wisdom of her words.

*   *   *

Deputy Schoer led his two companions, Everett and Donald Fellows, up the southern bank of the Elkhorn. The Fellows were cousins and only slightly younger than Schoer. Beyond Fontanelle, The men expected to run across far fewer refugees making their way eastward but they were surprised how absolutely deserted the landscape appeared. The first farmhouse they came upon was intact and looked well kept. When they looked about for its residents, none could be found. A few chickens pecked about and a cat peered lazily out the kitchen window but no persons, alive or dead, could be found. The deputies moved onward.

Within the hour they made out a faint line of smoke and hurried towards it. They found a burning farmhouse and barn. Two goats were lying in the pen with their throats slit and it appeared other livestock had been stolen or run off. The barn had been burning for at least a day and was nearly completely consumed. It appeared that the farm had been a significant livestock operation and a great deal of feed grass remained smoldering. It seemed as if the clapboard house had been partially burned but the arsonists could not get the green planking on the roof to ignite. Schoer felt the house might be salvageable.

The men pressed on riding up the riverbank. After another hour or so, they once more spied a trail of smoke lifting north of the Elkhorn's far bank tree line. Deputy Schoer knew they were nearing Dead Timbers and should push on but curiosity got the best of the three. The closer the men got the heavier the smoke appeared. Could Indians be still at the farmstead? They discussed the possibilities and the urge to be heroes got the best of them. They crossed the river and hobbled the horses. Schoer split the men up. Each man would approach from a different direction and sneak up on the renegades.

Schoer had the greatest distance to travel to approach from the west so he set off immediately. He expected all three to meet up again at the cabin's front door. Everett was to advance from the east and had the least ground to cover, but he did not seem to understand timing. He crabbed upstream until the cabin was within sight. He was making his way through the grass when he suddenly saw an angry face staring back. He leapt up and turned to run in the opposite direction, unfortunately his boots got caught up and he fell flat on his face. The savage would surely be upon him so he pulled his gun and began to fire toward the face. The deputy got off two shots before his revolver jammed. He began to shout, "Indians! Indians!"

Donald came toward the house from the north. He had heard the shots and shouts of desperation and drew his gun thinking the worst. He ran up the stairs and saw the front door was completely shot up and a dead Indian was sprawled across the threshold. He heard footsteps running behind him and turned and fired at the figure making a mad dash towards him.

Had the running figure been an attacking Indian the frightened deputy could not have made a quicker and more accurate shot. The bullet entered Deputy John Schoer's forehead killing him instantly.

The moment Donald recognized his friend was one of horror.

"Oh God, Everett! I just shot John!"

His cousin returned and reported that he had also not been shooting true as the face that had startled him was another Indian body. It was apparent both Indians had been dead for some time. The deputies had stumbled upon the Moore homestead.

Donald wiped his brow in consternation and yelled at the deputy's body. "To hell if this isn't a dreadful experience. It's your fault John . . . runnin' up like that!"

"Donald, what are we gonna tell the sheriff?"

"Let me think on it, Everett. Ohhh . . . damn it all if we ain't in a hell of a fix!"

Chapter 6

July 5, 1859

The Pawnee met with the *Omahaw* on the northeastern bend of the Elkhorn River. The Pawnee called the river the *Kicita*. The *Omahaw* had another name for the stream but both tribes thought of the river as a brother. The river was running deep and slow. The *Kicita* had neither the rapids nor channel cutting power of either of its cousins, the Platte or Loups to the south. It had a smaller watershed than the Platte and its headwaters started in the Sandhills so mountain snowmelt did not tear at its banks. The water drained lazily to the Missouri; as if it had all the time in the world. It seemed to be mindful and deliberate, but always steady.

The *Omahaw* camped quietly knowing game would be plentiful in the days ahead. The tribes met and the Calumet pipe was smoked. The *Omahaw* chiefs announced the Ponca would meet with the tribes further up along the river. The hunting was expected to be excellent as scouts reported enormous herds grazing south of the Missouri River. All of the Pawnee celebrated the renewal of good relations with the tribes that had recently been so strained.

Petalasharo asked each chief in person, alone if possible, if they knew why braves had been leaving the hunting party. "This cannot continue. We must be mindful of our task to feed the people." Each chief denied knowledge but doubted that the Great Chief's concerns were unfounded. *Petalasharo* took the explanations in good faith and did not push the issue. It was not the time to complicate the tribe's plans. There were so many feelings of goodwill it would have done no good to promote worry and discontent. The Great Chief thought now the memories of the devastated village could be put behind the Pawnee as excitement for the summer hunt would grow.

The Great Chief's dream could still not be forgotten or washed away with a Calumet ceremony so he sought out the great mystic, *Tahirusawichi*. He found the old man within his sister's teepee dutifully at his prayers, blessing the new alliance with the *Omahaw* and the Ponca. The medicine man welcomed the Great Chief and tobacco was found to aid in their conversation.

"The Great Chief honors my lodge as our new friendships with the *Omahaw* and Ponca honor our people." *Tahirusawichi* said after his pipe stem flowed with sweet flavored smoke. "Come my friend, we should enjoy the beauty of this day."

Petalasharo graciously took the pipe and soon was enjoying his own draws. "My mind is troubled on this day. Last night the spirits sent me a dream and I have not yet concluded its meaning. Shall we discuss it?"

Tahirusawichi nodded and the Great Chief began to explain.

"I do not know whether in my dream I was a spirit, or a bird, but I looked down upon the prairie from a great height. The land was endless and yet I saw the grassland with great detail. I saw rocks and shrubbery, the tops of great trees and the bend of a small creek. The land was brown and green and warm. Far below I saw a precise stretch of cranes and could hear their gentle cries. Their flight was pleasant to watch and they soared as they often do with an unhurried purpose. It was then I spotted a great eagle slightly below me. He cuffed his wings and dropped with great speed. I then knew the eagle's purpose. It tore the last crane from the flock and dropped to the earth killing it with its talons. I then saw it lift once more without its prey. This mighty eagle again achieved great height and plummeted to the cranes taking the next trailing bird. I then saw the eagle was not on a hunt for food and I shouted a warning to the cranes but could not be heard. They did not hear my anguished cry and I watched as they died. I looked down and suddenly the dead cranes were warriors killed and burned. It was as if I saw the dead of the Big Sandy Creek from long ago. The bodies were all of red people, Sioux and Pawnee, Otoe and Osage; I knew there were others. Somehow I understood I was within the dream world and struggled to wake up. I woke within my robes in a great sweat. All about me was dark and quiet. It is this dream that I bring to you."

Tahirusawichi sat quietly through the telling of the dream. Once the Great Chief had concluded the old medicine man thanked him for the insight into the spirit world.

The old man began to speak. "The world of dreams is separate from the world of men but there are times when the worlds connect. During the times of this connection," he explained, "It is difficult to see what is in a dream and what is not. What is a dream and what is within the world of men?"

Both chiefs took long thoughtful drags upon the pipe and *Tahirusawichi* continued. "The crane is eternal and he is not often among us. The crane comes with the spring. He comes with the warmth in the air and the trees on the leaves. He is not here now but neither of us doubts the crane will return with his season. He goes we know not where. The crane then returns at the proper time and place."

Petalasharo nodded and agreed. *Tahirusawichi* pointed toward the sky. "The eagle is always with us. It matters not the season to him. He is a hunter of opportunity. He will kill, or he will feed off a corpse, again it matters not to him."

Petalasharo nodded thoughtfully. He understood the man's wisdom.

"Seldom should we prefer the hunter or the hunted. Are not both spirit animals and sacred? But in your dream the eagle was a killer and not a hunter. That is dark and not the way of their spirit. I fear for our people for this message is dark. I fear all our brother people. They are as the cranes."

"What is it I can do for the people? I fear for them as well!"

"You are a great man, *Petalasharo* and you are our Great Chief. Did the cranes heed your words within the dream? Could they even hear your words? There is nothing more for you to do then to travel the path already set forth. Cry out when you see danger. Give good counsel when you are asked. Speak the truth even if no one hears the words. Sleep well at night for the future is not in your hands. It is not in my hands. It is only for us to remember the Pawnee and our bothers are like the cranes. The Pawnee and all our brothers and sisters are eternal. We will die but will return with the proper season."

The two men sat and smoked in silence. *Tahirusawichi's* words were not what the Great Chief had expected or wished for but they were soothing. Nothing lay before the men this afternoon except to enjoy the good tobacco and the beauty of the day.

*   *   *

Had Donovan been a betting man he could have made some money. Eliza was not at the docks waiting for her husband when the *Colorado Queen* landed. Samuel was perplexed but he knew it would only be a matter of time, and it was. She was at The State House. He saw her just before he went into the council chambers located to the north side of the governor's office.

The council meeting contained none of the dramatics expected by Black and Donovan. The tone of the meeting was quiet and respectful. No one even questioned the governor's absence the last few days. When Black asked who gave the order for the militia to march, Secretary Morton stood solemnly and reported that he had. He thought it best having heard the reports from General Thayer and the heart rendering tales of the refugees. The secretary then stated the only reason he had taken such drastic action was he knew where Black's heart was and Morton was confident the governor's first priority would be the safety of innocents.

Samuel eyed the secretary suspiciously but was grateful no further inquiries to his whereabouts were being raised. He sensed second guessing Morton was an impolitic thing to do. Donovan thought Black had improved remarkably since arrival. The governor stopped belching and his eyes did not seem so bloodshot. Donovan only noticed that he kept his hands folded or behind his back, presumably to hide the shakes.

"Gentleman, I cannot say that I would have done anything otherwise. Your quick and decisive actions could have saved hundreds of our citizen's lives. I only wish that I could have arrived sooner to march forward with our brave men in arms. Have we received word on General Thayer's progress?"

Morton eagerly responded, "A courier was received this morning bearing dispatches of Thayer riding to the aid of Fontanelle. The general intends to thoroughly raconteur the area and proceed with haste to Dead Timbers. He hopes to provide succor to the town in two days' time."

"My only objective at this point is to meet up with the general as soon as practical. Prepare a speedy rider and ask General Thayer to make camp and hold his position."

Morton looked about. The secretary had not expected this. "Do I understand you, governor? Do you intend to ride forward with the men?"

"I intend to command them. It is only proper. I am the militia's commander in chief."

"Surely it is best if an experienced Indian fighter such as General Thayer lead the troops?"

"Mr. Secretary, General Thayer is an experienced Indian watcher. What our boys need is a soldier to lead them. A soldier is not a watcher, nor is a soldier necessarily a fighter."

"But, Governor Black . . ."

"My word is final on this, Mr. Secretary. We need no further discussion." Black shouted. "Joe!"

"Yes, sir."

"I hereby commission you as a first sergeant in our militia. Find out why our brilliant General Thayer did not take the cannon. I intend to have artillery if it comes to fighting."

Secretary Morton spoke up. "I know Thayer did not take the gun because he felt the militia could cover more ground faster without dragging it along. People may be dying out there, Governor Black. This is not the time for your federal chest thumping!"

Black stared hard at the secretary. He said in a low gravelly voice, "Morton, I will not take your military counsel! We need the gun!"

"But . . ."

"Have you ever crossed a field without artillery support? I thought not! And neither has Thayer. This is not some bill you are calling due and we will have no further discussion!" Black's voice rose in emphasis and even the formidable secretary was cowed. "Sergeant, you have your orders!"

"Yes, sir!" Donovan saluted and quickly exited the room.

Black stood up and bowed. "Gentlemen, we all have necessary matters to intend. I thank you for your advice in this matter. It is appreciated. I understand this meeting was called on short notice. If you excuse me I will be off to my command."

Standing outside of the council chambers were newsmen and dozens of concerned citizens. Samuel noticed Eliza standing against the far wall quietly surveying the bustling scene. Her hair was pulled back and tied in a bun and she was wearing a solid blue dress. Eliza always impressed Sam how she could seem so aloof and dignified within a public storm. Almost as if she was a different person than the sharp-clawed female who would berate him for drinking. Black pushed his way through the reporters and gruffly told them he had nothing to say that was permissible to print. He took his wife by the arm and escorted her within his office stopping only to shut the door on the nosy press.

Black noticed his office was much the same as he had left it, papers stacked in a pile waiting to be reviewed, his old swivel chair pressed up back against the far wall, his desk with a thin sheen of dust. He struggled against the thought of digging into his right hand drawer and locating his bottle of Pennsylvanian gin. He decided to fight the urge and merely leaned against the wood of the desk.

"I suppose you have ideas of joining our brave militia." Eliza snapped. She was already on the attack. "Do what you want Samuel. You are not hurting me. I only ask you to think of our children who will grow up fatherless if you are killed."

Samuel dropped his head sadly. "I expected this manner of welcome from you Eliza but what makes you think I aim to march off to the militia?"

"You are like Julia's boy, Samuel, terrified of thunderstorms but cannot help playing in the rain."

Black nodded in agreement and quietly said. "You know it is my duty."

Eliza took a kerchief out of her case and absently began dusting a table. "Keep telling yourself it is your duty; but do not tell your wife. She knows the truth. You go because Samuel Black has decided to go and he listens to no one."

The governor sighed. "What do want me to say, Eliza?"

Her eyes grew red as she beat back tears. It was too much and she rushed into his arms. "I do not want you to say anything damn you! Please stay safe, Samuel. I could not lose you!"

Their hug lasted but a moment but Samuel could feel his wife's body shaking in suppressed sobs. He truly did not know what to say.

There was a knock on the door and Donovan announced the governor was needed in the yard.

"One moment please, sergeant." He gently pushed Eliza away and showed her to the door. Black lowered his voice and whispered, "I do not intend for there to be fighting. Nobody knows what will happen, probably nothing more than ill-timed maneuvers; could end up being no more danger than a Sunday ride. Tell the children I will see them presently."

Eliza paused before she walked out the door. "I will not tell them that Samuel. For someday, I know, you would make a liar of me."

"Ma'am" Donovan said as he saw her exit.

Before Donovan could enter Samuel closed the door behind her. The governor walked over to his saber hanging on the wall and strapped it on. Under his breath he muttered the old dirge of his officer's corp. "Draw me not without cause. Sheath me not without honor." Black chuckled to himself. "What epic pig shit!" He then approached his desk and located his gin. "Now Lieutenant Colonel Black, thus fortified, you are ready to ride forth!"

Chapter 7

July 6, 1859
Dead Timbers, Nebraska Territory

Sheriff Pattison did not particularly believe the full story he got from his two forlorn and addled deputies as they rode into Dead Timbers with John Schoer's body draped over the back of his horse, but he knew accidents happen. He knew the cousins were good people; well-meaning and all, he could not blame them for being inept. Whoever had sent them on a scouting mission should be questioned severely. If the men's advanced age did not convince someone of their unsuitability to competently spy on hostiles surely the Fellows' spectacles should have been a clue. As it was, the townsfolk greeted the men as conquering heroes, particularly when word got out that Schoer had been ambushed at Moore's cabin and it was only through the heroic action of the Fellows cousins that his body was retrieved.

Pattison bit his tongue when Everett declared, "I could not allow Deputy Schoer's body to be desecrated by the savages and so I went in with both guns blazing. John deserves a Christian burial!"

Before the younger Fellows could begin relating his own heroics, Pattison quietly drew the men aside. He admonished them. "Now boys, we all know it did not happen like that. Those Indians we came across had no firearms and they were skedaddling. Let's cut the crowing before I mention that John was shot by a caliber similar to your pistol, Donald."

The cousins looked at one another sheepishly and did their best from then on to downplay their roles in the second battle for Moore's cabin.

Chapter 8

July 8, 1859
Pebble Creek

"They were camped here for sure, General Thayer." O'Kelly announced. "This is a wide campground and the grass has been beat pretty flat. The Indians must have remained here a few days."

"How far are we from Dead Timbers?" Thayer asked.

"Not far. The town is six miles upriver on the far bank."

Thayer nodded considering his options. His mind was going in a number of different directions. Where could the Indians be now? Could they have scattered? "How long ago were the Indians here, lieutenant?"

O'Kelly smiled and answered, "General, I sure couldn't tell you that. Maybe if we have a fur trader in the van he might be able to give us a better idea. Although, I do think it has been awhile. The campfires are cold ash and the pony dung has dried some. It sure wasn't yesterday, but that's all I could say."

"That will do, lieutenant."

"General! General!" hollered a worn out scout as he rode up on a sweating horse.

"What is it man? Spit it out!"

"Colonel Robinson from Fort Kearny is riding up to join us! He sent me forward sir as soon as we heard of your whereabouts."

"What is this?" General Thayer asked after he looked at O'Kelly. "So our riders got through to the fort and they decided to give us a hand. Well bully for the army!"

"That's not all the news, general. We heard some terrible story and hope that you can confirm it was just a rumor."

"What is it, private?" O'Kelly asked. "What have you heard?

"Oh it's a bad one general, but mind you nothing has been confirmed."

"Well spit it out, private." The general ordered.

"Dead Timbers, sir. We heard it was burned all to a cinder and nothing alive remains!"

"When did you hear this? Who told you this?" Now it was O'Kelly demanding an answer.

"Don't rightly know where the reports came from, sirs. And mind you, we did not see it ourselves, but word is going around the town was a burnin' and everyone was killed and scalped, men women, children, even the horses and dogs."

O'Kelly and Thayer looked at one another and both were trying to decide whether they were being told a tall tale.

"Where is Colonel Robinson now?" O'Kelly finally asked.

"When I left him he was two, three miles south of here. He will be coming up over that hill line. He has half-dozen dragoons with him. They're good men too sirs."

O'Kelly continued, "If they're such good men why did they not march directly to Dead Timbers?"

"Well the colonel thought about it, he did. I can vouch for that. But we came up through Columbus and with our numbers he decided to join up with you first."

General Thayer began to get nervous. The army sent troops? This was the first time he thought that he may be going up against Indians who might actually whip him. He remembered talking about how tough Indians could be. Thayer began to look as if he seen a ghost. He took a quick breath. "Lieutenant, what would you suggest in this situation?"

O'Kelly looked west and then looked back at cold campfires and Indian pony dung in the grass. "I don't believe it general. I mean the tale of Dead Timbers. A whole town burned? If the Indians just passed through here the time frame just don't match up. If Dead Timbers was burned a few days ago it would still be smoldering and we're close enough to it to see some smoke . . . No general . . . I don't reckon its true, although I am thankful the army is coming." O'Kelly walked over to the rider. "The private here looks worn out. I'll take him to the camp and we can send some men to guide the colonel this way. Come here, private. You look like you could use a good meal."

"I would be much obliged, sir."

"Don't worry, general. Those army dragoons will come in mighty handy. I will question the private fully once he has had a bite."

"Very well, lieutenant. That is precisely what I would do." Thayer gave the private a full and much too formal salute. O'Kelly could tell his superior's confidence was slightly restored but he was glad for the wild rumor. The militia was moving entirely too fast and it was a good excuse to be cautious. Thayer would not lose face by waiting for the army dragoons.

The private saluted back weakly. His mind was still on the dinner that was promised.

Chapter 9

July 9, 1859
***Taa Zuka* Plain**

It was on the wide flat bed plain called *Taa Zuka* the Pawnee and *Omahaw* set up camp for the lighting of the council fire.[28] The Ponca rode in from the southwest after hunting light game, antelope and prairie hens in the Sandhills. They were proud and joyous from their bounty and were greeted by their friends, the *Omahaw*, with gifts and dancing. The Ponca were friendly to the Pawnee but still doubled their guards about their horse herds. They were now allies but old habits often die hard.

With a waxing slice of moon beaming upon the members of the tribes, the council fire was lit and the chiefs shared the sacred tobacco of the Calumet. It was a gathering of 5,000 Indians and each tribe celebrated a renewal of their ancient friendships. Scouts had reported large herds of buffalo along the high divide just south of the great Missouri but Sioux were also reported to be lurking to the southwest. It was decided that the tribes would set up lookouts within a day's travel for mutual defense. The *Omahaw* would move to the north and push the herds westward. The Ponca would enter the buffalo hunting ground and begin preparing kill zones and surrounds. The Pawnee, the largest and strongest of the three tribes, would move directly west, keeping the animals from escaping and watching for Sioux encroachment.

Yellow Sun and his boys had yet to rejoin the Pawnee. They remained along the Elkhorn distributing their booty and repeating Little Anger's caution that raiding must cease. Yellow Sun put his sons in charge of

---

28   Near modern Norfolk, Nebraska.

tampering down news and reports of past raiding. The old warrior did not personally feel it was necessary to boast of past deeds, but who was he to tell how a man must speak his words?

*   *   *

"What was it like down in Mexico, governor?" Donovan asked as he added more kindling to the fire.

"Terrible from what I remember." Black answered. "The damn fools had a different word for everything."

Donovan chuckled. "I expected that. I mean what was the fighting like? You saw action at Cerro Gordo and Pueblo right? Weren't you injured?"

Now it was the governor's time to chuckle. "Do you want to hear of my injury? Now that is a genuine hero's tale."

"I heard it happened at Cerro Gordo."[29]

"Yes it did my good man. Cerro Gordo." Black nodded as he thought back. "Do you know what a beautiful country Old Mexico is? What is amazing is the worst fighting in that war actually took place in the prettiest locales. Cerro Gordo. Magical place; green and bountiful it was. They have trees with fruit that hang so low you could reach up and pick it off with your hands. Not a jungle but certainly not a desert either. High palm trees, gentle breezes and shade trees. Mountains were off in the distance and they had birds of every color I could have imagined. The sky was a deep blue and it surprised me how warm it was at that altitude. We had disembarked three days earlier at Veracruz and marched straight up into the highlands."

Black checked the level of his bottle. "I was with my home regiment. We ran into the Mexican army holding a strong defensive position within a gorge. Winfield Scott had his artillery moved up and he blasted their forward positions to pieces. Actually my Pennsylvanians weren't in the initial fight although we could hear the battle off on our left flank. I served with some good men but our full-bird colonel was a blundering oaf. The company was marching down an arroyo when we saw some

---

29   The Battle of Cerro Gordo pitted the American army of Winfield Scott against the Mexican army of Antonio Lopez de Santa Anna. It was fought on April 18, 1847, and resulted in American victory.

of Santa Anna's peasants dash right before us and run for their lives. I expect they had enough of the pounding Scott was giving their redoubts. The poor bastards were in full retreat. Of course, the Colonel Full Bird, forget his given name but Full Bird is apt, sends us boys forward and we were all full of vinegar. I tell you . . . Too full of vinegar as it turned out. The men naturally outran their officers but they were too green to know and we were too drummed up with glory to care. We would have chased those peasants to Mexico City but one of our lieutenants started calling a halt. Fortune showed on us. That man was the only one to have his head attached because he could tell we had outdistanced the artillery umbrella. Of course, he sent word to us officers to get the men back . . . we could only get the stragglers and some infantry to return. We watched as the bulk of our cavalry rode forward into a low widening of the land. Good ground for a counter attack and we saw Santa Anna did have some professionals."

Black took a swig of his gin. Miles back, after he had noticed Donovan's rectitude to stop him, he drank more openly. "They were lancers and well trained. It was like watching cats being kicked by old town delinquents. You can't fight damn lancers in formation with sabers and they were too quick for the pistols. We watched our cavalry butchered and then the lancers rode toward our infantry. The boys were spread out in a long ragged line and it was useless trying to form up. Most were spitted in the back as they tried to run. Now it was our turn to scat and we made for the high ground."

Black thought back and then showed a faint but ironic smile. "Just then I got the most god awful bloody nose I ever did have. Doesn't that sound ridiculous? Blood seemed to be pouring out of my head like I had an endless supply. Dropped my damn saber right there trying to plug my nose while me and the boys were riding hell bent for leather. No use. I bled like a stuck pig. Thought my brains were leaking out. A bullet took my horse out and we rolled. He was a kicking too much for good cover and I had to slit his throat. Once his death throes stopped I drew my pistol and started firing at those lancers. My god, can you imagine shooting in that blood? I can tell you I can't shoot worth a damn with blood in my eyes, my mouth, hands sticky as hell and the trigger slippery."

"Once again we were lucky or they would have finished us off. We just made it to where the artillery could help and the lead balls started falling. We were barely in range and that shot would skip along the ground. The artillery broke the charge and many of those Mexican horse's legs. I saw one open up the belly of a mount and the horse kept tripping over his own entrails. The damn lancer was still trying to push him forward."

Black took a swig. "I just sat there holding my nose closed like a school boy. I could not stop the blood from clogging up my throat. Believe it or not, I was just as fearful of drowning on that arid battlefield as getting shot. The lancers, or what was left of them, fell back. It was a hell of a sight . . . a hell of a sight. I puked up clotted snotty blood for three days. The army continued to follow them but mind you—our company was a bit more cautious."

Donovan sat stunned. He did not expect to hear so much. Once Black opened up he began to talk like it was bottled up. Through it all he showed no emotion, or at least allowed no emotion to tinge his words.

"That was what I got my medal for Joe, a nosebleed. Reported my experience to the birded colonel soon as I could; he thought I looked like something from a slaughterhouse. I was truthful about it all but he put me in for an accommodation. Suppose the more heroes in his regiment the more heroic he looked himself. Too damn many medals handed out after that muddled fray if you ask me." Black looked down as if he were suddenly tired as hell.

"Why are we jawing about this, sergeant?" Black asked. "You did your part in that war."

"My part wasn't exactly heroic, governor. You said yourself . . ."

Black interrupted, "Are you talking about my comment in Nebraska City? Hell, I was drunk. The only bigger fool than a drunk talking is a fool listening to a drunk talking. Pay that no never mind! What else have I told you? Damned if you didn't do your part."

Donovan nodded but Black kept on, "Would Cuming say what you and he did wasn't heroic? Don't you think we needed the supplies and cannon, the food, the ammunition, the transport, the watching of prisoners and the evacuation of the wounded? Why do you think we won that war? Were we braver or loved our country more? Hell no! We had an infrastructure for war and we were smart enough to build it. Most of those poor Mexican peasants were half starved and still carrying the Brown Bess![30] Believe me, you did your part!"

---

[30] British Long Pattern Musket, the Brown Bess, was the standard infantry firearm of the British Army though the wars in the Americas and with Napoleon. It was considered obsolete by the Mexican-American War.

Black took another swig and handed the vile to Donovan. Joe took a sip. He decided to change the subject.

"You know we should be meeting up with Thayer and the militia soon. Do you expect Dead Timbers to still be there?"

Blacked nodded. "I expect so. I have heard of Indians attacking towns but Dead Timbers probably got fair warning and the citizens were able to build a defense. I have never heard of Indians mounting much of a siege." Black did not admit he was speculating, but he thought the reasoning sound. "If Dead Timbers has been sacked I expect that we will actually be due some justice. In any case, we'll sure find out in the morning."

Chapter 10

July 10, 1859
Dead Timbers, Nebraska Territory

The dragoons from Fort Kearny and Thayer's militia had met at Dead Timbers two days earlier. General Thayer was at first upset with the Fellows cousins for not returning with word the town was safe and the deputy's death at the cabin, but then he learned they were following Sheriff Pattison's direct orders.

"We knew you were coming in General Thayer. It seemed prudent to hold tight to avoid any further . . . er . . . casualties." Pattison explained.

This seemed to mollify the general, especially since the deputies' report of a death caused by the heathens added to the fervor of his militia and the righteousness of his cause. Thayer took overall command of the combined detachment with Robinson as his second in command. They set up an encampment just to the west of the town. O'Kelly was relieved he now had some professional military scouts that he could assign and organize systemic reconnaissance missions and he quickly began to arrange the men.

It was mid-morning before the governor and Joe Donovan rode into town. A few of the settlers recognized the governor and they were directed toward militia.

General Thayer was mighty surprised to see the man. "Why Governor Black, there is no need for you to be here; Colonel Robinson and I have matters quite in hand."

Black dropped somewhat awkwardly off his charger. "I have no doubt that is true general, however, I felt it my duty to march with the militia. I am sure you would agree."

O'Kelly saw the new arrivals and smiled when he saw Joe was wearing sergeant's stripes.

"Thought you boys could use a hand!" Donovan said as he shook hands with Pattison and some of the volunteers. O'Kelly gave the man a sharp salute much to the consternation of General Thayer. Pattison moved forward and offered his hand to Sam.

"Pleased to meet you, Governor Black, I'm Sheriff Pattison from Fontanelle. I saw you give a speech before the assembly last winter. Mighty fine talk you gave about the homestead issue although I could not disagree with you more."

"Nice meeting you, sheriff. Now gentlemen, if the general and I could meet to discuss our situation."

Thayer puffed himself up and looked back to his officers. "Governor, I had no idea that you would be arriving. Surely the ride was dangerous . . . If you would like to continue as an observer I would have to discuss it with my officers."

"Balderdash Thayer, don't you think I can lead this outfit?" Black put one hand up against his mount to steady himself. Donovan looked down, as he knew what the trouble was. The man was drunk again.

"Of course not sir . . . I am quite aware of your heroism. But sir . . . it is quite irregular. I am the commanding officer of the militia. I could not necessarily guarantee your safety sir."

Black's voice rose. "Damn it general, not one of these soldiers expects that. Guaranteeing my safety? What do you think I came for? Think I signed up for a pleasant excursion with a picnic basket under my arm? What is important is I am your superior! That is the brass tacks!"

Donovan came forward and grabbed Black's arm. Governor Black, General Thayer sir, should you have this discussion before the men?"

Black recovered his composure but he was unable to recover his total sobriety. "Quite right. You are quite right, sergeant."

"General Thayer, sir," Colonel Robinson stepped up. "Perhaps now might be the time to convene a war council and discuss our situation."

"Excellent suggestion colonel, where is your command tent?"

"This way Governor Black, Lieutenant O'Kelly can show you."

"By all means lieutenant, pray lead the way." The governor staggered a bit as he followed O'Kelly through the camp. Donovan was a bit unsure of what would happen and he felt as if the governor was still in his charge. Joe followed meekly behind. Seeing the small party cross the campground Thayer was struck with an idea.

"Lieutenant, please return once Governor Black is comfortable. I need you to carry some maps."

O'Kelly looked back slightly suspicious but he showed the governor to the tent and poured two cups of coffee. The men sat down around the map table and Black could tell Donovan was uncomfortable.

"Relax, sergeant! That is an order. You deserve to be at this officer's call more than that blowhard!" Black nearly shouted and caused Donovan to forget himself and put his finger awkwardly to his lips. O'Kelly looked hard at Donovan and both understood the governor was making a fool of himself.

"Drink up, Governor Black." O'Kelly offered. "I brewed this pot myself just this morning."

"Thank you, lieutenant. But what I am really hoping for is a bit of a nip like what we used to have in our war councils in Old Mexico. You should have tasted the fine barley corn we shared before the Battle of Pueblo."

Donovan spoke up. "Governor, it is a might early."

O'Kelly did his best not to answer. He nodded and said, "Governor Black, Sergeant Donovan, I must go see what is taking the general so long. Will you excuse me?" O'Kelly was about to get back with his prior project of organizing the scouts when Thayer ordered him over to speak.

"What did the governor say? Tell me lieutenant." Thayer and Robinson were huddled together like nervous conspirators.

"Well sir . . . He asked for a drink."

Thayer smiled, "The man is drunk isn't he?"

"I have seen him worse, sir."

"I told you, Colonel Robinson. That man is not fit to lead this expedition."

"What do you propose, general?"

"I propose that I not allow him to lead these fine men. Hard telling what drunken fool mistakes he would lead us into. Could be the Indians are creeping up on us right now trying to catch us napping."

"That is a fair point." O'Kelly offered. "I should be back getting the scouts set up to ride out."

"Not yet, lieutenant," Thayer ordered. "We need to settle this."

"Settle what?" the colonel ejected. "If you supplant the governor it is mutiny. I will not be a party to a mutiny."

O'Kelly sighed. He did not want to offer insight into the dilemma but he felt it was his duty. "General, the Nebraska Organized Militia's field regulation has a provision that can only be resorted to with a detachment operating in the field. It states that an incompetent officer may be relieved from his duties by his superior or, if the officer in question is the superior, he may be relieved by a written document signed by a unanimous agreement of all subordinate officers."

Thayer's eyes began to grow large with excitement. "Did I hear you right lieutenant? Just the three of us could remove the man."

"I believe so, general. We would need to determine he was incompetent for command. Then we would need to hold an officer's call and draft an appropriate document."

Thayer slapped O'Kelly on the back. "What are we waiting for? Lieutenant fetch your valise, we have some drafting to do!"

"Hold on, general!" The colonel held up his hand. "The man may have had something to drink but I cannot say he is incompetent."

"Colonel Robinson I assure you the man will be roaring drunk by the noon hour."

"Don't mean to throw cold water on this idea," the colonel said, "but perhaps we should let this matter rest until then, general?"

Thayer saw that he was losing ground so he feigned indifference. "Oh very well, we all have things that must be attended to. Let us look to our duties."

O'Kelly saluted his superiors and returned to the scouts. Colonel Robinson joined his men. Thayer discretely made his way back to the command tent and sat down with Donovan and Black. He began asking questions about what was occurring back at the capitol and if they had been seen by Indians on their journey. Thayer then pointed out on the field map where their best guess was as to the location of the hostiles. As Black began to study the map, the general ordered Joe to find out whether O'Kelly needed any assistance. Donovan saluted and as soon as the sergeant was out of earshot he began to cajole the governor.

"Governor, I could sure do with a sip of brandy. Would you join me?"

Black continued to look at the map but he lifted his eyes for a moment. "Splendid idea Thayer, it was a dusty ride!"

*   *   *

Sergeant Donovan found O'Kelly speaking with one of the volunteer scouts deeper into the camp. The lieutenant was planning to send out parties in roughly the same direction as he had before, but this time he would assign relay messengers to report their findings and movement. After O'Kelly was through giving the man his instruction he went over to Joe.

"Did you two stop in a brewery this morning? I think the governor's drunk again."

"I don't know where he gets his liquor, Brady. I figured he had a flask leaving Omaha City but he must have had more than that. Our governor has a problem for sure."

"Well he is going to have more of a problem if he keeps it up. Thayer is fixing to take command and I can't say I would disagree." O'Kelly thought for a moment. "Still we may be somewhat of a quandary. We came across a campsite of Indians we are chasing. There could be thousands of them. Larger than a regiment as close as I can figure and I don't think Thayer has any idea what we could be up against."

"Well he's the general. I expect he has fought Pawnee before."

O'Kelly rolled his eyes. "Don't fool yourself, Joe. He's made some arrests and negotiated some captive exchanges but we've never had a toe-to-toe fight with numbers like this. When I first saw you and the governor ride in I was feeling hopeful. If Black would lead us I would feel better because I am confident that we would not blunder into anything; but he is a mess."

"He was not like this yesterday evening but then I hit the sack early. He told me some tales about the fighting in Mexico. Our governor has seen some hard fighting. I expect it may have rattled up his head some. Probably why he drinks."

"I know Thayer is my general but I do not respect the man. I respect Black but can't hide my eyes from him being a drunk."

Donovan nodded sadly. "We should find out what is ahead of us regardless who leads us. Mind if I sign up as one of your scouts, lieutenant?"

Brady smiled. "I was just going to suggest something along those lines!"

Battle Creek

Chapter 1

Early Morning July 11, 1859
Battle Creek

Moving west the Pawnee found a low plain south of the Elkhorn that was traversed by a small creek flowing north. The stream was cool and clear, a wonderful place to camp. They crossed the creek and set up an encampment on the western rim. Two braves rode into camp and announced large herds of antelope were sighted in the tall grass hills in the southwest. Antelope meat and hides were nearly as valuable as the summer buffalo. Nothing was finer for a Pawnee morning meal than antelope stew. *Petalasharo* decided this was a good place to rest. He sent his messenger boy to gather the priests and medicine men to conduct dances that would insure the success of an antelope hunt. Scouts were sent out to find the exact locations of the pronghorn and the elders were summoned to begin the quiet but joyful blessing of the venture.

As the Great Chief was about to begin making his way to *Tahirusawichi's* teepee to begin the ceremonies, Little Anger made an unexpected visit. He entered Red Turtle's teepee and immediately addressed *Petalasharo*.

"Great Chief, we must share words."

Petalasharo raised an eyebrow. Seldom had the Little Anger called him Great Chief since his elevation. "Certainly *Sharitarish*, come have some tobacco."

Little Anger quietly took a seat by the fire while the clay morning pipe was prepared. He seemed unusually quiet. A social a visit by the younger chief was always unusual. Red Turtle did not know why he visited their teepee after so many harsh words. She did not trust the man and glanced sideways at her husband. The Great Chief tried to hide his

213

confusion as well but offered Little Anger a seat of honor. For a moment there was an uncomfortable silence. *Petalasharo* decided it was best to let Little Anger speak in his own time. The Great Chief's patience was rewarded, for after the pipe was handed to Little Anger, he immediately began to speak. "Great Chief, there has been raiding by our people. I remember you were concerned a number of our braves have not been accompanying the people along the trail. This is true. Many of those braves, more than I know, have been stealing from the whites. They have been burning crops and homes of the whites. I fear there was a battle. Some whites killed three young men at a cabin and injured a few more. The foolish boys have been tending to their own wounds for fear of your wrath. One is badly injured. He may still yet die. I sent him to the doctors for medicine; there has been enough foolishness . . . . Still . . . I fear the white men's blood runs hot against the Pawnee. I fear that our braves have not forgotten our village and they still want revenge against the whites."

Petalasharo began to puff at his pipe and looked downward. Little Anger wondered what seethed hotter, the tobacco or the Great Chief's temper. When the Great Chief spoke Little Anger was surprised by the measured tone of his voice. He only had a question.

"Has the raiding stopped?"

"Yes Great Chief, at least I have not heard any more tales."

Petalasharo then began to speak quietly, "This is my fault *Sharitarish Tiki*. I should have learned from your father that our young men needed a release for their angry spirits. I knew their blood was hot after *Pah-Huku* was burned and I did nothing."

Little Anger was shocked. The Great Chief was not looking for recriminations or seeking to blame others. Guilt arose in the Little Anger and he spoke up, "I am to blame too, Great Chief!" He nervously looked up at Red Turtle fearful that he had recriminated himself. Seeing she was not listening into their conversation he continued. "I mean all the chiefs must share this responsibility."

"Yes, that is true. We are all responsible and we shall share the fate of our people. If the whites wish to punish the Pawnee, the chiefs must protect the people and take the punishment if that is just."

Little Anger was feeling the burden of his conscience. He decided he should tell of his role. "I must speak further, Great Chief."

The Great Chief shook his head and held up a hand. "No. You need not speak more *Sharitarish Tiki,* unless what you say will stop future mistakes made by our people. If the raiding has been stopped, and you believe it has, nothing more needs to be done. I do not seek to blame anyone for these acts. I only ask they not be repeated. The past is what it is. The future is where we must lay our eyes to protect our people. Now let us enjoy this smoke before we join the medicine men. After the ceremony we must visit this foolish young man and offer what assistance we can for his family."

The Great Chief drew the fragrant tobacco in deeply and closed his eyes. He let some smoke waft through his nostrils and pulled the curling wisp over his black hair. He released the smoke and offered the pipe to Little Anger.

"Enjoy the tobacco my friend, it comes from strong seed. The joys of life are as many as our tobacco puffs, unfortunately joys must be enjoyed within the moment, for they disappear as quickly as the smoke touches the air and is seen no more.

Sharitarish nodded. He did not know what to say.

Chapter 2

Late morning July 11, 1859
North Bank of the Elkhorn River

The militia was ignorant of the fact, but they were closer to the Pawnee than they knew. They rode through yesterday's heat and finally made camp on the north side of the Elkhorn opposite a large copse of ancient cottonwoods.[31] Black was hardly seen by the men of the militia. The governor seemed to disappear into one of the freighter wagons and was quiet as a mouse. Every man in the detachment knew that a high ranking person was riding in their midst, yet they found it disturbing he chose to remain alone. Black had taken up with a bottle. Joe felt it was best not to call attention to the governor.

Early the next morning Joe and Brady ate breakfast together and then rode out east of the camp following the quiet but steady river.

"Do you know this country at all?" Donovan asked O'Kelly.

The lieutenant gave him a hard look back and shook his head. "Never been this way although I was with the general when he visited the Pawnee at their agency four years back. You can bet they know the land. These Pawnee know it like they know their babies' bottoms. If they know we're coming the warriors could ambush us and there would be hell to pay."

Despite the difference in their ages and ranks the men were comfortable with one another. The two old friends discussed the directions of each scouting sortie Brady sent out. The lieutenant had a lot of things running roughshod in his mind and he enjoyed the quiet

---

[31] Somewhere in modern Stanton County, Nebraska.

moments. He enjoyed time with Donovan; sitting on their mounts trying to sort through the questions.

Donovan's horse was getting skittish with the inactivity and his rider understood. Joe spoke up, "There is another thing I don't figure makes sense. If these Indians are bent on raiding why are they moving in this direction? There aren't many settlers out this way."

O'Kelly nodded. "I am worried. Could be they are running from us, but I'm still worried about their numbers. I want you to ride out front, follow the path of this big trail up river. I expect those Indians to be close and most likely where I am sending you. I'll send with you a couple of militia boys I trust."

"Thanks Brady, but I can probably move faster and quieter without anyone. Your little army will need all the boys it can keep if these numbers stack up."

"Agreed, but how will you get word back to us?"

"Don't worry. I'll make it back with word. You just make sure the militia stays together and no one takes foolish chances. If you can sober Black up a little he's the man I would trust to lead in a pinch."

O'Kelly nodded and looked upriver. The sun was beginning to beat down with mid-morning heat and carp were jumping in the stream. "You make it back here, Sergeant Donovan." He said with a smile.

Joe smiled a boyish grim back and saluted, "Yes, sir!" Donovan kicked his horse and whipped him forward. O'Kelly watched his friend ride off until he lost sight of him through the foliage along the rolling river bend. He stood for a moment longer than he needed. This whole campaign was beginning to eat at him. He prayed that they were not on the edge of committing a terrible wrong even if they did all get out of this without losing their scalps. He tried to calculate when he last heard Mass. No matter. He knew he was long overdue for a full confession. Finally, he decided he'd best get back sure to be needed at the camp. He turned his horse and made his way to the command tent.

Chapter 3

July 12, 1859
Battle Creek

At sunset the hunters returned with a rich harvest. Laid upon the backs of small ponies were dozens of fat antelopes ready for skinning. With trills of excitement the women and children began to unload the carcasses and prepare for the skinning and butchering.

The temporary encampment now lay in a great half circle along the eastern bank of the stream. The water still ran cool and clear with runoff and the elders knew it would shrivel to nothing as the days grew longer and hotter as the summer wore on. The horse herd was settled along the western bank and they nibbled the soft grass in the evening air. The younger hunters were quick to find their favorite maidens and the grounds they chose for their skinning pegs. The animals were stretched upon the earth and the butchering began. Laughter and flirting followed as the braves jostled through the busy girls seeking attention and pointing out which bucks they had brought down. The Great Chief looked over the encampment and decided it was a wise decision to delay the march to the buffalo hunting grounds and hunt smaller game. The people needed rest. They needed replenishment for the hard and much more dangerous work of hunting and harvesting the big bison.

Chapter 4

Militia camp
North Bank of the Elkhorn

"Yes sir." Donovan reported. "There is a big camp west of here. About six miles south of the bend of the Elkhorn that shows on this map." Joe pointed his finger down on the old fur trader's chart. "Their camp is on the near side of a creek that's not shown on this map but it is there."

O'Kelly, Robinson and General Thayer listened intently to what Sergeant Donovan found on his scout. The air was still and musty in the command tent. The men were uncomfortable standing so close together, but their curiosity was greater than their concern for social graces. All eyes were fixed upon the map while they were trying to ignore their rank odor. This far into the campaign everything began to smell like wood fire and tobacco; the tents, the bedding, their own bodies.

"You say more than a thousand Indians?" The general anxiously clarified and Donovan nodded.

"That's more than we should take on sir without waiting for more help from the army." O'Kelly added.

Thayer looked at Robinson. The colonel spoke up. "My men and I are the only help that's coming from Fort Kearny. Remember boys, we have to look at national priorities and policing the Overland Road takes precedence. The army is not unsympathetic mind you, that's why we're here, but you're lucky you got us. I will tell you, I am not cowed by these numbers as long as can surprise the lot of 'em."

Donovan looked around and noticed the governor was absent. "Where's Governor Black?"

"He's in the tent over yonder sleeping a hard night off." Thayer pointed indifferently.

"What happened?" Donovan asked looking at O'Kelly. The lieutenant simply nodded sadly. "I did not know he had any booze left."

"Never doubt the resourcefulness of a wastrel, sergeant." Thayer stated dryly. "Our governor actually asked Colonel Robinson to procure more spirits."

The colonel nodded. Joe was beside himself.

"But don't mind him." Thayer said. "The colonel and I will be handling operations on this campaign."

Robinson spoke up, "Sergeant Donovan, could you tell whether the Indians are wise to our presence."

"I doubt it sir. They seemed pretty intent in hunting and skinning."

"So there are women in the camp, eh?" Colonel Robinson asked.

"Yes sir, and some children too . . . or at least young boys. I saw them watching the horse herd. Good sized herd and I may not have seen all of them. About a thousand head of animals."

"Could it be these aren't the Indians the militia has been tracking?" Robinson asked looking at Thayer. "We don't want to make a mistake here."

O'Kelly spoke up. "It's the right Indians, colonel. Too many solid trails run to that encampment Donovan found." The lieutenant looked right at Joe and asked, "They were Pawnee, right?"

Joe Donovan rubbed his face and stepped back from the map. He wished he did not have to answer the question; but he did. "Yes sir, they were Pawnee."

Thayer stood up and slapped his riding gloves on his thigh, "There you go. That decides it. We need to ride to those rascals and attack before they know we are onto them!"

O'Kelly held his hand up. "Sir, we will still be outnumbered even if most of that camp is noncombatants. I think we ought to think this through. Remember what those *Omahaw* Indians told us today, the Pawnee are aiming to do some hunting and that large encampment may just break up. Maybe we should wait or at least come up with a plan."

The militia had come upon a small party of *Omahaw* who had been with the Pawnee and Ponca earlier that week. The *Omahaw* proved cooperative with valuable information. It was lucky Robinson's dragoons had come upon them first and the Indians were correctly identified. If militia scouts had come upon the little group gunplay may have resulted from over eager ignorance.

"He is right, general. It is best if we have a plan. We don't want to tie into a thousand Indians without a plan." Robinson's agreement surprised O'Kelly as he had seemed as gung-ho as Thayer.

Thayer sighed; slightly miffed his show of determination had not inspired his men to immediate action. He relented. "Very well, I will order an officer's call. Sergeant, thank you for this timely information. You are dismissed."

Joe gave a tired salute to the officers as O'Kelly suggested he find something to eat. Donovan only nodded knowing he should find some grub but wanting to talk to the governor. He was silently concerned the man would not be capable of conversation. He wandered over to the tent hoping the officers would not notice his destination. Joe approached the entrance quietly.

He whispered into the tent. "Governor . . . . Governor Black. Sir, are you awake?"

A quiet groan emitted out of the tent. Joe decided to enter. He saw the governor seated on his cot holding a feedbag full of syrupy vomit. Donovan shook his head and asked if he could sit down. Black nodded.

"If you are done sir, I should take that."

Sam did not argue. "Not sure I am done but here take it."

Donovan left briefly and poured the contents out beside the tent. He looked back at the officers and there was a heated conversation going on. He returned to the tent and sat on the other cot. Black had lain down with his fist covering his eyes.

"Governor, if you don't mind me saying, you are in a fine state of inebriation once again."

"I'm not bad, Joe. Leave me the hell alone."

Joe kept on, "Where'd you get the booze."

Sam opened his eyes and shook his head a little. "I don't rightly remember . . . maybe? Hell I don't know. Leave damn you!"

"Sam I will leave if you order it but they will remove you as governor if this keeps up. You have got to cut back the drinking."

"That's what damn Eliza tells me . . . nag . . . nag . . . don't drink so much . . . get the hell out of this tent. That's an order!"

Joe stood up. He nodded and said, "Yes, sir."

Just as he was about to stoop through the flap Sam began to talk again, mostly to himself, "Eliza Black says Samuel don't drink so much! Sergeant Joe Donovan says governor don't drink so much!" He sighed and then began a question. "Do you know what my children tell me, Joe?"

Donovan was somewhat embarrassed and said, "No, sir."

"They say daddy don't drink, not don't drink so much . . . They say don't drink!"

Donovan nodded and said, "Well governor then it must be you let them down most of all." He left and joined the men sitting around the campfire swapping stories about past scrapes they had been in with Indians, arguments with their wives, business and political feuds going on in their hometowns. The same type of discussions you get when you mix militia irregulars, volunteers, and part-time lawmen. The professional soldiers that had accompanied their colonel were the only ones who did not see this excursion as a grand adventure. They drank slowly and consistently, quietly brooding in the thought of how much longer they would remain enrolled. Donovan seemed most drawn to the militia and he sat down by two corporals who offered him a quick nip of dry mash. For some reason the thought of drinking did not appeal to him.

Sounds of a heated argument continued to emanate from the command tent and the militia looked about nervously.

One of the volunteers looked about and asked no one in particular, "Do you think we're going to see any action before this is all done?"

Another spit on the ground and gave an answer, "Doubt it. I think we are just letting the brass take their horses out for a stretch of their legs. Those Indians are probably across the mountains by now."

Donovan listened to the men's talk with indifference. He was somewhat miffed at the governor. After all, he could be home with his wife right now. Why was he was on this excursion when it seemed obvious to everyone about that Black took no interest in the events? Suddenly he felt a tap on his shoulder and he looked back and was truly surprised.

"Governor? Here take my seat sir."

At that point, the men were wise to Black's identity. They took him for a sot. Black had straightened his clothing and put on a jacket. His hair was slicked back and his beard was combed. His eyes, while a tad bloodshot, were alert.

"Now now gentlemen, I did not mean to stop the revival."

The men were very silent after Black joined them. Donovan was curious. Finally one of the men spoke up. "Can I offer you a drink from my flask, sir?" He was instantly ribbed by the man sharing the log. Several muffled snickers let out.

"The governor seemed completely nonplussed staring into the fire. "No thank you. But I shall see we share a draft upon returning to the capitol."

Black followed up the remark with a noisy belch. This emboldened the men who shared the fire and brought a smile to the face of the man who had spoken.

"The man who doubted that the Indians were near spoke up. "Governor, what do you think of this campaign? Will we get vengeance upon these Indian or what?"

Black pondered the question. "I don't know what will happen. What do you want to happen?"

The man answered back, "I want to get at them bastards and kill some. My wife knew Uriah and they came close to hurting him bad."

Someone else spoke up, "I knew the lady who was killed. She never did anything to those savages, always treated them as a Christian should. She needs some justice."

Samuel nodded in agreement, "We have had some trouble in these parts that's fair to say."

The men nodded and agreed. Black went on, "What if we do kill the guilty Indians but some of us die? Maybe you or the fellow sitting next to you, or all those boys from Columbus, and maybe a few soldiers too; some killed some not. Will we still get justice?"

The men sat back and began to look at one another. They had not given much thought to the possibility of their own demise. An uneasy silence fell upon the campfire.

Black spoke up. "I want to catch the rascals who caused this trouble. That is for sure; but I also want us to make it back home to our families. Each man who survives a victorious battle and survives unscathed will say the fight was worth it, but no battle ending in victory or defeat was worth fighting for the man who dies. He's dead for sure and no amount of fancy words or poems written in his behalf will change that." Black sighed deep. "There is the nub boys; we have to fight battles from time to time. It is a fact. The uncivilized so often prey on the civilized. Sometimes you have to sacrifice a dozen lives to save hundreds or even thousands. But you need to be very careful about sacrificing lives because it can get away from you. Soon you start turning killing into something else . . . Something else with just a new word attached like diplomacy or war craft. But it is killing just the same and it can turn into a habit."

Donovan spoke up, "Well sir, I know it won't turn into a habit for me . . . but I need to do my part as best that my gifts and abilities will allow. We all need to contribute up to our abilities." He looked knowingly at the governor.

Black smiled and nodded. He needed to start doing his part. The conversation began to grow down right depressing and the men did not know what else to say.

Donovan was amazed that the Black was so well spoken and polished. He seemed pretty wrung out less than a half hour before. Apparently, the man had gotten a second wind somewhere.

The governor and men continued to sit, smoke and listen to the increasing arguments of the brass going on behind them. The men talked about their training, or lack thereof, their officers, what type of grub they received, and opportunities for leave. A few aired various grievances they had with command. Governor Black listened quietly smoking a foul smelling cheroot. Donovan saw that he was very comfortable with the men and understood what was on the mind of both a commoner and soldier.

Just before the glow of sunset began to fade from the sky, Lieutenant O'Kelly called out to the sergeants to organize their companies for a night march. The militia needed to make good time tonight he shouted and he needed to get everyone mounted and lined up soon.

"I figure it is about time we find out exactly what General Thayer has in mind for our boys here." Black announced as he stood up and headed for the command tent.

Joe was immediately uneasy and asked whether the governor really wanted him to come along.

"Absolutely."

O'Kelly saw the two draw near and was immediately surprised by the presence of the governor.

"Sir?" He stepped back forgetting to salute. "I thought you were . . . er . . . unwell?"

"Feeling much better, lieutenant, thank you for your concern."

The three entered the command tent and Thayer took a step backward. Colonel Robinson was standing against the wall clearly upset with how the officer's council had gone.

"Good evening, gentlemen. Sergeant Donovan has informed me the hostiles have been located and that we are about to approach their encampment. Please provide me with the details as to how you intend the approach and disposition of troops at the point of confrontation."

Thayer finally gathered himself and spoke, "Governor Black? You really need not concern yourself with these military matters sir. The colonel and I have matters well in hand."

Black approached the table that had a commercial trader's map and a larger more detailed, yet less accurate, surveyor's map of the area unrolled. Pins and stones were laid out showing possible movements of both the hostiles and the troops. "I do not doubt that General Thayer, please humor me with the details. The cartography is still out so it should be easy."

Thayer looked at Robinson uneasily. The colonel looked back with a quizzical air. "Governor Black there really is not time, the lieutenant has just called the militia to mount up and time is of the essence."

The governor bent down on the map picking up on something that interested him. He spoke over his shoulder. "I know how long it takes to organize a detachment for a forced march, General Thayer. We can spare ten minutes. First, tell me about the approach. Will we have the men track single in file or by squad? Will you have the militia on the fore or rear guard? Where will the colonel have his dragoons within the line of march?"

"Sir really, this is unnecessary." Thayer stammered, thoughts of leading the men single handedly to a great Indian victory suddenly dimming.

Black began tracing movements on the map and picturing angles of fire within his head. "Now general, of course it is necessary, as surely you know that the entire chain of command has to have a firm grasp of the tactical priorities and dispositions in case any or all officers are not able to perform their duties."

"Governor, I assure you I intend to fulfill my duties and I will expect my officers to carry out their assigned tasks. They are well briefed in my chosen plan of battle."

"I understand General Thayer, but if I go down I want you to know what must be done."

An icy silence hit the room with a nearly audible crack. All in the tent realized at that moment Black was taking command.

"Governor Black, I wanted you to be kept unaware of this embarrassment but you have forced me. Pursuant to the enactment of the General Assembly and Militia Code sixteen six dash one, you have been determined to be unfit for the duties of your command because of wayward drunkenness."

Black stood up and approached Thayer. The general did not back down.

"This document has been signed all officers of this command." Thayer held up O'Kelly's hastily scribbled draft before Black's face. "I can place you under arrest for suborning us in our duties."

Black's eyes remained fixed on Thayer's and he said, "Colonel Robinson, this is not how you would approach the hostile camp correct?"

"Why no Gov . . ." Before the colonel had completed his sentence Black had snatched the paper away and torn it in two. He threw the shreds upon the ground.

"Vote again." Black dared the general. "Have your officers vote again. Have them vote this time in my presence."

The two men stood eyeing one another for a moment. Donovan and O'Kelly could not believe what was actually transpiring before them.

"John," the colonel spoke up using Thayer's given name. "Let's just hear the governor out. It appears he has some insight."

Black looked back at the colonel. "You were saying, Colonel Robinson, how you would handle the deployment prior to battle."

"Yes, yes governor I was . . . I would not do an envelopment sir. There would be . . . risks." I would send my regulars in the fore and place the general's militia on the right flank because we have Donovan's report that is where the horse herd is located . . . I would station the cannon on this plateau, approximately here, to fire within this angle of trajectory." The colonel placed the compass upon the map to show the field of fire. Black approached and nodded thoughtfully.

Thayer soon realized that he was beaten but he sheepishly returned to the table. Black looked up at the general and with no hint of anger in his voice he stated. "General, I do approve of your militia's approach. This order of march will allow the men to deploy in any contingency."

"Uh yes, governor."

"Gentlemen, here are my ideas: We should have three plans in place as frameworks for dealing with various contingencies. We will utilize both of your plans depending upon how we find the hostile encampment and its perceived strength. I will alter Robinson's proposed cannon placement because this topography does not look right and a deviant of the elevation here would shield the hostiles in the event that there are greater numbers scattered . . ."

O'Kelly was amazed at what he saw unfold before him. It was almost like watching a master of his craft perform. The governor explained in the clearest and most basic terms preferred tactics, possible risks, appropriate countermeasures and options of an unfolding battle. It was artistic and nearly beautiful in its design. Once the governor completed the war council he closed as he had seen Winfield Scott close each war council in Mexico. "Gentlemen, these plans are sound and I thank all of you for your thoughts and energies that went into these decisions. Remember once blood has been shed no one knows where it will flow. Look to your men and pray to our God. Our lives are in his hands."

The colonel saluted Black smartly and Thayer saluted him with only slightly less enthusiasm. "General Thayer ride with me if you will. We still have much to discuss."

"Yes sir."

As the officers left the command tent Black looked at Donovan with a knowing smile. "Do not look so surprised sergeant. My wife will tell you I have three talents. The first is drinking, the second is soldiering."

"Can I ask what that third talent is?"

"Lately I have had the talent of making her mad but it used to be something quite different."

Chapter 5

After midnight, July 13, 1859
Battle Creek

Pahaat Icas watched the stars whirl overhead through the clear smoke hole of her teepee. She snuggled against the Great Chief's back thankful that her husband had finally been able to nod off to sleep after so much tossing and turning. She could hear owls softly hooting to one another as they flew near the encampment looking for prey. The night was quiet and had the feeling of magic about it. She felt grateful that Indian men slept so much more silently than do the whites who would visit their villages along the Loups and Platte. Whether it was their ever-present burning water, thick active tongues, or great furry faces, their snores, coughs and emissions often kept entire horse herds skittish throughout nights such as these. She loved nights like this. Red Turtle giggled softly thanking *Tirawahat* for feeding the people and providing the Pawnee with such joyful evenings. She did not know what had troubled her husband this day, he had been distant since the unusual visit by *Sharitarish,* but she felt very content, very content and very safe.

*   *   *

The militia column rode double time and the trot the horses began to lope in caused the men to grow more anxious.

"The boys know we need to get somewhere in a hurry." Thayer mentioned to the governor.

Black nodded and agreed. "We best slow up after we cross the river and head along the southern rim of the valley. We need to pace the mounts."

The river crossing went well as there was a fordable sandbar just where Donovan remembered. The horses were brushed down and cooled off.

"Your militia boys have some good horse flesh general, my compliments."

"Lieutenant O'Kelly is the officer in charge of requisitions, governor. Of course I sign off on every purchase." Thayer informed him.

"If this moonlight holds out we may just reach those Indians before dawn. You were not much exaggerating on time being of the essence."

"Well sir . . . the cannon carriage is slowing us down. Perhaps we should leave it."

"Absolutely not general! I have plans for its deployment."

"Yes, sir."

Black continued with a question. "Who would be your best scouts, outside of Sergeant Donovan of course?"

"Perhaps I should inquire of Lieutenant O'Kelly? He has overseen our reconnaissance on this campaign."

"By all means, general."

O'Kelly was called forward and the three officers decided to send Donovan and two other men forward to get land measurements and scout the encampment. We will send them with spare mounts to insure the pace. Make sure Donovan returns with actionable information."

Without a cloud in the sky the stars and moon did cooperate that late evening and the militia made good time. It was a waxing gibbous moon that hung fat and bright in the summer sky. As it began to set in the west, the light became golden and it gave the prairie a bronze glow. Only one horse was lost with a leg break from stepping in a hole. Luck was with the detachment and the militia covered the miles unseen. Governor Black began thinking to himself that soldiering did have its enjoyable aspects; the camaraderie and teamwork of the unit, the acceptance and feeling of belonging, and the near intoxicating excitement of a determined ride across a magical landscape on a moonlit night. He also remembered, however, the sick in the gut understanding that war was murder. His thoughts came back to the present. He needed to concentrate on the trail and the task at hand. If he started thinking on things too hard, he may get an urge to open the vial he had in his saddlebag.

Chapter 6

Prior to dawn, July 13, 1859
Battle Creek

Dogs are always the earliest risers in a Pawnee hunting camp. Scampering about looking for an early meal or chasing large rowdy crows, dogs always found demands on their time. This morning they were especially taxed and busy licking the grass clean from the blood left from skinning and drawing antelopes.

Most Pawnee were still stretched out within their summer furs and skins. The tribe was enjoying the last few moments of quiet before the women would get back to the scrapping of the hides and the hunters would collect more game. They hardly noticed the intensifying barking of the hounds but they certainly woke up with a start as women began screaming near the creek. The first braves to look to the east saw dozens of riders heading straight for the camp. The dawn had not yet erased the gray mist from the ground and no one could determine who the riders were. They seemed to be closing in from the horizon and no one doubted they were not friends of the Pawnee.

"Aieee . . . wake the criers! Warriors arise!" Everyone poured from the teepees groggy with sleep. *Petalasharo* stumbled from his hides. He began to shout out for the men to secure the horse herd. He had been in the Pawnee villages often enough to understand early morning raids were common. They could be deadly, especially if the raiders were Sioux, but only two he had ever been a part of resulted in death.

"White men!" a woman screamed. "The white men are attacking!"

Those terrifying words changed everything. Suddenly there was confusion mixed with the fear. This changed the very nature of the attack. It was not a common raid. *Petalasharo* had never known the whites to attack an encampment this large. In fact, he had to search his memory for when the Pawnee and whites had been at war. He instantly knew this had to do with Little Anger's raiding. Most of the braves instinctively ran for the horse herd across the creek assuming the herd would be the first target. The Great Chief took a few moments to gather his thoughts. The whites were still a distance away. His mind went back to the Big Sandy Creek and his nightmare. The white raiders would not be going for the horses but to punish the people.

The Great Chief shouted over the chaos. "Stop! Stop, my warriors! We must remain in the camp to protect the women and helpless ones!"

The braves who had gathered their weapons looked to *Petalasharo* to decide what must be done. Many of the braves, who would not think of going into battle without a horse beneath them, continued to run to the herd. But most stayed and looked to his words. "We must meet them at the edge of the camp with our arrows ready. Now is the time for our hearts to be strong."

The Pawnee gathered at the line of teepees along the edge and drew their bows back. Once the soldiers were in range hundreds of arrows would be launched into their ranks. *Petalasharo* looked down at his staggered line of men. He thought was there any way to put an end to this?

Suddenly, as if the white men had crossed an invisible line, their racing steeds pulled up short. A few men dismounted and gathered before the troops. The Indians looked at one another uncertainly and glanced at the Great Chief. No one knew what would happen next.

Chapter 7

Indeed the sudden restraint shown by the militia had been planned in advance. Black wanted to rest the winded horses before leading them into the Pawnee encampment. Thayer had argued against the maneuver.

"We will lose the advantage of our surprise." He contended. "The savages will have time to put up a defense or get to their horses and scatter."

Black was adamant, however. "I have seen this work. A pause does nothing to lessen the surprise already achieved. If nothing else, it causes more confusion and consternation. When we make our charge toward the village I expect to be seen. We have arrived too late for the darkness to cover our approach. We will give our horses a breather and the Indians will not gain an advantage."

Colonel Robinson saw the sense in sparing the horses from even more exertion and together with O'Kelly; the general was persuaded to silence his thoughts. According to plan, and shockingly well executed without having practiced the maneuver, the detachment stopped on cue. The cannon had been rolled off to the right of the formation and it fired. The shot was aimed to land short and the bombardiers put the ball perfectly between the militia and the encampment. A burst of sand and dust showered the teepees.

The militia could see the confusion within the camp and many of the braves who were near the front broke away and ran into the camp for the horses.

Samuel masked his rising excitement well, but Thayer was beside himself. The general wanted to charge into the encampment with guns blazing.

"Steady men. Steady. Don't get greedy." Black shouted. O'Kelly was amazed how much volume was in his voice, yet the command seemed

232

nonplussed, almost casual. Even Colonel Robinson looked as if he were torn between continuing the charge and maintaining the line. The men standing just out of bowshot of the Pawnee looked on at their prey and began to hoot in derision. The pause was having a desired effect on the Indians as they seemed to be disappearing within the camp. Only the officers with their telescopes observed that the Pawnee were not running but retreating toward the horses. Soon only a half dozen remained along the edge of the encampment.

"Hold the line, men! Not one step forward." Black shouted with his arm still held upward. "We go when I say!"

Sergeant Donovan watched the commotion of the encampment before him while both militia and their horses literally chewed at the bit to be unleashed. Whatever the governor had planned it sure seemed to be working. The cannon had only fired once and it appeared as if the Pawnee defenses were crumbling before them. What would happen next was only guesswork. Was this what war was like when everything went perfectly? How did the governor know the Indians would react like this? Donovan then saw what seemed like hundreds of Indians making a dash to the south. Were the warriors trying to flank them? Robinson had his eye-piece out and took a good look at the Indians running from the camp. The colonel put his telescope down and looked at his fellow officers.

"It is their women governor. Can't see they have any warriors. The squaws are making a break for it."

"Hold steady, men. No one break for the camp until I say!" Black continued to shout over the neighing of the sweating horses. "Calm your ponies, boys. They need to rest up some!"

O'Kelly looked over and noticed General Thayer was now holding his arm into the air as well. Wasn't he putting on a show?

"What are we waiting on, governor?" The colonel asked, "Looks to me that the Indians may be able to get away if we hold like this for much longer."

O'Kelly was surprised at the colonel's question. He figured the man had had enough experience on the frontier to realize the Indians could not get far without their horses. He figured that the governor was watching the horse herd. He was right. After the line of Indians standing guard along the camp had melted away to next to nothing the horses began running away from the encampment toward the north-west. Once the governor saw the ponies fleeing from the encampment he dropped his arm and shouted, "Charge!" A mighty yell rose from the boys and spurs were dug into the horse's flanks. This is it, thought Donovan. This is war.

*   *   *

Red Turtle had drawn the women and children about her trying to determine where the safest place was for them to go. The fact that the attackers were white seemed to add terror to all their hearts. No one knew what to expect. Indian raids could often be beaten off with only lost horses and a few dead and wounded, but with whites? All of the Pawnee had heard about the mighty Sioux encampment at Blue Water wiped out and the people drug off to imprisonment at the soldier forts. Could this be the dreaded Squaw Killer returning for the Pawnee?

The women gathered about her eager for guidance as to what needed to be done. The entire camp was on the edge of panic since the thunder wagon had spoken and sent a ball so near to the camp. The warriors had run away from the encampment and left the Great Chief with only a few braves to stand the whites off. It was not courage they lacked; the Pawnee simply could not comprehend fighting without their horses beneath them. The explosion they heard made many braves fear the horses would stampede. How was a man to fight without a horse?

Red Turtle and the women quickly crossed the creek and ran toward the hills southwest of the camp. They ran as long as they could and as far as they could. It was only after they had struggled to the crest of the first hillock they looked back and saw that the soldiers were not in pursuit. They were exhausted. The women dropped their bundles and began to keen their songs for battle. It was a cry for the warriors to protect them. They knew as long as one Pawnee heart beat within the chests of their braves they would not be abandoned.

Like a dam bursting the horse herd tore away from the camp. The first horses released were rider less but soon they were followed by horses with braves clinging to the backsides. Red Turtle saw that the Pawnee warriors were now in rapid retreat. She looked vainly for her husband. The women gave a gasp as they saw the braves explode out of the village with the horse herd. How far would they run? Suddenly, across the morning air, the women heard the sing-song blare of a soldier trumpet. The whites were once again riding directly for the camp. This time there was nothing to stop them.

* * *

Black had unleashed the militia once he saw the horse herd make a break from the encampment.

"Forward! Forward men!" He shouted.

The distance was quickly crossed and soon the militia was within the deserted teepees and smoking breakfast fires. The horses' hooves trampled through the debris and foodstuff of hundreds of uneaten morning meals and crushed the skinning framework of drying hides.

"Forward men! Continue forward! Now is not the time to stop!" The bugler continued to sound for the men to charge and only a few volunteers dawdled with thoughts of pilfering the Indian's belongings. The militia passed through the encampment in moments and plunged across the creek. They were hard on the heels of the fleeing braves. When they were approximately one hundred yards beyond the encampment, Black shouted another order.

"Column left oblique!"

The bugler called out the signal and the militia headed directly for the women on the hill top. The maneuver was performed flawlessly by the dragoons and the militia followed as Black knew they would. He could see many braves were looking behind them to see how closely the militia men were following. Black knew that their plan was to the lead the militia away from the women and the encampment and exhaust them in a merry chase through the dissected hills and valleys in the west. He had thought this out before hand and he was determined that the militia would not play by Pawnee rules.

* * *

"Do the whites intend to attack the helpless ones?" Little Anger gasped as he looked back horrified at what he saw.

"We must return! We must!"

The Pawnee braves turned their mounts about, but a stampeding horse herd could not be so easily turned. The horses slammed and broke against one another making it impossible to maneuver in a concerted attack. Small pockets of horses ran off in all directions and the boys who were responsible for the herd scattered hoping to return the ponies.

Little Anger could not comprehend the magnitude of what was happening. Was this what he had wished for at one time, conflict with the white man? Is this what it has come down to? He needed to do something.

Little Anger was a chief and needed to protect his people. "Let us go, my braves! We must return. Who are the white men to drive us from our homes and threaten our helpless ones? They will see our wrath!"

With wild shouts of encouragement the warrior began tearing their clothes from their bodies in preparation for battle. The Pawnee succeeded in gathering their strength and attempted to force their way through the frightened horses back toward the encampment. It was perhaps the worst thing the Pawnee braves could have done at the moment as the riderless horses were still moving in the opposite directions. The horses thudded and bit at one another in confusion and rage with their riders hanging on desperately.

When Black saw the Pawnee warrior's turnabout and the bedlam along the hillside, he ordered the men to halt and form a rough skirmish line. The horse herd was still pouring into the Pawnee charge which was a lucky break for the militia who had trouble forming up. The braves gave up the charge and fanned out. Eventually a rude line of battle was formed and the opposing lines had a chance to stare at one another.

"We should continue the attack, Black! We had them on the run!" Thayer shouted.

With all of the confusion and tromping of horse's feet the militia heard a sharp pounding drum coming from the camp. Behind them *Petalasharo* was walking out to the militia wrapped in a large American flag. Beside him was old *Tahirusawichi* beating a hand drum and chanting some ancient incantation. Many of soldiers turned their guns upon the chiefs and were about ready to fire when Black shouted "Hold your fire!"

All was silent in the valley except for the soft rhythm of the drum.

Thayer looked at Black. "We should continue our attack and keep them running!" Black just gave the general a cold stare and pulled his revolver from his belt.

"We attack when I say. Is that understood, general?"

"Governor, if you had as much experience with Indians as I have you would continue our attack!"

"General, if you had as much experience with warfare as I have you would understand my reluctance to follow that course. Waging war is not near as entertaining once blood begins to be shed and I plan on staying entertained for a while!"

Colonel Robinson rode up. "It appears that chief wants to talk."

Governor Black nodded to the colonel and said, "You are correct and we will oblige the gentleman. Colonel, you keep your eyes toward those warriors on the hillside. As long as we remain equidistant from the noncombatants on our flank I am quite certain they will not attack."

The general and colonel looked around. They were very impressed how Black seemed to maneuver everything into place. The militia set upon an undulating field ideal for setting up a defensive perimeter under the sweep of the cannon or setting upon the warriors on the hillside.

Petalasharo and his companion continued to approach. Both chiefs walked forward, neither looking to the left or right. Soon they were in the midst of the troopers and the horses shied away from them as they continued their slow march. The Great Chief approached Black and made gestures known on the plains for peace. Both Robinson and Thayer recognized the movements and conveyed the thought to the governor.

"Well boys, seems to me we ought to hear this gentlemen out since he is dressed like a patriot!"

Robinson demurred to Black and it appeared as if Thayer reluctantly agreed. "Is there anyone here who can speak this man's tongue?" The governor asked.

"I can, general." O'Kelly stepped forward.

"Well, lieutenant." Black said, "You are a man of many talents!"

Suddenly a shot rang out. One of the dragoons had fired a pistol at one of the chiefs approaching from the hill.

"Hold your fire!" Shouted Black and he was echoed by all of the officers. The Great Chief gestured frantically and his eyes communicated a great wish to avoid bloodshed. The chief who had been approaching continued forward and upon reaching the militia the soldiers saw his horse had been wounded. He was allowed to join his companions and O'Kelly asked for all to sit.

"Why is it our white brothers come to do us harm?" The weary Great Chief asked.

General Thayer spoke up angrily, "I remember you, Man Chief. You spoke words of peace when we met before, then you set your braves upon stealing my dinner. You Pawnee are a thieving lot and nothing's changed!"

Black did not even give the lieutenant time to translate the general's words. He spoke directly at Thayer. "General, I'll be damned if we are here to discuss your lunch! Pipe down and mind your place!"

Black announced that before they got too far and commenced with formal introductions he needed to know if they could call a formal truce to parlay. The question was asked of the Great Chief and he spoke back.

"It is good for us to talk for we shall not fight the white man. Your guns cause our women to fear and we must be assured no one will attack our helpless ones while the chiefs share words."

Thayer leaned over and whispered, "This one is wily. He wants to buy time for his braves to gather their horse herd. We should not lose our advantage."

Black looked at the general and gave the man a hard stare. Thayer understood that he had said too much.

"I will have our men stand down. Your women are safe as long as we talk. I assure you that we are not savages."

After O'Kelly translated this, *Petalasharo* spoke some to *Tahirusawichi*. The medicine man began to beat on the drum and walk out of the circle. O'Kelly explained that the old man was being sent to quiet the braves and reassure the women. Both Robinson and Thayer looked at one another and then at the men who began to mill about anxiously.

"Donovan go, quiet the men. Explain to them the officers are trying to settle this thing."

"Yes, sir." The sergeant readily replied.

The sun was now rising into the sky and the grass was losing its sticky dew. It was going to be a hot day and Black was determined that their guns would remain silent. Still he knew wrongs had been committed and the men would be steamed if they returned to their families without getting some answers.

Black looked back at *Petalasharo* and wondered if this man knew what a tight spot they were both in. He wondered if it was going to be possible to get out of this creek valley without the shedding of blood. The governor thought that it was a good sign that the chief was wearing an American flag. He knew *Petalasharo* understood it was a powerful symbol.

"I am Governor Samuel Black of this territory. These are my officers, Colonel Lawrence Robinson of the U.S. Army and General John Thayer of the Organized Militia." There was a pause while O'Kelly translated the words.

Black continued slowly, "We are here to stop your people from attacking us." Little Anger looked at the Great Chief. *Petalasharo* continued to look straight ahead.

"My militia and I have just followed a path of destruction for over a hundred miles all along this river. Settlers have been attacked, homes burned, crops and livestock destroyed. We know the Pawnee have done this." O'Kelly continued with a solemn translation.

Both chiefs remained silent and now it was the turn of the whites to look at one another.

Thayer spoke up. "Lieutenant, do you think they understand? Have you told them why we are here?"

"I told them sir."

"Why aren't they speaking?"

Black put up his hand, "Easy gentlemen, give them some time."

Finally the Great Chief drew the flag back from his shoulders and began to reach for an object he had tucked in his clothing. Thayer instinctively grabbed at his revolver and Robinson became very uneasy. Even Black was fearful he had made a mistake in allowing the Indians to get so close before he saw the chief had brought out a short stemmed pipe.

As the chief began to pack his pipe with tobacco he asked how many of the white had been killed by his people.

Thayer looked at Black wondering if he should report the woman killed at Fontanelle. Black looked straight at the chief. "There have been casualties."

The Great Chief lit the pipe and then offered it to Black. The governor took a few puffs and then returned the pipe. As *Petalasharo* handed the pipe to Little Anger, the Great Chief spoke. "My people have lost young braves too. Our old village has been burned. It is the will of the gods that this misfortune has come upon our peoples."

The white men shook their heads.

Black looked sideways. "Man Chief, there were no gods causing this trouble. It was your people that need to be taught a lesson."

Petalasharo began to puff on the pipe. O'Kelly translated this and the chiefs looked confused. Black began to understand they may not understand what lesson he could be referring to. After the Great Chief and Little Anger spoke among themselves for a moment, *Petalasharo* began to talk.

"I am sorry that this has caused you to travel so far. I am sorry for what may have been done, but let us not set upon one another because of past bad blood. There must be some other way. The Pawnee have been friends to the white man before. We wish to remain your friends."

Black looked around and saw the men beginning to mill about. He saw the warriors gathering on the far hillside looking down at the militia. There seemed to be more of them than before and he saw they were no longer crawling over their horses in confusion. His mind went through a quick array of questions: Could they take the Indians? Should they try? What would that even solve if they could take the field and inflict some punishment? What would it solve if the militia left quietly? Would it be taken as a sign of weakness? What if the Indians overwhelmed them?

The governor decided they need to continue to talk. "Chief, if I understand you, you're not denying that your people participated in these outrages?"

Petalasharo spoke. "What has been done has been done. My people have lost braves as well. Perhaps if I were a great warrior chief such as yourself, my young men could be controlled. Our people have me as I am. I must apologize to you and to them for being as I am. I must apologize for my failures."

Black looked at the Great Chief with a smile of curious amusement. Who was this man with such strange words?

"Was it you chief who ordered these depredations?" O'Kelly gave the translation.

The Great Chief answered, "No one orders the Pawnee to do such things. Each brave decides his own paths."

Black sighed and said, "We will need the braves responsible for this trouble."

"We can punish our own for bringing this trouble to our peoples. I tell you again we have lost several braves. Mothers and fathers have lost sons. Sisters have lost brothers. Many campfires will see fewer braves gathered by its warmth."

Black shook his head, "Many of your braves have violated the peace between our peoples. They need to see justice. I assure you they will get a fair trial."

"We can punish our own."

"Your braves violated our law. They need to be tried by our courts. They will get a fair trial."

"The red man never receives a fair trial in a white court."

"We will not discuss that now. We will have those responsible or there will be war between us." As Black said this he nearly regretted the harshness of his language. Did the Indians have guns? He hoped not. He thought not. Probably a few, but then, how to be sure?

Petalasharo and Little Anger discussed the matter briefly in a softened tone. After some discussion the Great Chief spoke.

"Will you allow me to return to my people? This is not an easy thing you ask. *Sharitarish* will remain as a hostage."

"We do not take hostages, chief. You may both go as long as we understand that you will not attack."

"We will not fight the white man." The Great Chief affirmed.

Chapter 8

The Great Chief offered *Sharitarish's* horse as a token of good faith to the whites and they accepted. *Petalasharo* said that it was a custom of his people but he made the gesture more as a way to stall the proceeding. Something told him the heat of the day would sap the blood thirst of the whites. The chief's walk up to the braves on the hill took longer than the two expected, and that was good.

"I am worried how this will end, Great Chief." *Sharitarish Tiki* admitted.

"It is right to worry. The white men have many guns."

By the time that the chiefs arrived and were surrounded by the braves, the sun had travelled well into the morning sky. Anxious faces looked upon them and few were eager for a fight. They could see down by the creek the whites were well armed. All seemed grateful that the whites had stopped their charge toward the women.

Horse Chief came forward. "What is it the whites want? Do they wish to attack us because of the troubles that the braves have been speaking of?"

The Great Chief nodded.

Little Anger said, "If it is to be a fight we should prepare. Every warrior who has a gun must join us." The warriors who had guns were already toward the front and they were so few. The Pawnee looked at one another. Some faces showed anger, some eyes showed sad determination, but none of the men showed apprehension.

"Are these the men that burned *Pah-Huku*?" Hose Chief asked.

The Great Chief shook his head. "No, but they do not care for our village or Pawnee grievances. They are here for a war."

Horse Chief spoke up. "A war is not a hopeless thing. We are strong!"

The whites have suggested another path." *Petalasharo* said. "We will need to give them the young men who struck at the settlers. If we do that their war chief will not insist upon a fight."

Tahirusawichi shuddered. Horse Chief took a step backwards. "How could we do such a thing? Do they know what they ask?"

Petalasharo gazed over at the women who had begun to keen songs and prayer. The sound sounded soft and rhythmic as it carried across the warm morning breeze.

"What will happen if we refuse?" Little Anger asked clearly recognizing the Great Chief's leadership in this matter.

"I do not know but it is safe to say they have not travelled this far to be denied."

"If the whites attack many of the women will die. Perhaps all the braves will die too."

"Yes." The Great Chief said as he nodded. "But we cannot give up our braves. A chief could not give up one of his people. No one can choose another man's path for evil or for good."

"Then we must fight. We have no more decisions to make." Horse Chief said. "The white men are rabid dogs. They will not stop until we have killed them."

Knife Chief shook his head, "yes but more white men will follow."

"That is true. I will go and speak with the white men again." *Petalasharo* offered.

"You should not go alone. I will go too." Little Anger stated.

"No." The Great Chief said firmly. "You must lead the warriors if the helpless ones are attacked. I go alone." The Great Chief wrapped the flag about him closely and began to walk down the hill.

As the soldiers saw him approached a few began to raise their rifles. "Stand down!" Shouted Black, then motioning to O'Kelly he began to march up the hill to meet the chief. After meeting half way the Great Chief sat upon the ground and Governor Black did likewise. O'Kelly decided to bend down upon one knee.

Petalasharo spoke first, "I will go with you and your soldiers."

Black looked sideways at the lieutenant a moment then spoke. "If you participated or incited the raids you must go with us. But if you did not we will not take you. We will not take you alone whatever the case. There are other Pawnee who were guilty of breaking our laws and my command will have all of them."

"I will not give up my people. There must be another way." O'Kelly kept up translating the words.

"The other way is for us to have a battle here and now. We will have those responsible."

"This is not the way for us to have peace between our peoples. I will not fight the white man but I cannot give up our braves."

Black shrugged trying to look indifferent. He hated himself for what he was about to say. "Then we will attack your people and take the guilty." His mouth was dry and his head pounded in pain. He knew his body wanted a drink.

The Great Chief looked incredulous. He was shocked at the words he was hearing. "There is always a way for peace. Let us find out that way."

Black answered coldly, "Man Chief, give me the guilty parties."

"We will have war here on this day. We will defeat you and kill your soldiers. Do you not see this? There must be another way. A great chief could find another way." *Petalasharo* stopped speaking beginning to think he was pleading and losing his dignity.

Black glared at his Indian counterpart feigning indifference.

The Great Chief thought they could come to an arrangement but it looked as if blood would be shed. "There must be another way. We should have peace between our peoples. Are you so sure that we will not defeat you and sing our victory songs?"

Once again the governor shrugged, "We will have the guilty parties. Your braves know who they are. If you do not give them to us we will have a war here."

"Are you not a chief with your people? Can you not find a way for peace? Must it be that you deprive the Pawnee of their dignity or force them to war?"

O'Kelly continued to translate. He was shocked that Black was being so rigid and terrified they were on the edge of a tragedy.

Black rubbed his forehead. He looked down. "You may see me as a chief but I am a soldier. We will have the guilty parties or we will have a war on this day. There is nothing more to say."

The governor stood up. He looked at O'Kelly and began to motion to leave but then stopped. "Man Chief, I do respect you. Once this is over I hope you survive and lead your people back to their agency."

Petalasharo lifted himself from the ground. "If the gods will have it, I will lead my people. I am a chief and I know there are always ways to peace. I will be a chief even if I can do no more than comfort the fearful on the way to our destruction. I have paths before me and there is always a path to peace. All of my braves have their own paths before them. They see paths to peace as well. They are chiefs of their own spirits. It is only you and your followers who see no paths but ones to war. I respect you as well; but I would not smoke the peace pipe with you again. Your spirit is ill."

The Great Chief turned and, continuing to wear the flag about him, returned to his people. O'Kelly felt nauseous. He was not a coward but he was fearful. This was not what he had expected and felt as if they were in the wrong. He made a quick sign of the cross and then saw Black looking at him.

"I am sorry sir." O'Kelly said. "My family is Catholic."

"No need to apologize lieutenant. Keep praying to God but let us begin to prepare for war."

*   *   *

"The white men are bent towards war. There can be no other way." The Great Chief sadly reported to the Pawnee braves.

"Then we must fight them." Horse Chief observed.

Tahirusawichi began to offer prayers to the directions. "The braves must again strip for battle."

Little Anger, who had been silent for some time, spoke up. "I think there is another way. We can speak with the braves and tell them the paths before the people. It will be a service the brave can make for his people, to surrender for their good. I will go with the white man. There will be others who will walk this path."

Tahirusawichi then spoke, "Your choice will be honored by the people."

Petalasharo looked hard at *Sharitarish*. "The people will fight to protect all. You do not need to do this."

Little Anger shook his head.

"This is a brave thing that you do." The Great Chief said as he put his hand upon *Sharitarish's* shoulder.

"No one knows how much I need to do this. I only have one question. What is a fair trial?"

Knife Chief spoke up. He had much experience living closely to the whites. "A fair trial is where the whites gather to talk in front of the Indian before they decide the Indian should go to hang from a rope."

Little Anger understood the gravity of his decision. He paused for a moment, but only for a moment. "A chief must protect the people."

The Great Chief nodded. Never had he seen Little Anger stand so proud and determined. Was this was what the first *Sharitarish* had been like so many years before?

*   *   *

"How long do you intend to have us wait here, governor?" Thayer asked.

Black was looking up at the Indians through his scope. "It appears they are still discussing the matter. We can give them more time."

"They could be talking about sneaking up behind us and attacking too."

"General Thayer if we keep a sharp lookout that should not be a problem."

"I don't like this waiting. We are beginning to look like fools."

"I stopped worrying about looking foolish long ago." Black said under his breath.

Colonel Robinson spoke up. "I don't like this either, governor."

"No man needs to concern himself. Remember I am the governor."

"Yes sir." Thayer grumbled.

*   *   *

Sharitarish went out among the braves. Many he knew had been raiding but he chose to speak with only a few. Among the few he chose were the ones he knew had done the most damage and the ones who were the oldest and most responsible for their actions. One of the braves Little Anger approached was Yellow Sun.

"I asked you to go raiding my friend and now we shall do a better service for our people. We must go with the white men."

The stone faced warrior looked intently into Little Anger's eyes. He showed less emotion than a tired ox. He simply nodded, mounted his horse and began to follow the chief down the hillside. His sons cried out when they saw their father and the others led away. They followed the sad group despite Little Anger's suggestion they return. They refused to turn back. The sons of Yellow Sun would not allow anyone doubt their devotion to their father.

The Great Chief led thirteen Pawnee down the hill to the white men. They rode slowly and proudly. The trip down lasted even longer than had the journey up. With the movement of the Indians down into the valley the militia began to look towards the governor. Black just sat upon his horse watching intently for any sign of trickery.

Among the women gathered upon the hill *Eerit Ta* saw her love once more descend into the valley toward the white man. There was great fear and confusion among the women who pitifully could only sing prayers against their people's plight. When word was received from runners that the braves involved in the raiding would surrender and the whites leave in peace, she became hopeful. She knew *Sharitarish Tiki* had not left the hunting band on raids. It would not be in her love's nature. Why should he not accompany the Great Chief in these negotiations? After all he was a great chief in his own right, the eldest son of *Sharitarish Malan*. It was when it was reported that her love was one of the ones that would surrender she joined in the fear of her Pawnee sisters. What was to be the fate of the surrendering men?

This could not happen, the maiden thought to herself. He could not leave her. There must be a way to rescue her man.

The Return Trail

Chapter 1

July 15, 1859
Militia Encampment along Shell Creek

The militia had moved south immediately following the surrender of the captives. Of course, no one had prepared for the contingency of taking prisoners. With thirteen captives the number was too many to be watched singly. It was also debated how to transport the Indians as the freight wagons had been left back at the Elkhorn River. No one had chains or shackles so Donovan was told to make do with some thick herding rope. He was able to fashion some crude binds and the prisoners were moved south on foot. The rode was long, slow and dusty.

It was the second day of their captivity and the Pawnee spoke quietly among themselves. Many were regretting the decision to surrender themselves to the whites but all were too proud to attempt an escape. Yellow Sun's boys would certainly not separate from their father who, as usual, appeared indifferent to his fate.

The army regulars had ridden off the prior day with thoughts to get back to Fort Kearny. Discipline was lax. The militia men had finished eating their breakfast and they were about to strike camp. All of the men were tired and tempers were short. Random and petty arguments could be heard throughout the camp. The volunteers went about packing the tents and equipment haphazardly and no one seemed intent to their duties. The warm dawn had broken with a heavy cloud cover and fog still lay outside of the camp. All were thinking of home but not anxious to ride the hard miles to get there.

General Thayer had been trying to incite O'Kelly and many within the militia to return to Battle Creek and take more prisoners. "Are we expected to believe all this trouble was done by a baker's dozen braves?"

He argued. His words fell on unenthusiastic ears. Most men wanted to get back to their wives and dinner tables. They had had enough of sleeping on the prairie grass.

Black retreated into his tent and the liquor he had been able to secret from a few of the enlisted men. His mood was oddly melancholy. Now he had to return to his role as governor and face whatever lay in the future. He was confident that he had acquitted himself well in the field and he would stand beside all the decisions he had made, but he knew his drinking was being discussed. Damn them politicians he thought, damn them.

*   *   *

Seeing Deer crept through the grass. So far she had not been seen but her luck was sure to run out. The girl had never been so close to a camp of soldiers and she was very much afraid. How would she free *Sharitarish*? She wished for a moment that she had accompanied raiding parties in the past so she knew how this could be done. But then she knew it was rare for a Pawnee girl to do such things. She would simply have to remain quiet. The Indian captives sat in a half moon rubbing their sore ankles and trying to loosen the tight ropes around their chaffed red skin. Little Anger was the first to see her crawling forward. Anxiously he looked at the guards. Asleep! The girl's timing was good! As she approached she took her knife from her belt and blew whispered kisses. Soon she was working on her lover's ropes. After the bounds were cut she scampered back to the grass. She was angry and terrified when Little Anger did not follow but began cutting the binds of the others. He cut Yellow Sun free first and the aged warrior simply looked on impassively. His sons were the next freed and they quickly set to work on the others.

"Quickly, quickly!" *Eerit Ta* whispered with a note of panic in her voice.

The guard looked up as the last man was freed and the Indians scattered. His shot went wide but soon there were more wild shots fired in the direction of the fleeing Indians Little Anger was struck in the back and the bullet broke his spine and pierced his heart. Seeing Deer was shot in the leg as she was trying to get back toward her love. She was kept from him by Yellow Sun's strong right arm that held her easily by the waist.

His eyes were focused on the high hill that lay north of the creek floor. He chose his foot falls carefully as he bore his angry broken heartened burden away. Two other Pawnee had been shot in the backs making their bid for freedom. As the detachment recovered from its confusion, it found three Indians had been killed making their escape. No one seemed anxious to track down the fugitives. After all the demands of vengeance only Thayer had been disappointed the militia had lost their catch. When Black heard the news he shrugged and rolled over. "It will save the expense of a trial to the territory. We could ill afford one hanging let alone thirteen."

Donovan was ordered to dig the graves and O'Kelly decided to help. They had no idea what to use for a marker and thought it inappropriate to fashion a cross. O'Kelly dug into his satchel and came up with the turtle pedant bestowed upon him by his father. He draped over the pendant's cord a stick in the middle of the three graves. He said a short prayer. Donovan nodded and the two hurried off to join the detachment.

Aftermath

The militia trudged back to Omaha City and a small "Victory Parade" was held on the grounds of The State House. The General Assembly authorized "Nebraska Medallions" be struck and handed out to the returning heroes. The governor refused his ribbon and was not present when the others were given out. Secretary Morton agreed to hand out the medallions and the ceremony was even better attended then the "Victory Parade".

Samuel Black remained a loyal appointee of President James Buchanan after he returned to The State House. Following directives from Washington, Black vetoed an extremely popular and widely supported bill proposed by the Nebraska General Assembly outlawing slavery within the territory. This veto forever tarnished his legacy. Black saw the bill as a minor symbolic gesture that was ill conceived during the time of great national division. He also continued to toe the line and remain consistent with federal administration policy to do nothing that would antagonize the southern states.

On October 16, 1859, John Brown led an armed uprising to seize the federal armory in Harpers Ferry, Virginia. The U.S. army crushed his brief but violent revolt within 36 hours and the man was executed by hanging in December of that year. The passions and issues that inspired Brown to such extremes eventually exploded into an American Civil War after the election of Abraham Lincoln in 1860. Lincoln's election had immediate consequences for the federal politicians of Nebraska. The Democratic Party men, such as Samuel Black, were relieved of their positions and replaced by Republican job seekers. In 1861, Nebraska Territory had its first Republican governor.

Black was drinking heavily his last months in office and was disenchanted by the American public's choice for president. He looked on with bitterness as Abraham Lincoln was elected and the election results triggered the most violent conflict seen in the Western Hemisphere. Governor Black was chagrined by the prospect of war. He was disgusted by the Democrat's inability to stop the momentum for war. The Union declared war after South Carolina forces fired on Fort Sumter in the spring of 1861.

Samuel Black was nothing but a patriot, and he supported the integrity of the Union above all. He was also fearful of creditors and had few friends in Nebraska so he returned to Pennsylvania to organize a brigade. Eliza saw him once again march off to war. He had sworn off liquors for the duration of the conflict and he even impressed himself by his determination and success. The conflict drug on and the war lasted longer than his fortitude. He first drank during McClelland's Campaign on the Peninsular. The man was drinking with gusto when a bullet at the Battle of Gaines's Mill killed him on June 27, 1862.

Eliza Black never remarried. She is buried beside her husband.

Commissioner James Denver was appointed Governor of Kansas Territory but also joined the army following the outbreak of war. After the Confederacy was crushed he went on to become a powerful western politician. The city of Denver, Colorado was named for him. He reportedly visited the city once but left after he felt that the citizens had not shown due respect and affection.

Horace Greeley continued to develop a powerful and influential media empire. He was fundamental in reporting on American expansion into the frontier and popularizing the settlement of the west. Ever a staunch Republican he was instrumental in reporting and shaping public sentiment throughout the Civil War and into the period of Southern Reconstruction. He died a wealthy man in 1872.

Lieutenant O'Kelly served in the 1st Nebraska Regiment in the Civil War as a brevet colonel. He served with distinction until he was shot in the arm at Fort Donelson, Tennessee in 1862. He returned to Nebraska fight with the home militia against the Sioux in the summer of 1863. He was able to survive both wars. He married in 1872 and farmed in Iowa until his death in Grinnell.

Black's old political crony William Richardson remained a lifelong Democrat. After returning to Illinois he was appointed to fill Stephen A. Douglas's senate seat in 1860. Following the Civil War he retired from politics and spent the rest of his life in journalism. He died in Quincy, Illinois in 1875.

Joe Donovan could have sat out the war on his Lancaster farm but the longer the fighting lasted, the guiltier he felt about remaining out of the conflict. He enlisted with the federals in Omaha in early 1863 and was shipped to Jackson, Mississippi. Donovan was immediately recognized as a man with significant mechanical and engineering skills and was put to work fixing ironclads for the western flotilla. He was killed in December of 1863 when a boiler he was working on exploded. His body was never returned to Nebraska and he was buried in a non-segregated Union cemetery on the edge of Jackson.

Julius Sterling Morton had a spectacular political career with the Nebraska Democratic Party. He served in a number of positions and becoming a leading voice for rural concerns and was President Grover Cleveland's Secretary of Agriculture in the 1890s. The enormous mansion he built and designed in Nebraska City became the centerpiece of Arbor Lodge State Park. He is widely regarded as Nebraska's preeminent founding father.

General Thayer has had a more controversial legacy. He remained the general of the Nebraska Organized Militia until he was mustered into the federal service at the outbreak of the war. Sensing that the local Nebraska authorities wanted to keep the militia within the territory to protect the frontier Thayer quickly marched them to St. Louis where they were incorporated into the massive Union Army marching on the Confederacy. He finally found the combat he sought at Shiloh and the Siege of Vicksburg. After the war, President Grant briefly appointed him the territorial governor of Wyoming. He returned to Nebraska and was elected the state's seventh governor in 1886.

Thayer successfully completed two terms as governor, but was defeated when he ran for a third term. He had grown increasingly heavy-handed and was extremely unpopular when James Boyd defeated him in the election of 1892. Despite the election results indicating he had lost by a significant number of votes, he refused to surrender office and barricaded himself into the capitol building with some armed partisans. The governor elect had to take the matter to court and a district court judge ruled in Boyd's favor. While the militia remained neutral, the Lancaster County Sheriff mustered a force to evict the renegades off government property. Sensing Thayer's cause was hopeless, and unwilling to shed blood, his supporters melted away. An embittered Thayer retired from political life and devoted the remainder of his days to literary pursuits.

For Nebraska, the two most consequential federal projects both came about with the Lincoln administration; the long sought after Federal Homestead Act of 1861 and the Union Pacific Railroad Act of 1862. Both changed the state forever and embittered the tribes toward steadily encroaching white settlers.

The Pawnee remained on the tract of land set aside for them through the Treaty of Table Creek until 1875. *Petalasharo* remained a wise ruler for his people until he was killed under mysterious circumstances while crossing the Loup River. Whether it was an accident, murder, or suicide has never been determined for certain. *Tahirusawichi* was killed at the Battle of Massacre Canyon in 1873. Knife Chief made the trek with his people to Indian Territory and helped with their difficult adjustment onto the reservation in present day Oklahoma.

Perhaps the most disturbing destiny of the Pawnee belonged to Yellow Sun. In 1869 he was found guilty of murdering a white man on an island within the Platte River to the west of the agency. Due to jurisdictional issues the case made it all of the way to the U.S. Supreme Court where his conviction was upheld and he was sentenced to life imprisonment. He served it in an Omaha prison. Although most authorities at the time, both white and Indian, did not doubt his guilt, his time spent in incarceration was harsh even by the standards of the era. He was denied food and medical assistance. The man was locked away and friendless surrounded by enemies, both Indian and white. He brawled with his fellow prisoners and was often injured.

Eventually, Yellow Sun became so desperate with pain from a toothache he attempted to self-administer a root canal with a sharpened kitchen utensil. It is probable that he died of severe infection after the procedure. It is not know where Yellow Sun was buried, although it is probable he was laid to rest in an unmarked prison grave.

Eerit Ta died from an infection caused by the wound in her leg two months after she had been shot. Her mother held her burial ceremonial along Looking Glass Creek on the Pawnee Agency.

Who had burned *Pah-Huku*? That was destined to remain a mystery. However, there was a report by a settler, Jeremiah Garret, who saw dozens of heavily armed warriors camped along the banks of the Salt Creek in late April of 1859. A few of these Indian approached his home begging for food. They were put off but then Jeremiah grew fearful of their presence and he and his wife took a large basket of biscuits out to the group. They ate the bread eagerly. None of the Indians spoke English but

Jeremiah did engage a friendly boy who appeared to be with them. He knew some sign language and was clever about communicating thoughts. The boy indicated they were Comanche from the south. He pointed to his eyes and kept asking "Pani? Pani?" Garret got the impression the Comanche were looking for Pawnee. The settler pointed to the north hoping for the Indians to move on. He got his wish. The next morning there was no trace of the warriors. Only a basket was left. Inside the basket were a neatly folded napkin and an old Spanish style Rosary.

It was one of the last times renegade Comanche were seen in the Lancaster area. Did the Comanche burn the ancient Pawnee village? Was it white men? Could it have been the Sioux? No one knows who burned the *Pah-Huku* village and triggered The Pawnee War.

Fort Atkinson Treaty Of Unorganized N.w. Territory

Louisiana

September 30, 1825

FOR the purpose of perpetuating the friendship which has heretofore existed, as also to remove all future cause of discussion or dissension, as it respects trade and friendship between the United States and their citizens, and the Pawnee tribe of Indians, the President of the United States of America, by the United States' army, and Major Benjamin O'Fallon, Indian Agent, with full powers and authority, specially appointed and commissioned for that purpose, of the one part, and the undersigned Chiefs, head men and Warriors of said Pawnee tribe of Indians, on behalf of their tribe of the other part, have made and entered into the following Articles and Conditions; which, when ratified by the President of the United States, by and with the advice and consent of the Senate, shall be binding on both parties—to wit:

Article 1.

It is admitted by the Pawnee tribe of Indians, that they reside within the territorial limits of the United States, acknowledge their supremacy, and claim their protection.—The said tribe also admit the right of the United States to regulate all trade and intercourse with them.

Article 2.

The United States agree to receive the Pawnee tribe of Indians into their friendship, and under their protection, and to extend to them, from time to time, such benefits and acts of kindness as may be convenient, and seem just and proper to the President of the United States.

Article 3.

All trade and intercourse with the Pawnee tribe shall be transacted at such place or places as may be designated and pointed out by the President of the United States, through his agents; and none but American citizens, duly authorized by the United States, shall be admitted to trade or hold intercourse with said tribe of Indians.

Article 4.

That the Pawnee tribe may be accommodated with such articles of merchandise, as their necessities may demand, the United States agree to admit and license traders to hold intercourse with said tribe, under mild and equitable regulations: in consideration of which, the said Pawnee tribe bind themselves to extend protection to the persons and the property of the traders, and the persons legally employed under them, whilst they remain within the limits of their particular district of country. And the said Pawnee tribe further agree, that if any foreigner or other person, not legally authorized by the United States, shall come into their district of country, for the purpose of trade or other views, they will apprehend such person or persons, and deliver him or them to some United States' superintendent, or agent, of Indian Affairs, or to the commandant of the nearest military post, to be dealt with according to law. And they further agree to give safe conduct to all persons who may be legally authorized by the United States to pass through their country, and to protect in their persons and property all agents or other persons sent by the United

States to reside temporarily among them; nor will they, whilst on their distant excursions, molest or interrupt any American citizen or citizens, who may be passing from the United States to New Mexico, or returning from thence to the United States.

Article 5.

That the friendship which is now, established between the United States and the Pawnee tribe, shall not be interrupted by the misconduct of individuals, it is hereby agreed, that for injuries done by individuals, no private revenge or retaliation shall take place, but instead thereof, complaints shall be made, by the party injured, to the superintendent, or agent of Indian affairs, or other person appointed by the President; and it shall be the duty of said Chiefs, upon complaint being made as aforesaid, to deliver up the person or persons against whom the complaint is made, to the end that he or they may be punished, agreeably to the laws of the United States. And, in like manner, if any robbery, violence, or murder, shall be committed on any Indian or Indians belonging to said tribe, the person or persons so offending shall be tried, and if found guilty, shall be punished in like manner as if the injury had been done to a white man. And it is agreed, that the Chiefs of said Pawnee tribe shall, to the utmost of their power, exert themselves to recover horses or other property, which may be stolen or taken from any citizen or citizens of the United States, by any individual or individuals of said tribe; and the property so recovered shall be forthwith delivered to the agents or other person authorized to receive it, that it may be restored to the proper owner. And the United States hereby guaranty to any Indian or Indians of said tribe, a full indemnification for any horses or other property which may be stolen from them by any of their citizens: Provided, That the property stolen cannot be recovered, and that sufficient proof is produced that it was actually stolen by a citizen of the United States. And the said Pawnee tribe engages, on the requisition or demand of the President of the United States, or of the agents, to deliver up any white man resident among them.

Article 6.

And the Chiefs and Warriors, as aforesaid, promise and engage that their tribe will never, by sale, exchange, or as presents, supply any nation, tribe, or band of Indians, not in amity with the United States, with guns, ammunition, or other implements of war.

Done at Fort Atkinson, Council Bluffs, this thirtieth day of September, A. D. 1825, and of the independence of the United States the fiftieth.

In testimony whereof, the said commissioners, Henry Atkinson and Benjamin O'Fallon, and the chiefs, head men, and warriors, of the Pawnee tribe, have hereunto set their hands and affixed their seals.

Benj. O'Fallon, United States agent Indian affairs,

- Esh-ca-tar-pa, the bad known chief, his x mark
- Shar-co-ro-la-shar, the sun chief, his x mark
- La-cota-ve-co-cho-la-shar, the eagle chief, his x mark
- La-tah-carts-la-shar, the war eagle chief, his x mark
- La-ta-le-shar, the knife chief, his x mark
- Scar-lar-la-shar, the manly chief, his x mark
- La-ke-tar-la-shar, the partizan chief, his x mark
- Lark-tar-ho-ra-la-shar, the pipe chief, his x mark
- Esh-ca-tar-pa, the bad known chief, republican band, his x mark
- Co-rouch-la-shar, the bear chief, his x mark
- Ah-sha-o-ah-lah-co, the dog chief, his x mark
- La-ho-rah-sha-rete, the man who strikes men, his x mark
- Tah-rah-re-tah-coh-sha, the singing crow, his x mark
- Lah-ro-wah-go, the hill chief, his x mark
- Ta-rah-re-tah-nash, the big horse stealer, his x mark
- La-shar-pah-he, the tranquil chief, his x mark
- Ah-re-cah-rah-co-chu, the mad elk, his x mark
- Ta-lah-re-ta-ret, the partizan that strikes and carries his bird on his back, his x mark

- Ta-lah-re-we-tail, the crow that strikes, his x mark
- Lo-lah-re-wah, the horse stealer who suffers his prize to be retaken, his x mark
- Ta-hah-lah-re-esh-lah, the handsome bird, his x mark
- Ah-sho-cole, the rotten foot, his x mark
- Ah-shar-o-ca-tah-co, the poor man, his x mark
- Cha-nuck-cah-lah, the partizan that strikes, his x mark
- Ta-lah-we-cah-wah-re, the man that is always at war, his x mark

In presence of—

R. Woolley, lieutenant-colonel, U. S. Army., John Gale, surgeon, U. S. Army., John Gantt, captain, Sixth infantry., S. MacRee, aide de camp.,Thomas Noel, adjutant, Sixth regiment., J. Rogers, lieutenant, Sixth infantry., R. Holmes, lieutenant, Sixth infantry., M. W. Batman, lieutenant, Sixth infantry., J. Nichols, lieutenant, Sixth infantry. W. W. Eaton, lieutenant, Sixth infantry., G. H. Kennerly U. S. S. Indian agent., A. L. Papin.,William Rodgers.

Fort Childs Treaty Of Kansas-Nebraska Territory

August 6, 1848

Treaty with the Pawnees; articles of agreement and convention made this sixth day of August, A. D. 1848, at Fort Childs, near the head of Grand Island, on the south side of the Nebraska or Great Platte River, between Lieutenant-Colonel Ludwell E. Powell, commanding battalion Missouri Mounted Volunteers, en route to Oregon, in behalf of the United States, and the chiefs and head-men of the four confederated bands of Pawnees, viz: Grand Pawnees, Pawnee Loups, Pawnee Republicans, and Pawnee Noisy, at present residing on the south side of the Platte River.

Article 1.

The confederated bands of the Pawnees hereby cede and relinquish to the United States all their right, title, and interest in and to all that tract of land described as follows, viz:

Commencing on the south side of the Platte River, five miles west of this post, "Fort Childs;" thence due north to the crest of the bluffs north of said Platte River: thence east and along the crest of said bluffs to the termination of Grand Island, supposed to be about sixty miles distant; thence south to the southern shore of said Platte River: and thence west and along the southern shore of the said Platte River to the place of beginning.

The land hereby conveyed is designated within the red lines of the following plat:

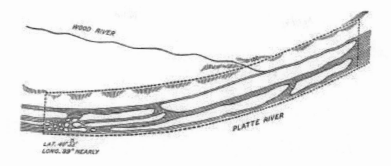

Article 2.

In consideration of the land hereby ceded and relinquished, the United States has this day paid, through Captain Stewart Van Vliet, assistant quartermaster United States Army, under an order from Lieutenant-Colonel Ludwell E. Powell, commanding battalion Missouri Mounted Volunteers, to the said four bands collectively, on the execution of this treaty, the amount of two thousand dollars in goods and merchandise, the receipt of which is hereby acknowledged. The bands hereby agree to retire and reside within the Beaver Creek reserve and or the forks of the Loup in peace and perpetual quite enjoyment of the lands except as to be provided with hunting, fishing preservation rights and egress to effect the same.

Article 3.

.The United States shall have the privilege of using any hard timber that may at any time be needed, situate upon Wood River, immediately north of the land hereby conveyed.

Article 4.

The Pawnee Nation renew their assurance of friendship for the white men, their fidelity to the United States, and their desire for peace with all the neighboring tribes of Indians.

The Pawnee Nation, therefore, faithfully promise not to molest or injure the property or person of any white citizen of the United States, wherever found, nor to make war upon any tribes with whom said Pawnee tribes now are, or may hereafter be, at peace; but, should any difficulty arise, they agree to refer the matter in dispute to such arbitration as the President of the United States may direct.

Article 5.

These articles of agreement and convention shall be binding and obligatory from this sixth day of August, A. D. 1848.

In testimony whereof, the said Lieutenant-Colonel Ludwell E. Powell, commanding battalion Missouri mounted volunteers, and the chiefs and headmen of the four confederated bands of Grand Pawnees, Pawnee Loups, Pawnee Republicans, and Pawnee Noisy, have hereunto signed their names, and affixed their seals, on the day and year aforesaid.

Ludwell E. Powell, Lieutenant-Colonel Commanding Battalion Missouri Mounted Volunteers.

(XX)   Chief Sha-re-ta-riche,Ma-laigne, Principal Chief of the Four Confederated Bands.
Chiefs of—
Grand Pawnees:

(X)   Ah-tah-ra-scha.

Pawnee Loups:

(X)   Ish-Ka-top-pa,
(X)   French Chief,
(X)   Big Chief.

Pawnee Republicans:

(X)   La-lo-che-la-sha-ro,
(X)   A-sha-la-la-cot-sha-lo,
(X)   American Chief.

Pawnee Noisy:

(X)   La-pa-ko-lo-lo-ho-la-sha,
(X)   La-sha-pit-ko,
(X)   Ta-ra-re-tappage.

(To each of the Indian names is affixed his mark.)

Executed and delivered in the presence of—

Thomas J. Todd, adjutant, battalion Missouri Mounted Volunteers, secretary.

WITNESSED HERETO:

W. Sublette, captain, company A., J. Walker, A. S., U. S. Army., W. H. Rodgers, captain, Company L., David McCausland, captain company B.,Stewart Van Vliet, captain and acting quartermaster, U. S. Army.,D. P. Woodbury, lieutenant, Engineers.,J. W. kelly, second lieutenant, commanding Company C., Saml. J. lingenfelter., Ant. Le Faivre., Peter A. Carnes, forage master., J. B. Small, A. S., U. S. Army.,F. Jeffrey Deroine, interpreter.

Table Creek Treaty Of Nebraska Territory

SEPTEMBER 24, 1857

Articles of agreement and convention made this twenty-fourth day of September, 1857 A.D. at Table Creek, Nebraska Territory, between the Federal Republic of the United States of America, James W. Denver, Commissioner of Indian Tribes and Relations, and the Chiefs and Head-men of the four confederate bands of Pawnee Indians, viz: Grand Pawnee, Pawnee Loups, Pawnee Republicans, and Pawnee Noisy, and generally known as the Pawnee Tribe.

Article 1. The confederate bands of the Pawnee aforesaid, hereby cede and relinquish to the United States all their right, title, and interest in and to all the lands now owned or claimed by them, except as hereinafter reserved, and which are bounded as follows, viz: On the east by the lands lately purchased by the United States from the Omahas; on the south by the lands heretofore ceded by the Pawnee to the United States; on the west by a line running due north from the junction of the North with the South Fork of the Platte River, to the Keha-Paha River; and on the north by the Keha-Paha River, to its junction with the Niobrara, L'eauqi Court, or Running Water River, and thence, by that river, to the western boundary of the Omaha cession. Out of this cession the Pawnee reserve a tract of country, thirty miles long from east to west, by fifteen miles from north to south, including both banks of the Loup

Fork of the Platte River, the east line of which shall be at a point not further east than the mouth of Beaver Creek. If, however, the Pawnees, in conjunction with the United States Agent, shall be able to find a more suitable locality for their future homes, within said cessation, then, they are to have the privilege of selecting an equal quantity of land there, in lieu of the reservation herein designated, all of which shall be done as soon as practicable; and the Pawnee agree to remove their new homes thus, reserved for them, without cost to the United States, within one year from the date of the ratification of this treaty by the august Senate of the United States, and, until that time, they shall be permitted to remain where they are now residing, without molestation.

Article 2. In consideration of the foregoing cessation, the United States agree to pay to the Pawnees the sum of forty thousand dollars per annum, for five years, commencing on the first day of January, eighteen hundred and fifty-eight, A.D.; and after the end of five years, thirty thousand dollars per annum, as perpetual annuity, at least one-half of which annual payments shall be made in goods, and such articles as may be deemed necessary for them. And it is further agreed that the President of the United States may, at any time, in his discretion, discontinue said perpetuity, by causing the value of a fair communication thereof to be paid to, or expended for the benefit of, said Indians, in such manner as to him shall seem proper.

Article 3. In order to improve the condition of the Pawnee, and teach them the arts of civilized life, the United States agree to establish among them, and for their use and benefit, two manual-labor schools, to be governed by such rules and regulation as may be prescribed by the President of the United States, who shall appoint the teachers, and, if he deems necessary, may increase the number of schools to four. In these schools, there shall be taught the various branches of a common-school education, and, in addition the arts of agriculture, the most useful mechanical arts, and whatever else the President may direct. The Pawnees, on their part, agree that each and every one of their children, between the ages of seven and eighteen years, shall be kept constantly at these schools for, at least, nine months of the year; and if any parent or guardian shall fail, neglect, or refuse to so keep their child or children under his control at such school, then and in that case, there shall be deducted from the annuities to which said parent or guardian would be entitled, either individually or as a parent or as a guardian, an amount equal to the value, in time, of the tuition thus lost; but the President may at any time change or modify this clause as he may think proper. The Chiefs shall be held responsible for the attendance of the orphans who have no other guardians; and the United States government agrees to furnish suitable housing and farms for said schools, and whatever else may be necessary to put them in successful operation; and a sum not less than five thousand dollars per annum shall be applied for the support for each school, so long as the Pawnee shall, in good faith, comply with the provisions of this article; but if at any time, the President is satisfied they are not doing so, he may, at his discretion, discontinue the schools in whole or in part.

Article 4. The United States agree to protect the Pawnees in the possession of their new homes. The United States also agree to furnish the Pawnee:

First, with two complete sets of blacksmith, gunsmith, and tinsmith tools, no to exceed in cost seven hundred and fifty dollars: and erect shops at a cost not to exceed five hundred dollars; also five hundred dollars annually, during the pleasure of the President, for the purchase of iron, steel, and other necessaries for the same. The United States are also to furnish two blacksmiths, one of whom shall be a gunsmith or a tinsmith; but the Pawnees shall agree to furnish one or two young men of their tribe to work constantly in each shop as strikers or apprentices, who shall be paid fair compensation for their labor.

Second. The United States agree to furnish farming utensils and stock, worth twelve hundred dollars per annum, for ten years, or during the pleasure of the President, and for the first year's purchase of stock, and for erecting shelters for the same, an amount not exceeding three thousand dollars, and also to employ a farmer to teach the Indians the arts of agriculture.

Third. The United States agree to have erected on said reservation a steam-mill, suitable to grind grain and saw lumber, which shall not exceed in cost six thousand dollars, and to keep the same in repair for ten years; also, to employ a miller and engineer for the same length of time, or longer, at the discretion of the President; he Pawnees agreeing to furnish apprentices, to assist in working the mill, who shall be paid a fair compensation for their services.

Fourth. The United States agree to erect dwelling-houses for the interpreter, blacksmith, farmer, miller and engineer, which shall not exceed in cost five hundred dollars each; and the Pawnee agree to prevent the members of their tribe from injuring or destroying the houses, shops, machinery, stock farming utensils, and all other things furnished by the Government, and if any such shall be carried away, injured, or destroyed, by any of the members of their tribe, the value of the same shall be deducted from the tribal annuities. Whenever the President shall become satisfied that the Pawnee have sufficiently advanced in the acquirement of a practical knowledge of the arts and pursuits to which this article relates, then, and in that case, he may turn over the property to the tribe, and dispense with the services of any or all of the employees herein named.

Article 5. The Pawnee acknowledge their dependence on the Government of the United States and promises to be friendly with all the citizens thereof, and pledge themselves to commit no depredations on the property of such citizens, nor on that of any other person belonging to any tribe or nation at peace with the United States,. And should any one or more of them violate this pledge, and the fact be satisfactorily proven before the agent, property taken shall be returned, or in default thereof, or if injured or destroyed, compensation may be made by the Government out of the annuities. Nor will they make war on any other tribe, except in self-defense, but will all matters of difference between them and other Indians to the Government of the United States, or its agent, for decision, and abide thereby.

Article 6. The United States agent may reside on or near the Pawnee reservation; and the Pawnees agree to permit the United States to build forts and occupy military posts on their lands, and to allow the whites the right to open roads through their territories; but no white person shall be allowed to reside on any part of said reservation unless he shall be an employee of the United States, or to be licensed to trade with said tribe, or be a member of the family of such employee or licensed trader; nor shall the said tribe, or any of them, alienate any part of said reservation, except to the United States; but, if they think proper to do so, they may divide some lands among themselves, giving to each person, or each head of a family, a farm, subject to their tribal regulations; but in no instance to be sold or disposed of to the persons, or not of the Pawnee tribe.

Article 7. The United States agree to furnish, in addition to the persons heretofore mentioned, six laborers for three years, but it is expressly understood that while these laborers are to be under control, and subject to the orders, of the United States agent, they are employed more to teach the Pawnee how to manage stock and use the implements furnished, than as merely laboring for their benefit; and for each laborer thus furnished by the United States, the Pawnee engage to furnish at least three of their tribe to work with them, who shall also be subject to the orders of the agent, and for whom the chiefs shall be responsible.

Article 8. The Pawnees agree to deliver up to the officers of the United States all offenders against the treaties, laws, or regulations of the United States, or the territorial sovereigns, wherever they may be found within the limits of their reservations; and they further agree to assist such officers in discovering, pursuing, and capturing any such offender or offenders, anywhere, whenever called upon so to do; and they agree, also, that if they violate any of the stipulations contained in this treaty, the President may, at his discretion, withhold a part, or a whole of the annuities herein provided for.

Article 9. The Pawnee desire to have some provision made for the half-breeds of their tribe. Those of them who have preferred to reside, and are now residing, in the nation, are entitled to have equality of rights and privileges with other members of the tribe, but those of who have chosen to have followed the pursuits of civilized life, and reside among the whites, are entitled to scrip for one hundred and sixty acres, or one quarter section, of land for each male of family unit. Said grant shall be bestowed, provided application shall be made within the same within five years from this time, which scrip shall be receivable at the United States land offices, the same as military bounty land warrants, and be subject to the same rules and regulations.

Article 10. Samuel Allis has long been the firm friend of the Pawnees, and in years gone by has administered to their wants and necessities. When in distress, and in a state of starvation, they took his property and used it for themselves, and when the small pox was destroying them, he vaccinated more than two thousand of them; for all these things, the Pawnees desire that he shall be paid, but they think that the Government should pay a part. It is therefore, agreed that the Pawnee will pay Mr. Allis one thousand dollars, and the United States agree to pay him a similar sum of one thousand dollars, as a full remuneration for his services and losses.

Article 11. Ta-ra-da-ka-wa, Head Chief of the Noisy Pawnee, and four other Pawnees having been out as guides for the troops of the United States, in their late expedition against the Cheyennes, and having returned by themselves, were overtaken and plundered of everything given them by the officers of the expedition, as well as their own property, barely escaping with their lives; and the value of their services being fully acknowledged, the United States agree to pay to each of them one hundred dollars, or in lieu thereof, to give each a horse worth one hundred dollars in value.

Article 12. To enable the Pawnees to settle any just claims at present existing against them, there is hereby set apart, by the United States, ten thousand dollars, out of which the same any be paid, when presented, and proven to the satisfaction of the proper department; and the Pawnee hereby and formally relinquish all claims they have against the United States under former treaty stipulations.

IN testimony whereof, the said James W. Denver, Commissioner as aforesaid, and the undersigned, chief and headmen of the four confederate bands of Pawnee Indians have hertounder set their hands and seals, at the place and on the day and year hereinbefore written.

James W. Denver   J. Sterling Morton
U.S. Commissioner   Territorial Authority

(X) *Pie-ta-na-sharo* or the Chief of Men in lieu of *Sa-ra-cherish Mal* or the Cross Chief, Chief in Principal

Grand Pawnees
(X) Te-ra-ta-puts or He who Steals Horses
(X) Sa-ra-cherish-ticki or Smaller Cross Chief
(X) Le-ra-kuts-a-na-sharo or Grey Eagle Chief

Wolf Pawnee
(X) La-le-ta-ra-nasharo or the Comanche Chief
(X) As-sa-na-sharo or the Horse Chief

Pawnee Republicans

(X) Na-sharo-se-de-ta-ra-ko or the One the Great Spirit Smiles On
(X) Na-sharo-cah-hiko or A Man but A Chief
(X) Da-lo-de-na-sharo or the Chief like an Eagle, Eagle Chief
(X) Da-lo-le-kit-ta-to kah or the Man the Enemy Steals From

Noisy Pawnee

(X) Ke-we-ko-na-sharo or the Buffalo Bull Chief
(X) Na-sharo-la-da-hoo or the Big Chief
(X) Nasharo or the Chief
(X) Da-ka-to-wa-kuts-o-ra-nasharo or the Hawk Chief

Signed and Sealed in the Presence of:
Wm. M. Dennison US Indian Agent, A.S.H. White, secretary to the Commissioner, N.W. Tucker, Will. E. Harvey, O.H. Irish, Samuel Allis, Interpreter

Bibliography

Non-fiction

Beadle, Erastus F., *Ham Eggs, & Corn Cake, A Nebraska Territorial Diary*, University of Nebraska Press, 2001

Becher, Ronald, *Massacre along the Medicine Road; A Social History of the Indian War of 1864 in Nebraska Territory*, Caxton Press, 1999

Bristow, David L., *A Dirty Wicked Town, Tales of 19th Century Omaha*, Caxton Press, 2006

Brooks, Juanita, *The Mountain Meadows Massacre*, University of Oklahoma Press, 1962

Burns, Cass G., *The Sod House*, A University of Nebraska Bison Book, 1930

Cleary, Kristen Mare'e, *Native American Wisdom*, Fall River Press, 1995

Coleman, Ruby Roberts, *Pre-Statehood History of Lincoln County, Nebraska*, Heritage Books, Inc., 1992

Dorsey, George A., *The Pawnee Mythology*, Bison Books, 1997

Dunley, Thomas W. *Wolves for the Blue Soldiers, Indian Scouts and Auxiliaries with the United States Army, 1860-90*, University of Nebraska Press, 1982

Gwynne, S.C., *Empire of the Summer Moon, Quanah Parker and the Rise and Fall of the Comanches, the most Powerful Indian Tribe in American History*, Simon and Schuster, 2010

Hafen, LeRoy R., *To the Pikes Peak Gold Fields, 1859*, Bison Books, 2004

Howard, James, H. *The Ponca Tribe, Second Edition*, Bison Books, 1995

Lesser, Alexander, *The Pawnee Ghost Dance Hand Game, Ghost Dance Revival & Ethnic Identity,* University of Nebraska Press, 1996

Mann, Charles C., *1491 New Revelations of the Americas before Columbus,* Vintage Books 2003

Philbrick, Nathaniel, *The Last Stand, Custer, Sitting Bull, and the Battle of the Little Bighorn,* Peguin Books, 2010

Phillips, Thomas D., *Battlefields of Nebraska,* Caxton Press, 2009

Sandoz, Maria, *The Beaver Men, Spearheads of Empire,* University of Nebraska Press, 1964

Stone, Irving, *Men to Match My Mountains, The Monumental Saga of the Winning of America's Far West,* Double Day, 1956

Zimmerman, Chaz *Centennial Reminiscing, Battle Creek,* Houchery Binding-Omaha, 1960—Battle Creek Lied Public Library

Fiction

Botts, Jack, *Whitestone, The Second Nebraska Cavalry,* iuniverse, 2003

Edwards, Lynn, *Bacon, Beans, Tobacco 'n' Whiskey,* WordsWorth, 2011

Esteleman, Loren D, *The Branch and the Scaffold, a Novel of Judge Parker,* Forge Books, 2009

Frazier, Charles, *Thirteen Moons,* Random House, 2006

Johnson, Terry C, *Blood Song,* St. Martins Press, 1993

Lee, BJ, *The Shores of Issyk-Kul,* 2009

Manfred, Frederick, *Lord Grizzly,* University of Nebraska Press, 1953

McMurtry, Larry, *Dead Man's Walk,* Pocket Books, 1995

Michener, James, *Centennial,* Fawcett Crest Books, 1974

O'Brien, Dan, *The Indian Agent,* University of Nebraska Press, 2004

Ross, David William, *Beyond the Stars,* Avon Books, 1991

Ross, David William, *Savage Plains,* Avon Books, 1996

Shaara, Jeffrey M., *Gone for Soldiers, A novel of the Mexican-American War,* Ballantine Books, 2000

Sommers, Jeanne, *Comanche Revenge,* Dell Publishing, 1981

Pamphlets, Magazines, Papers and Essays

Connelley, William Elsey, *The Provisional Government of Nebraska Territory and the Journals of William Walker,* (Lincoln, Nebr. 1890) Library of Congress Online

Stephen Potts, Nebraska History, A Quarterly Magazine, *North of "Bleeding Kansas": The 1850s Political Crises in Nebraska Territory*, Fall, 1992

United States Federal Reports, supplement, *Indian Treaties, Acts and Agreements*

David M. Johnson author, Nebraska State Historical Society, *Nebraska in the Fifties*

John B Dunbar, Magazine of American History Vol. V, No. 5; *The Pawnee Indians; Their Habits and Customs*, November 1880

John B Dunbar, Magazine of American History Vol. V, No. 5; *Pitalesharu-Chief of the Pawnees*, November 1880

John Thayer, NSHS Annual Meeting January 10, 1900 Address, *The Pawnee War of 1859*, Proceedings and Collection of the Nebraska State Historical Society, Second Series, Vol. 2, 1902

Critical Acclaim for End of Pawnee Starlight

Shawn Farritor has written an insightful book about the removal of the Pawnee Indians from their homeland and the American West. It would be so easy to ignore this part of our heritage because it was so painful and we would just like to forget these atrocities ever happened. It is obvious the author poured his heart into this book, and it is researched in precise detail and includes the use of maps and illustrations. He describes many of the battles in detail and it is as if the reader is right there, watching as if in a dream as history unfolds. If you're thinking it is merely a history book you would be wrong. It reads like a Western and the facts and storyline ring true. I would highly recommend this book. Farritor has forged new territory. What was most impressive was the fact that I felt drawn into the story and the characters emerged as lifelike and not just names pulled from the pages of history. You feel the emotions and conflicts of those characters as if you were right there with them. No history book could do this. In school we are taught about these events; but Farritor brings them to life in such a way that you will never see it as history again. It becomes part of you. If you thought this story had been forgotten or not worth remembering, you would be wrong. These characters live and breathe and I am fortunate to have stumbled upon this diamond in the rough.

BJ Lee—Author of The Shores of Issyk-Kul